Ed Garfield shook his head. "Look, Liz. Ms. Sullivan." He leaned forward, looking at me earnestly. "Let's let bygones be bygones. How about you come in just for today and tomorrow? That finishes the week, and Monday our receptionist should be well again."

I cleared my throat. "It would be uncomfortable to work at SoftWrite after what Clarice said this morning."

Ed touched my arm briefly. "Listen, she wasn't making any sense at all. We're so busy right now, nobody has time to think. And the phones are going crazy." His jaw was rigid, his hands tense. "Whatever it takes. Double what you usually get from temp work."

I could hear the sullen groans of the water heater from the back porch. It wouldn't last much longer.

"Okay. I'll be there in half an hour or so." Life was taking on a hectic tone. Office work for the next two days. That evening was Bridget's hen party. Then there was grocery shopping, laundry to do, puppy training, and garden tasks.

"Thanks, Liz. Ms. Sullivan." Ed had his face under control again. "We're all too busy to gossip right now. Probably no one will even notice you."

That sounded like famous last words.

By Lora Roberts
Published by Fawcett Books:

MURDER IN A NICE NEIGHBORHOOD
MURDER IN THE MARKETPLACE

MURDER
IN THE
MARKETPLACE

Lora Roberts

FAWCETT GOLD MEDAL • NEW YORK

A Fawcett Gold Medal Book
Published by Ballantine Books
Copyright © 1995 by Lora Roberts Smith

All rights reserved under International and Pan-American Copyright Conventions. Published in the United States by Ballantine Books, a division of Random House, Inc., New York, and simultaneously in Canada by Random House of Canada Limited, Toronto.

Library of Congress Catalog Card Number: 95-90031

ISBN 0-449-14890-4

Manufactured in the United States of America

First Edition: July 1995

10 9 8 7 6 5 4 3 2 1

For all the ladies—Jeanne and Elizabeth and Nancy,
Judy and Missy and Mom,
and especially for you, Mama

1 _____

I was sitting at a wrought-iron table in the sun, with half a cheese Danish on a napkin in front of me. Other tables, complete with umbrellas, occupied a wide second-story landing behind the offices of SoftWrite, Inc., in downtown Palo Alto.

It was ten A.M., break time in the office world. The sky was that soaring blue that Californians take for granted, and the June air managed to be warmed by the sun and cooled by a fresh breeze at the same time. Steps at the end of the landing went down to the ground-level alley behind the building. SoftWrite occupied the second floor of a big Spanish colonial; the first floor had several shops, including a coffee place that, judging from the burnt-toast odor, roasted its own beans.

Mindy Luccetti, across from me at the table, took a deep breath. "Smell those coffee beans. Just the aroma could keep me awake."

I preferred the scent of the lemon blossoms from the little tree growing in a tub beside us. Coffee is not my drink. I dunked a homemade tea bag up and down in my cup of lukewarm water. In a world of coffee achievers, tea drinkers can't even get the basic amenity of really hot water.

"So, Liz." Mindy set her coffee mug down after a satisfied swallow. "Do you do a lot of temp work, or is Soft-Write your first job?"

I pinched the tea bag out of my cup and took a cautious sip. "I've worked for several places, but I spend the most time at Tech Ware."

Mindy's forehead wrinkled. "I don't know a Tech Ware." She was a willowy young thing, with a mop of curly hair and oversized glasses that perched on her cute nose. I was sharing her office that morning, sitting at a spare computer to do data entry.

"It's a little place, started by Emery Montrose. His wife is a friend of mine."

"I see." Mindy pried the outside arc off the sliver of cinnamon roll she'd brought out with her. She had taken me under her wing in the two hours I'd worked at SoftWrite—introduced me to the computer, helped when I got stuck with the spreadsheet, hauled me outside for a break when the screen and keyboard seemed to be running together.

Over the past few months I'd made the transition from typewriter to computer—probably the last person in Silicon Valley to do so. I had used the typewriter to make a scanty living as a freelance writer. The computer was useful to a writer, too, but so far its main benefit was in giving me the skills to be a member of the pink-collar workforce. Much as I disliked it, temporary office work filled holes in my budget that freelancing hadn't touched.

"I've often thought temping might be kind of fun," Mindy said, breaking the layer of cinnamon roll into several tiny pieces. "Going to a new place, meeting new people. Do you work through an agency?"

"I'm signed up with one." They didn't call me often because I liked to pick and choose. And just then I had another job in the afternoons. "But this job came from Emery recommending me to someone here. Most agencies don't want to be involved in part-time arrangements."

"That's right, you're just giving us mornings." Mindy nibbled one of the little pieces of roll. I picked up my cheese Danish and took a healthy bite. Okay, so I'm not willowy. I'm short and stubby, with nondescript hair. And on my budget, free Danish is something to be celebrated. After the two hours of steady keyboarding I'd put in, I felt I deserved it.

2

"Yeah, I've only got mornings free, and I may not be needed tomorrow. The mailing labels are almost finished."

"That was fast." Mindy blinked at me behind her glasses. "You're a real keyboarding whiz."

I had learned to be accurate the hard way, on an old manual portable. It was practically a museum piece. Compared to it, a computer keyboard was like the difference between a push lawn mower and the riding kind. "Thanks, but you deserve the credit for showing me how to jump the fields." I drank my rapidly cooling tea and tried to keep the conversation going. "I noticed from the company mailing labels that a lot of SoftWrite employees live around here. I would have thought more would come from the South Bay or from Redwood City."

"We're encouraged to bike to work or take the train, because there's not much parking downtown." Mindy started dissecting the next layer of cinnamon roll. "This is a nice area—safer, you know. And if you have roommates it's not too pricey. I live in a group house near Stanford." She looked at me. "Do you live nearby?"

"Yeah." I didn't go into it. A year ago I had lived wherever my VW bus was parked—it had been my living room, dining room, and bedroom. I woke up each morning encased in the narrow confines of my vehicle, like human toothpaste in a rusty tube.

The miraculous gift of a house near downtown Palo Alto had taken me off the streets. Now I woke in the (comparatively) vast expanse of an old brass bed, in a bedroom with plaster only slightly cracked, watching the dawn through a tall window's wavy glass. My bathroom had a big claw-foot tub, enamel only slightly chipped, and a shower with usually dependable hot water. I could hardly wait to wake up these days.

Mindy set her coffee mug down. Unlike the plain white cup I'd been given, Mindy's was personalized with a cartoony drawing of a deranged female stomping through a lilliputian town, crushing cars and waving fistfuls of small,

3

terrified men. Underneath was the caption: ATTACK OF THE 50-FOOT PMS WOMAN.

"Nice cup," I said.

Mindy regarded it morosely. "My boyfriend gave it to me. My ex-boyfriend."

There didn't seem to be any more to say. I savored another bite of the cheese pocket. Mindy dissected another ring of her cinnamon roll, working toward the center.

The back door opened and a couple of women joined us at the table. Mindy introduced me. "Clarice, Jenifer, this is Liz Sullivan, the temp who's catching us up with data entry."

Clarice nodded without really looking at me. She was a statuesque blonde, about my age of early thirties, with careful makeup and beautifully styled hair.

Jenifer smiled and offered her hand. She couldn't have been more than twenty-three or twenty-four; her reddish-brown hair rippled naturally down her back. She had warm brown eyes in the kind of face that was meant to be open and guileless, but there were smudges of purple beneath her eyes and lines of strain around her mouth, dimming the glow of her youthful skin. Even so, she made Clarice's maquillage look overdone.

Mindy examined her with concern. "You don't look too good, Jenifer. Hope you're not getting this major stomach thing that's going around."

"That's what I told her," Clarice exclaimed. "I said, Get some fresh air, Jenifer, you can't stay chained to that keyboard all day, no matter what Ed says."

Jenifer tilted her face to the sun. "It's a beautiful day," she murmured. "After a couple of years in Seattle I'll never take this weather for granted again."

"Does it really rain as much as they say?" Mindy lifted a raisin off her napkin with her finger. "I thought that was a myth."

"It's not." Jenifer lifted her hair off the back of her neck, as if it had grown too heavy. "There's a lot of inter-

4

esting stuff there, of course, but nothing makes up for the weather."

"Were you working there, or going to school?" I took a bite from my Danish.

"Working," Jenifer said shortly. A vertical line appeared between her eyebrows.

Clarice rummaged in her purse. "Here, honey. Take some aspirin. Your headache's getting worse, isn't it? Maybe the sun's too bright out here."

"It's fine." Jenifer accepted the pills Clarice handed her, washing them down with a gulp of her soda, and changed the subject. "So have you heard where the company picnic's going to be this year, Mindy?"

"I don't think they've decided yet." Mindy stirred her coffee. "Maybe Ardenwood Farm, maybe someplace in Santa Cruz."

"So far away," Clarice said. Her voice was slightly nasal and had a constant undertone of complaint. "Too much driving."

The back door opened again, and a tall, casually dressed man stuck his head out. "Jenifer, Ed's looking for you."

"Thanks, Keith." Jenifer pushed her chair back and got up.

"Just like Ed." Clarice sounded seriously annoyed. "Can't he let you take a break? He should be doing some of this himself, or let Suzanne do it."

"Well, he's put me in charge," Jenifer said, but a shadow crossed her face. She hurried back into the building, her hair catching the light.

Clarice watched the door close. The bright sun on her face showed the petulant lines clearly under her makeup. "Poor girl. She's really wound up about this new software release."

Mindy toyed with the last triangle of her pastry. "It stands to reason. She's been given a lot of responsibility for someone her age, hasn't she? I heard she was doing all the stuff Suzanne normally does."

Clarice sniffed. "Well, Suzanne's such a fuddy-duddy. Af-

5

ter all, when you're over forty in this valley, you're definitely over the hill. And she always holds on to the product much too long. You've got to get it out to the marketplace before someone else beats you to it."

"Now you sound like Ed." Mindy laughed.

Clarice wasn't laughing. "Even an asshole can make sense once in a while," she said, and stood up. "I've got to get back to work." She stalked into the building.

Mindy looked flushed. "That Clarice," she fumed when the door shut behind the other woman. "She's so touchy!"

"Who's Ed?"

"Ed Garfield." Mindy glanced around, making sure no one else had come out to enjoy the sun. "Our illustrious founder and head honcho. He and Suzanne started Soft-Write a few years ago, and now we're at more than fifty people."

"Ed's the big boss? Jenifer works for him?"

Mindy corrected me. "Technically, Suzanne's the veep of software, the one that thinks up the products. As a software engineer, Jenifer works for her. But this new release is something Ed dreamed up—him and Jenifer, or that's the story. She's very bright." Mindy snickered a little. "A couple of the guys say she's the new Suzanne—in more ways than one."

"Why? Is Suzanne going to retire?"

The back door opened to let out a noisy trio of young men who tossed a hacky sack around as they clattered down the stairs to the alley. Mindy pinched her lips together primly. "We'd better get back to work, too."

Picking up my cup and napkin, I followed her into the cool interior. Despite the immense skylight far above, taking up most of the ceiling space, it seemed dim inside after the dazzle of sun on the landing. To one side, along the exposed brick of the back wall, was a counter full of domestic machinery—coffeemakers labeled "Leaded" and "Unleaded," a microwave, a hot plate with a carafe of lukewarm water, and assorted canisters and jars bearing minatory warnings about unauthorized use. The big box on the counter that had held the pastries was almost empty. Some people at one of the tables that clustered in the open space were wadding up napkins and tossing them at the wastebasket, cheering loudly at any success.

Mindy pointed out a refrigerator, where I could leave my lunch if I brought it, and led the way out of the lounge area and into the maze of head-high partitions that created work cubicles for most of those fifty people.

The partitions were the pale gold of ripe wheat, stretching everywhere under the vast skylight. Here and there people had set plants on filing cabinets inside their cubicles to spill over the walls, creating oases of greenery. Occasionally a "Far Side" or "Calvin and Hobbes" cartoon was pinned up outside an opening in the maze, like a graphic name card. The hum of computers and the sound of voices mingled in a low-level, brain-dulling roar.

Until I started temping a few months ago, I'd spend most of my working time alone. Meeting so many new people, being surrounded by them, wondering if one of the chic-looking women was the previous owner of the denim skirt I'd picked up at Goodwill, all gave me a massive feeling of insecurity. I almost welcomed the enclosing walls of Mindy's cubicle, shutting away excessive stimulus.

After the yeasty turmoil of the marketplace, where the buying and selling of talent and skill was upstaged by the tangle of interpersonal relationships, my solitary work, when I could afford to get back to it, would seem very peaceful.

2

"GET off my driveway." The man did not yell. He didn't have to. The cold expression in his pale blue eyes was forceful enough.

I backed up a step and clutched my government-issue black shoulder bag closer. "My name is Liz Sullivan." The ingratiating smile that had been recommended during training felt wrong on my face. "I just wanted to ask you a few questions for the follow-up census—"

"Get out." He moved a step, and I backed up again, onto the smooth lawn that bordered his driveway. It was very green for Palo Alto, where water use is carefully monitored. My feet in the demure-looking but torturous black heels sank slightly into soggy turf.

"It will just take a—"

"Get off my lawn!" His voice rose a notch. I inched back onto the driveway, deciding that I would forget about completing a form for this house—just as I had for the last three houses I'd tried.

"I take it you don't want to participate." Keeping a wary eye on the man, I edged down the driveway toward the sidewalk.

"Don't come back." His voice was softer again. The woman who stood beside him didn't speak, didn't even blink.

They'd just gotten out of the big 4×4 that stood on the drive when I'd approached, smiling my cheery, pasted-on Census Bureau smile, and requested a few minutes of their time. No smile from either of them, no chitchat. Blankness from her, hostility from him. I might have been from the IRS instead of the Census Bureau.

"Have a nice day." Whenever I used the government-issue smile it seemed to generate such inanities. I would have despised me, too, just as this fun couple did. The man glared, the woman ignored. I faded away, leaving the smile behind.

My feet ached in the demure shoes, which was probably the reason why they'd been at the Junior League Thrift Shop in the first place. I sat down at the nearest bus-stop bench and eased my toes out of them while consulting the register of names and addresses assigned me by the chirpy local census supervisor.

Despite missing my lunch to work during the noon hour, only a couple of the eleven doors I'd knocked on so far had been opened. One of those doors had been slammed in my face. The other one had belonged to a lady who seemed to believe that I *was* from the IRS, judging from the way she'd complained about her tax dollars. I'd spent more time in her living room listening than asking questions.

The Census Bureau probably wished it were the IRS, too—at least the latter had an enforcement arm. I had been hired along with other financially desperate people to plod around with clunky black briefcases because when the census had been taken a few years ago, the bureau had muffed it big-time in California. Headlines had proclaimed that millions of people had gone uncounted; along with the rest of the nation's taxpayers, I'd marveled at the incredible inefficiency of our government, and especially of the Census Bureau. If your mandate was to count, you should know how.

Now I was getting a different picture. In California, it seemed people didn't want to be counted. And some of them could be downright unpleasant.

At least the Census Bureau had been realistic about that when they'd made up the forms I was supposed to fill out for each household. There was a place for indicating the uncooperative. I'd filled that space in a lot. Now I blacked

9

it in with my official Census Bureau pencil for Mr. and Mrs. Fun Couple and tried to decide if this gig was worth the money. It paid a little better than temp work, but the aggravation level was much higher, too. If it hadn't been for my sweet little house, I wouldn't have put up with it for a minute.

My house had been a wonderful, unlooked-for gift. But, though free, it was needier than a deadbeat husband. Right now it required a new hot water heater; before that it had been the roof. The property tax bill I'd paid in April had been unpleasantly large; another payment was due in November. Generally I make enough money freelancing to scrape along, but I hadn't had a sale for a while, and things were getting tight. That's why I'd been temping mornings for Emery and anyone else he dug up; that's why I spent the afternoons going door-to-door for the U.S. Census Bureau, asking nosy questions no one wanted to answer.

I had applied months ago for the census job, when it was first advertised, but I hadn't expected to be hired—having once been an inmate in a correctional facility, even if it wasn't a full-scale prison, is not a good recommendation. After just a couple of afternoons and evenings as a government employee, I'd realized that no one with any sense would go around to houses where people had refused to cooperate with the census the first time around, and ask them to reconsider.

I smoothed the skirt over my knees and hoped that the hem wasn't too puckered and uneven from my inexpert attempt to re-tailor it. Whoever had owned it first had been taller than me—four or five inches, anyway. I think of myself as totally nonthreatening. Yet people didn't want to talk to me.

During the census orientation, we were encouraged to look nice. We were spoon-fed platitudes, led through some totally inadequate role-playing, given our black briefcases, registers, and pencils, and sent into the world. The job would last several weeks, if I could stick it out.

A man shambling up the street collapsed on the bus-stop

bench where I sat licking my wounds. He had the kind of stubble on his chin that isn't photogenic, and clothes that hadn't been within churning distance of a washing machine for a while. His blank gaze passed over me while he pulled a paper bag–wrapped bottle from inside his ragged overcoat. He smelled bad and looked worse, but I welcomed his appearance as a reminder to quit whining. I had my ground-level ivory tower, only slightly dilapidated, and a nice big vegetable garden. I wasn't homeless, nor would I starve. I wasn't dead, despite a close call or two.

The bus came along. The driver looked irritated when neither I nor my odoriferous benchmate wanted to ride. Resting on county property is not encouraged.

I stood on my aching feet and walked on. My territory was an area of Palo Alto that was unfamiliar to me, a neighborhood of small houses and apartment buildings off El Camino Real, one of the main drags in our fair city. Some of the houses were being remodeled, which is the major leisure activity of home-owning Palo Altans. Some of the houses, the rentals, were sliding downhill. The apartment buildings ranged from older, smaller duplexes or sixplexes to featureless monoliths like large-scale anthills. My register covered just a couple of blocks at a time, but I was beginning to feel that there was no end in sight. The secondhand pumps resumed their torture of my toes; I was tempted to climb into my VW bus, drive home, and not come back.

Instead, I plodded on down the street, approaching the next apartment house. It was a fiveplex, facing another like it across a driveway-courtyard. Each building had two units on the ground floor flanking the parking slots, and three across the top. Since the big earthquake of 1989, buildings like this have been suspect; the covered parking areas are often inadequately shored up to support the weight of apartments above them. But optimists still live in them.

Apartment 1, according to my register, was occupied by a Wanda Sorenski. It was on the ground floor. In front of the door was a small, tiled porch, surrounded by waist-high stucco walls with flat tiles on top. Ms. Sorenski, or some-one, had set plants along the wall, trailing Swedish ivy and something with pink-spotted leaves that I didn't recognize. A plastic pot with the price sticker still on it held a baby Venus's-flytrap, complete with youthful fangs.

The screen door was locked. Before I could ring the bell, a woman opened the door, obviously planning to go out. She pushed the screen door open as well, ignoring me so completely that if I hadn't dodged, the screen would have crashed into my face. She towed a small, snuffling child.

"Hello," I began, catching the screen before it caught me. "I'm with the U.S. Census Bureau—"

"Move," she snapped. The child, curious, forgot to sniffle while he peered at me.

I stepped back, and the corner of my clunky black brief-case brushed the plastic pot with the Venus's-flytrap. It teetered on the edge of the wall and then toppled, spilling its dirt on the porch at my feet.

For a moment I just gaped at it. "I'm sorry—"

"Look what you've done!" She spoke in the same voice she probably used to chastise the boy. He cringed a little, glancing at me sympathetically. "Pick that up, right now!"

Obediently I knelt at her feet, sweeping the dirt back into the pot with my fingers. The little plant's root ball appeared to be undamaged.

"It'll be all right." I tried a placating smile. "Are you Wanda Sorenski?"

"None of your business." She locked her front door and grabbed the little boy's hand again. "Get off my porch."

It was certainly my day to be ordered around. "I'm here for the Census Bureau," I said, standing my ground.

"I don't care if you're from the Publishers Clearing House." She elbowed me aside. "Come on, Bobby."

Bobby dug in his heels, but she yanked him along behind her.

"I just need to ask some questions," I tried, following them. "Would this evening be a better time?"

She turned at the sidewalk and faced me, flicking a

scornful glance over my Goodwill ensemble. "Bother me again and I'll call the cops."

"It's really for your benefit," I said quickly, before she could leave.

"Yeah, sure. The less the government knows about me, the happier I'll be. Now stop bugging me." She dragged the little boy away, and I watched her go. Yet another one for the uncooperative bubble on my census form.

The sunshine seemed concentrated on my head; that cool breeze of the morning was gone. I wished for a comfy old T-shirt instead of the stiff blouse that went (sort of) with the skirt. I wished I'd gone home for lunch before trying to find people at home; daytime was not the best time to be going door-to-door, but I had hoped to get it over with. Now I would have to come back in the evening, trying to catch up with people who weren't home until then, trying to get a few more forms filled out. I trudged across the courtyard to see if anyone was home in apartment 2.

Amazingly, someone was. A familiar someone—Jenifer from SoftWrite.

I gaped at her for a moment, wondering if it really was her. She was wearing a faded plaid robe, open over leggings and an oversized T-shirt.

"Jenifer?"

She rubbed her head. Her eyes were heavy. "Yes?" She looked at me blankly for a moment. "Oh, yes. Liz from the office. Were you bringing me some papers or something?" She frowned. "I don't think I can get anything done right now. I'm not feeling well."

"I'm sorry to bother you." The faint purple smudges under her eyes were more pronounced. I did feel bad—I must have gotten her out of bed. "I actually have a different hat on this afternoon—I'm a census taker, for the follow-up census."

She flapped one hand weakly, as if to push me away, and yawned hugely. There was a scrabbling noise behind her, and a puppy squirmed around her ankles, trying to escape.

It was a cute little thing, black and white, with floppy ears and big brown eyes. She scooped it up and held it.

"Does it have to be now?" She started to edge the door closed.

"It won't take too long." I felt like a heel, pestering a sick person.

"I guess I could answer some questions." She glanced behind her, hugging the puppy to her tightly. "If it's fast."

She didn't ask me in, so I just dove into it while standing there. "Your name is Jenifer, right? Last name?"

"Paston." She spelled both names for me, yawned, and gave me her date of birth and occupation—she was twenty-four, and a software engineer. But when I started asking about the apartment, she got restive.

"Why does the government need to know that?" She squinted at me. Her eyes were a little red and swollen—allergies or tears. I decided it was allergies.

I explained that the Census Bureau wanted to count housing units as well as people. "Do you have two bedrooms here, or one?"

"Two." She looked over her shoulder. I thought I heard someone stirring around, but whoever it was didn't say anything.

"And do you live here alone?"

"I have a roommate." The puppy whimpered a little when she squeezed it. I reached out to stroke one silky ear.

"Can I speak to your roommate? I'm supposed to fill out a form about everyone."

"She's still at work." Jenifer yawned uncontrollably. My jaws ached with the effort of staying closed. "Look, Liz, I'm sorry. I have to lie down now."

"I'll come back this evening, okay? I can get your roommate then, and I won't have to bother you."

"Yeah, sure." She was closing the door.

"Sixish okay?"

"Later—seven." The puppy struggled to get out of her grip. "Sorry. We'll talk later."

As the door closed, I thought I heard another, deeper

voice. Perhaps the roommate was there, but didn't want to talk. Pausing at the stairs, I wondered if I should go back. But I felt kind of funny taking census data from people I knew, even if only slightly. Maybe there was a regulation against it; maybe I should send another agent to talk to Jenifer and her roommate.

While I stewed about that, I plodded up the stairs. No one was home at any of the upstairs apartments. I trudged the length of the walkway, which projected out over the parking area below, ringing doorbells and knocking. I sat on a bench beside the door of apartment 5 to write the last little notice that said I would call again that evening.

Somewhere below me a door creaked open. Brisk footsteps walked away; a car started. The puppy began yapping. The wind blew the fronds of the pepper tree in the center courtyard; the long strands of pepper berries rattled together like little pink castanets.

I was tired, hot, and my feet hurt. And it was long past lunchtime. My little house beckoned. I would go home and soak my feet, have lunch, and do a little work on the census forms before trying again in the evening. I could also finish up a couple of query letters.

Walking the two blocks to where I'd parked the Volkswagen bus was agony. I added Number 48 to Liz's Rules for Survival: Never wear cruel shoes. I climbed through the side door and collapsed onto the backseat, the sofa of my traveling living room. The table was folded down and everything tucked away. Old habits die hard. I kept the bus ready to take to the road at any minute. You never know when you might need to escape from something—bill collectors, earthquakes, an abusive ex-husband.

I kicked off the toe-torturers and filled a plastic Woolworth glass with water from the sink. It tasted a little stale from being in the reservoir for a while, but my dry throat appreciated it just the same. I rooted in the cupboard beside the door for the old pair of sandals I kept for garden work, then went forward to the driver's seat. The bus seemed smaller to me since I no longer lived in it. I nearly bumped my head on its ceiling.

The engine made a strange coughing sound at the stoplight. I would have to spend time that afternoon delving into its guts to see if I could fix it. I've learned its peculiarities over the years, since there aren't that many mechanics who will work on '69 buses for a price I can afford. But when it makes these noises I always worry that it's the end. Aside from the expense of replacing it, I'm attached to the old heap.

My place is in north Palo Alto, a few miles from the scene of my census humiliations. It's on a flag lot, so called because it's tucked behind another house; the driveway is like a flagpole, and my lot is the flag. At one time my cottage was an adjunct of the larger house in front, but when I'd inherited the two houses, I could only afford to tend one. Paul Drake, a detective with the Palo Alto police department, was buying the one in front. His payments were a nice regular income, since my own house needed incredible amounts of deferred maintenance. I also tried to make regular contributions to an IRA. I didn't want to be dependent in my old age.

When I turned into the drive, Drake's car was parked in the graveled area between his backyard and my front yard. Every weekend we planned to plant a hedge beside the parking area; every week something got in the way of doing it.

Drake had probably come home for lunch. His meals were of great importance to him. Sometimes he invited me for dinner, and I enjoyed the fancy cooking he did as a hobby.

I stopped the bus in front of the garage, which I'd retained as part of my territory. Just beyond it was my cottage. It looked, to me, like the cozy home the fisherman's wife had extorted from the Magic Fish, before she got greedy. When I was a child, that story had seemed to imply that everyone deserves this much in life—a little home with some modest but important conveniences. Having it made me feel, as the fisherman must have felt, an incredulous sense of thankfulness to whatever magic exists in our cruelly unimaginative world.

I lavished it with attention—Drake called it the pride-of-ownership trap. I had given it fresh slate gray paint, French blue shutters, a new, expensive green roof when my own reshingling hadn't quite done the trick. A little matter of flashing had been my downfall the winter before—seems I'd neglected to use it in the right places. The roof had been replaced after leaks warped the hardwood floor in my living room. I was sanding that down, a little at a time.

Drake was standing in my front yard, which was unusual. Even more unusual was the girl who sat on my front porch. She had hair of many colors, chopped off raggedly on one side and shaved above her ear on the other side. Her lips were black, her eyebrows were black, and her face was dead white. What clothes she wore were skimpy, though her attributes were not. Being cursed with a large bosom myself, I could have sympathized, but her boobs were obviously on display, spilling out of a black tank top tucked into torn black shorts. Droopy black socks and black Doc Martens completed her getup. Something about her brown eyes was familiar; I wondered if they reminded me of Jenifer's puppy.

I also wondered why Drake had brought her to me, but his bemused expression when I jumped out of the bus told its own story. She had turned her back to him. When I appeared she got up, dragging an immense black leather pouch or backpack behind her.

"Hi, Drake." I reached into the bus for the horrid shoes and shut the door. The girl had approached a few feet, then stopped, staring at me with unnerving intensity. I stared back. "Hi."

She cleared her throat. "Hello, Aunt Liz."

I looked at her blankly, then at Drake. His air of bemusement had deepened. He was gazing at my new roof, obviously disassociating himself.

"You're—" I couldn't dredge up any names. I had been

17

estranged from my family for almost fifteen years. This could be the little niece born just before my disastrous marriage cut me off from them, but I couldn't for the life of me remember her name. Or figure out why she'd turned up on my doorstep.

"Amy Sullivan. I've come to stay with you for a while, if you don't mind."

3

"SO where did you dig her up?" I was in the kitchen whispering to Drake while I got Amy the drink she'd requested. She wandered around the living room; I could see her rooster-colored hair flashing near the book-case.

Drake leaned against the counter, holding back a smile. "I didn't," he said, moving aside so I could get some ice cubes. "She was sitting on your doorstep when I came home for lunch. I thought it was only neighborly to inquire who she was and what she was doing there." He added plaintively, "She doesn't seem to like me."

"Did you tell her you're a cop?" I took a big tub of plain yogurt out of the refrigerator. After some hesitation, I also got a little dish of raspberries I'd culled from my small patch. I had planned to eat them all myself in solitary gluttony, but it didn't look as if I was going to be solitary.

"I might have." Drake looked hungrily at the raspberries. "Where did you get these lovely things?" He picked one out of the dish and inspected it with reverence before popping it into his mouth.

"My community garden plot." I slapped his hand away when it came back for more. "Don't you have your own lunch at home?"

"You want me to go." He straightened to his full five-foot-eight and edged away. "Okay. I'll leave you here with your long-lost relative. If she tries to drink your blood, yell. I might hear."

He got as far as the kitchen door, then turned back.

"Bridget called and asked me to remind you about her party this evening."

"Thanks—I had forgotten." Bridget Montrose is a local writer. I'd met her a few years ago, when I was new in the area and she only had two children. Now she had four, and had graduated from poetry to prose; her first novel was coming out soon. "What time?"

"Fiveish. Mixed, she said."

Bridget had these parties every couple of months—not cocktail parties, she was careful to say, because that implied a hostess who would supply fancy drinks and hors d'oeuvres, instead of jug wine and cheese and crackers. Mixed meant that her husband Emery was also using the occasion to further Tech Ware, his little software business. Besides the usual complement of writers and poets, drinking, arguing, and devouring every crumb, there would be computer nerds and entrepreneurs.

"Hackers and hacks." I mumbled it to myself, but Drake picked up on it. He sometimes goes to the poetry readings, though he hasn't been persuaded to admit that he writes poetry.

"I'll have to remember that. Hackers and hacks." He laughed.

"So I'd have time afterward to get back to the census work." I was talking to myself, a bad habit. Drake heard me.

"Look, axe the census stuff." He spoke gruffly. "You shouldn't be knocking on doors after dark."

"Can it be that one of Palo Alto's finest thinks the streets aren't safe?" I put one hand to my forehead melodramatically. "Alas, if someone should mug me for my stylish government briefcase."

Drake was not amused. "I know the streets aren't safe despite what we can do. Cruising around in the dark is just asking for trouble."

"I can take care of myself." His concern was touching, but I had, after all, a closer acquaintance with the streets than he would ever get from a patrol car. I gave him a big, sticky-sweet smile. "Thanks for sharing that, though."

He smiled reluctantly in return. "I'm leaving before you start getting in touch with your inner child." He sauntered out, exchanging a few words with Amy as he left. I put the yogurt and berries on the rickety kitchen table, added ice water and a couple of bowls and, as an afterthought, a box of whole wheat crackers. Teenagers, I'd heard, eat heartily.

When I looked up, Amy was standing in the kitchen door, her black-edged eyes bright with interest. "Is this your whole house? Just that one teeny bedroom? Where will I sleep?"

I tried not to cringe. My privacy, my space, were precious. I didn't want to relinquish them. "We can talk about that later." I gestured to the table. "Want some lunch?"

She bounced into a chair, which, as rickety as the table, groaned under the assault. "Okay. Where is it?"

I opened the yogurt and spooned some into my bowl, topping it with some of the raspberries, which I suspected would be as so many pearls before her youthful swinishness. "Right here," I said, stirring. "Help yourself."

There was a moment of silence. I didn't look at her.

"Cool," she said finally. "You're, like, dieting. It's fresh."

"The berries are fresh," I said with modest pride. "I picked them myself early this morning."

"No, no." She put a small spoonful of yogurt into her bowl, and then added most of the remaining berries. "It's fresh that you're working on your body. I mean, I can respect that. I'll diet, too."

I laid down my spoon. "Amy," I said, watching the dainty way she conveyed the tiniest possible amount of yogurt into her black-rimmed mouth. "What are you doing here?"

"We could talk about that later, too," Amy suggested, digging into the cracker box.

"Let's talk about it now. Does Andy know you're here?"

She sniffed. "Daddy barely knows he's alive. He's, like, totally away from real life, from the street. I didn't even know you existed, Aunt Liz. When Gramma got your letter and everyone started talking about you and what a disgrace you were to your upbringing . . ." She smiled at me sunnily. "I thought you might be a good relative. I mean, not like Uncle Dan or Aunt Molly."

It was strange to hear my sister and brothers spoken about this way, portrayed as rigid adults. What I mostly remembered, growing up the youngest in a loud Irish household, were the incredible arguments that would last for days, with people changing sides right and left.

About some things, however, there was no argument possible. I had been given the opportunity of a college education. My older siblings had spurned such time-wasting foolishness, but that didn't stop them from complaining about the unfairness of it. My brothers, when they could spare time from their construction jobs and the drinking and brawling that went with them, thought my parents' money could have been better spent setting them up in business for themselves. And they were right, it seemed.

I had put all these people and their various disappointments in me out of my mind for quite a while. To hear them spoken of so dismissively, to hear the negative things I'd always felt about my family verbalized, stirred a strange mixture of recognition and regret. It took away the good moments, too, the times when I'd felt loved and nurtured, before everything I did began to be wrong.

Despite her black lips, I empathized with Amy. "You're sixteen?"

"Seventeen," she said, tossing that iridescent hair. "Almost."

"And you just lit out, without telling anyone?"

"I copied the return address on your letter, and then I left," she said scrupulously. "Is there any soda?"

My budget doesn't allow for soda, when water comes right out of the faucet. I said as much, and she seemed concerned.

"Are you poor, Aunt Liz?" She looked around the kitchen, at the worn Formica countertops and the small, ancient refrigerator, the elderly gas stove and the scuffed wood floor. "I didn't think—I mean, I just figured you must have made good or you wouldn't have written Gramma."

"I did make good," I said dryly. Writing that letter had been spontaneous; I'd been cut off for so long from my family that the need to communicate had welled up and spilled over one day. And the Palo Alto address, no matter how shabby the house, meant something. I hadn't told my mother that it was the first time in years I'd had a street address. I guess what I really wanted was something besides junk mail.

What I'd gotten was Amy. My mother had never answered my letter. I hadn't even been sure she'd received it. So much for being the prodigal daughter.

Amy looked confused, but I didn't bother to explain that the move from VW bus to house had definitely been upward mobility. Thinking about the bus, I remembered that funny noise. "I've got to change, Amy. Would you put away the lunch stuff?"

"Sure, Aunt Liz." She jumped to her feet. At least she didn't mind pitching in. I went into my teeny bedroom, hung up my skirt and blouse in my teeny closet, and pulled on jeans. I would have to wear those irritating "work" clothes again after Bridget's party, when I went back to try and fill in my Census register with reluctant names. The panty hose did not come off unscathed; a run slithered down my leg when I brushed against the bed frame. My next thrift-store trip would involve pants, not skirts.

Amy trailed me out to the garage, chattering about her friends in Denver and how much my brother and his wife had hated them, and how she'd wanted to move in with her friend Lisa but Lisa's mom had called her mom and her dad had dragged her home and forbidden her to hang out with her friends and how she'd just decided to leave and caught the bus three days ago and how she'd been riding it ever since. She didn't sound at all concerned that she was now out of money and throwing herself on the mercy of a

23

person her family had declared to be lost to all family feeling.

It gave me a cold chill to listen to her. I am no stranger to the street, and a lot of the young people who live on it started out the way Amy had—leaving home, cutting ties, failing to find that succor they'd looked for, gradually reduced to selling drugs, selling their bodies, losing their souls.

While I tightened belts and regapped spark plugs and tested connections, I listened to Amy's artless prattle and knew I couldn't boot her out or send her back—not yet, anyway. She wasn't ready to go back. But I wasn't ready to be responsible for a sixteen-year-old.

She was silent for a little while. I crawled out from under the bus to find her looking as pensive as a person with black, raccoonlike circles under her eyes could look.

"Amy," I said, cleaning the oil off my hands with a rag, "you have to let your folks know where you are."

Her lower lip stuck out. "They won't care."

"They will, and you know it." I watched her for a moment, but she wouldn't meet my eyes. "Did you leave a note?"

She shook her head, turning away a little.

"So they're probably frantic by now." I hesitated, trying to conceal my reluctance. "You can tell them you'll stay with me for a while. It's summer—you won't miss school."

She turned back, beaming. "Aunt Liz—"

"Wait a minute." I held up one hand. "There are rules. I am, as you noticed, poor. I don't have extra money. It's a struggle for me to get by, let alone support a teenager. You'll have to get a job and contribute to the living expenses, plus take care of anything you need. Jobs aren't easy to get around here. If you can't find work, you'll have to go home. I can help you with a bus ticket, but that's all the spare cash I have."

She thought about this, and gradually her lower lip returned to its place. "I'll find a job," she said optimistically. "I've been a waitress, you know. And a manicurist, for a

24

little while. Can you believe they fired me just for taking a tiny little break to fix my own nails? I mean, I wasn't away from my station more than a nanosecond. What kind of manicurist has a chipped fingernail?" She held up her black and white talons for inspection. "See, on the bus trip the polish chipped again."

"Do you type?" I was signed up with a temp agency, although the woman who ran it didn't seem to like me. Working for Emery wasn't so bad—at least he saw me as a person. The jobs I was offered through the agency were for faceless cogs willing to be ground away by the big machine. I hated those jobs. Sometimes, if I'd sold an article, I turned them down. Maybe that's why Mrs. Rainey didn't like me.

"With these nails? You've got to be kidding." Amy inspected the chipped polish anxiously. "Hey, how far is it to the Pacific Stock Exchange?"

"I don't know." I squatted down to finish tightening the new belts I'd installed. "Did you want to check your portfolio?"

"Actually, yes." She sounded on her dignity. Peering out from under the bumper, I could tell I'd hurt her feelings. "I did some investing for a school thing, and I, like, have a talent for it. My picks all went up. Maybe I'll get a job on the floor."

With a great effort of will, I refrained from pointing out the statistical likelihood of that plan. It was pleasant in the sun. The gravel crunched under my knees and the bees hummed in the lavender that edged the drive. Amy's voice rose and fell, telling me about PE ratios. At first I thought these had to do with gym class, but it turned out they involved some complicated investment formula. I was impressed by Amy's knowledge, but my attention wandered in the warm sunshine.

My cottage has a small green lawn in front, old turf dotted with little daisies and clover and chamomile that I'd sown that spring. The daffodils I'd planted along the front walk were long gone, of course, but forget-me-nots were blooming there, and I'd bought a couple of bareroot roses at the very end of the season, getting them cheap and soaking them for a couple of days to help them recover from the plastic bag. Now they had big blooms, and I could smell them over the engine oil—the dark, seductive fragrance of Oklahoma, my favorite hybrid tea, and the fruitier scent of Amber Queen. The sun, the scents, were transcendently peaceful.

Even Amy was affected by it. Her voice died away. She tilted her dead-white face to the warmth and closed her eyes. I cleaned the battery terminals and replaced the oil filter.

"So what did you do that was so bad, Aunt Liz?" Amy sat up straighter, opening her eyes. "I'm dying of curiosity."

"Didn't they tell you?" I don't like talking about my past, even with relatives.

"You got married to a jerk." She inspected a ladybug that had crawled onto her knee. "But I don't see what's so big about that. My mom and dad yell at each other all the time. Once he slugged her, and she broke the turkey platter over his head." Amy shrugged, elaborately nonchalant. "They're both jerks sometimes, so why did they get so mad at you?"

I wasn't surprised that my brother was capable of domestic violence. My dad had knocked my mom around a bit, after the accident that took away his work with the big cranes. She'd been stoic about it up to a point, but when she handed down the ultimatum, he'd stopped. As far as I knew, which wasn't far. At least Renee, Amy's mother, could defend herself.

"I don't know, Amy. I married a middle-class jerk instead of a working-class one. Maybe that was why." I certainly didn't want to talk about my ex-husband. I'd come to grips with all that, and as far as I was concerned, that part of my life was over. I handed Amy the ignition key. "Would you start it up real easy? I'll tell you when to turn it off."

The bus hummed sweetly, like a giant bee. I try to keep it from developing major problems that would be beyond my power to fix. It was coming up on the big 200,000—a lot more zeros than I saw in my savings account. A new used car would wipe me out. Besides, I was attached to my bus. We'd been through things together I hadn't shared with any human.

Amy turned it off. I wiped my hands once more and carried my tools into the garage. She followed, examining everything with great interest. "It's really radical that you can fix your car," she said, watching me put the tools away.

"I can maintain it, but if the engine blows I'm sunk." I stripped off the old coveralls I keep in the garage for car work and hung them on their hook.

"You probably need a new car anyway." Amy looked back at the bus, and I looked, too—at its faded blue and white paint, the dents I had inexpertly filled, the dimpled bumpers and duct tape–patched seats. Even thinking about a new car was disloyal.

"This old bus has some great attributes," I told her, shutting the garage doors. "For one thing, I'm absolutely safe from carjackers. For another, I never have to lock it."

"True." Amy nodded wisely. "It's kinda Zen—less is more, and all that."

"Very philosophical." She glanced at me sharply, and I tried to rein in my sarcasm. "Actually, that's my point of view. It works. That's what matters."

Amy looked up at the blue, blue sky. "It's so different here," she offered. "Warmer, for one thing. The air is wetter, somehow. And—oh, I don't know—thick or something. Not smoggy," she hastened to add. "I mean, it looks clear and all that. But it must be the altitude."

"Or lack of it." I hadn't lived in high altitudes for a long time. The Denver I remember had its share of polluted air, made worse by the thinness.

She breathed deeply, nearly coming out of her T-shirt, and scrutinized the back of Drake's house. He had painted the place and hired a mow-and-blow crew to take care of the yard, so it was considerably trimmer than when he'd moved in. My driveway looked directly out on the street;

we could see the occasional car going by. "So is that guy your lover?" Amy said casually.

"Who? Drake?" The sheer unexpectedness of her question rattled me. "Is that any of your business?"

"Guess not." She didn't seem put off by my reply. "I just wondered if he was going to show up in the evenings or anything."

"He might show up, but not for sex." I could feel a blush rising on my face. It was embarrassing to have her speculate on my love life. Not, of course, as embarrassing as it would have been if I'd had a love life. "We're friends. Neighbors."

"He's a cop." She looked disapproving. "I'm surprised at you, with your record and all."

"So you know about that, do you?" I turned toward the house.

She followed me. "I heard Aunt Molly telling Mom something about it. Don't you hate the police for putting you in jail?"

"It was better than the alternative." I sat down in the living room, gesturing Amy into the shabby, overstuffed chair by the fireplace. I didn't want to talk about it, but obviously she did. "I spent some time in minimum security. It would have been better if I hadn't felt the need to try and kill my louse of a husband, but actually I'm for people being locked up when they shoot other people. That's Drake's job, and he has my support for doing it." I took a deep breath. "He's not—we're not involved in anything but a neighborly relationship. If it's all the same to you, Amy, I would prefer not to be quizzed about all this. How would you like it if I asked about your sex life?"

"I don't have one," she said frankly. "I mean, I had sex once, but it wasn't at all what I thought it would be, so I'm a virgin again."

"Virginity can be regained?" I stifled a laugh, not wanting to hurt Amy's feelings. If renouncing sex made you a virgin, I could qualify.

"Why not?" Amy didn't find it troubling. She yawned.

"Gosh, I slept and slept on the bus, and now I'm sleepy again!" She looked at the sofa I was sitting on. "Is that a Hide-A-Bed?"

I got up. "Yes. I hope you'll be comfortable there tonight, but you can use my bed for a nap. I've got some work to do in here." My computer sat in the corner on an old library table. There were several writing projects in neat stacks around it; I had lots to do.

"So I'll sleep here tonight?" Amy looked, for a moment, lost and waifish.

"Guess so. Before you nap, we'll go call your parents."

She stuck that lower lip out again, but she didn't say anything. I took my keys off the key rack by the door.

"Where's the phone?" She followed me out the door.

"We'll use Drake's—he's given me permission to do that. We'll leave some money to pay for it. I don't have a phone."

This, in Amy's eyes, was an even bigger problem than the smallness of my house. She marveled over it all the way across Drake's yard. I opened the back door and let us into his kitchen. It was larger than mine and full of implements that hung from the ceiling and bulged from the cabinets.

Amy's mother answered—I could tell by the high-pitched, frantic quacking that came out of the phone when Amy identified herself. She rolled her eyes at me while she tried to get a word in edgewise. "Mom. Mom—I'm okay. Of course not! Mom, listen! I'm at Aunt Liz's." More quacking. "Liz. Yes, in California. I took the bus." She scowled into the phone. "I didn't tell anyone! She says I can stay. So I'm going to." More than a hint of bravado colored her voice. She crossed her arms, cradling the receiver between ear and shoulder, and sullenly examined her chipped nail polish. "I'm going to get a job," she said finally. More eye-rolling. At last she held the phone toward me. "She wants to talk to you."

I wasn't well acquainted with my sister-in-law. She and Andy had gotten married not long before I did, and Amy's birth had followed in six months or so. She had been very shrill about denouncing me, though, perhaps because all the flap over my marrying and quitting school had diverted attention from her "premature" eight-pound baby.

Now her voice on the phone was frosty, as if I'd somehow enticed her daughter away. "You've offered Amy a place to stay for the summer?"

"That's right, Renee." Amy wandered around Drake's kitchen and through the archway into the living room. "She's spent all her money on the bus ticket, and I'm not too flush myself. She's going to get a job, and if she can't, I'll front the money for her to get back home."

"Just what kind of job?" Renee didn't sound overjoyed. "What kind of racket are you running there, Liz?"

My patience began to seep away. "Look, Renee. Your daughter landed herself on me without a word of warning. You can come and get her or send her a plane ticket if you think she's in danger. Believe me, I wouldn't want a child of mine on the streets these days. I live very quietly, and a teenager is not my idea of a fun surprise, not to mention the expense. I don't have a phone, and this call is costing me. If you have anything else to say, be brief. Otherwise, you have my address."

Amy came back into the kitchen in time to hear this. Her eyes rounded.

"Settle your problems with Amy," I said, exasperated. "I'm not *in loco parentis*, and I make no guarantees beyond offering her a clean bed and a sympathetic ear."

Renee was speechless for all of thirty seconds. "Well! Really, Liz, I hardly think after what you did that you can set yourself up as some kind of example for an impressionable sixteen-year-old. What makes you think you can deal with an incorrigible young girl? Andy will have a few things to say about this! You must—"

At that point I gently cradled the phone.

"You hung up on my mother." Amy blinked. "She'll just call right back, you know."

"No, she won't. That's the beauty of not having a phone.

Annoying people can't reach you except by letter, and you can throw those away."

This viewpoint hadn't occurred to Amy before. She was thoughtful until we got back to my house.

"I could really use a shower." She picked up her knapsack and looked at me. "Would that be all right?'

"Certainly." I tried not to think about the hot water heater. It had only started acting up after I'd done what good homeowners are supposed to do and drained it. It seemed to miss all that rusty sedimentary fluid that had lurked in its depths for untold years. Now whenever I used hot water, it fired itself up with an angry roar, and then delivered water that varied from scalding to freezing in seconds. I warned Amy about that, and she went off to clean up.

I turned my computer on, determined to finish editing a rough draft intended for *Organic Gardening*. It was hard to concentrate on the details of seed germination, though. And even harder to think about going back to census duty later on, facing a multitude of Renee-like people without being able to hang up on them.

4 _____

"SO where is she?" Claudia Kaplan shrieked over the din in Bridget's living room.

"Who?" I screamed back.

Walking in the door, I'd been assaulted by the noise and the hunger-inducing smell of something barbecuing. Claudia, an imposing woman in her late fifties, semaphored her arms across the room toward the bank of audio equipment, causing the hibiscus blossoms on her caftan to billow.

"Turn it down!"

Her bellowed request was picked up by several other people in the room, and the scruffy-looking guy who'd commandeered the tape player finally obliged. There were audible gasps of relief.

"Greg's been experimenting with percussion as a background to his readings," one of the women standing nearby explained in the relative silence.

"That wasn't percussion," Claudia said, scowling across the room at Greg, who sheepishly tucked his tape into a pocket. "That was aural torment."

Bridget came bustling out of the kitchen. The crowd of people in there made a lot of noise, but nothing like it had been before. "That's better," she said, setting a stack of paper cups on the top shelf of a bookcase. "I was afraid for everyone's eardrums."

"Where are the kids?" Claudia squinted into the kitchen.

"I got rid of them," Bridget said frankly. "They're too young to worry about with so many people around." She came over and gave me a hug. "I'm glad you could make it, Liz. Paul said you were pretty busy working two jobs."

I offered her the bottle of plum brandy I'd brought, made by my own fair hands with the millions of tiny little plums that had appeared on a tree in my backyard a couple of weeks before. "Don't open this for a while," I warned her. "It needs time to mellow."

"Don't we all." Claudia looked past me and around the room. "Where's your niece? I don't see anyone who matches Paul Drake's rather fabulous description."

"She's not coming." I nipped a cube of cheese off the platter Bridget carried. "I told her she could, though I had my doubts, but she needed something from Walgreen's. I got the impression she really wanted to check out the scene downtown."

Bridget regarded me with worried eyes. She is one of the nicest people I know, and she mothers everyone. Four children ranging from seven years to nine months is enough to make a woman see the world through a haze of dirty fingerprints and skinned knees. "How are you going to cope with this, Liz?"

"Hey, how hard can it be? She seems pretty levelheaded, and she's going to get a job."

Bridget and Claudia exchanged the kind of look that unites those who are or have been parents in superior wisdom to those who haven't.

"Lots could go wrong," Claudia said darkly. She looked into her paper cup. "Just thinking about it makes me thirsty. I need a drink."

"You do, too, Liz." Bridget handed me a cup. "There's sangria in the kitchen."

"Sangria. Very upscale." Claudia raised her thick, impressive eyebrows. "When it's just us writers, you never go to so much trouble."

"I didn't this time," Bridget retorted. "Emery made it. At the last minute he wanted to invite some people, so he fancied up the refreshments. He also made some guacamole."

Claudia began to forge a path through the crowded living room. "I hope he put in enough garlic."

I followed her; I was hungry, and guacamole sounded good. Anything sounded good. After her nap that afternoon, Amy had finished off the crackers, both bananas, most of the bread, and the last of a jar of peanut butter. My cupboard was pretty bare.

The people in the kitchen were a different crowd. Most of them were men, some with ties pulled loose at the neck. They stood in knots, bottles of beer or mineral water clutched in their hands, jabbering as hard as the writers in the living room. One or two of the men had ponytails.

There was a traffic jam around the kitchen table. While Claudia and I waited, I overheard a man murmur, "Any viable multimedia platform needs a satellite DSP or an ASCI to get decent full-motion video."

"No, no," said the exquisitely dressed woman he spoke to. "The P7 has the raw horsepower to do the computations. The only question is what bus architecture you need to get the data flow rate."

Claudia and I looked at each other. She moved majestically through, parting the crowd at its thickest. The huge bowl that held the guacamole was already half empty. I managed to snag a chipful of it. There was plenty of garlic.

Claudia found a paper plate, shoveled a quantity of guacamole onto it, added a handful of chips, and went in search of the sangria. Her space at the table was immediately filled. I was hemmed in by guys, all busily scooping and munching and still managing to talk about C++ and AutoCAD and look-and-feel, which sounded quite risqué to me but evidently had something to do with software.

I must have looked bewildered. The twenty-something man next to me finished his beer and grinned. "So, what's your sine?"

His friend jabbed him in the ribs. "S-i-n-e," he spelled. "Not sign as in Aquarius, but sine as in geometry."

"Either way, I don't know." I smiled feebly. One of them was tall, one was short. Both had shaggy hair and were wearing short-sleeved plaid shirts and chinos. They didn't have pocket protectors holding lots of mechanical pencils in their shirt pockets—nobody actually wears those any more except the self-consciously hip nerdsters—but their pockets somehow looked naked without them.

"Do you work for Emery?" The tall one spoke through a mouthful of chips.

"Sometimes."

The short one said, "Do you write code or what?"

"I'm not in software."

"Are you one of the writers?" The tall one grinned eagerly. "Emery said there'd be writers."

"Do you like movies?" The short one pushed a little in front. "*Forbidden Planet* is at the Stanford."

I cleared my throat, feeling besieged. "I'm working nights—doing the census."

The tall one looked interested. "Online?"

"No, door-to-door."

"You mean, you use a laptop?"

"You enter the data remotely?"

I reached for another chip. "No, I ask questions and use a pencil to record the answers."

"Pencil?" The tall one stared at me.

"That's what's wrong with this country," the short one said passionately. "The government is still using pencils!"

"Say, there are lots of women in there," the tall one said, looking over the heads of the crowd toward the living room.

"Young ones?" The short one's voice was plaintive. They inched away from the table and disappeared.

I felt I deserved more guacamole, but the bowl was nearly empty. I stretched my arm to reach the bottom of it, and collided with someone else on the same errand. The man was trying to juggle his beer and a plate of chips. Most of the beer and half the chips ended on me.

"Oh, gosh, I'm sorry." He was nice looking, early forties, tall and lean, with blond hair falling over his forehead and blue eyes that were slightly shy. "So embarrassing."

"I didn't look where I was reaching." I brushed at the chips, and he dabbed my wet arm with a napkin.

"How can I make it up to you? Gosh, there isn't even any more guacamole to offer you." He craned over and peered into the bowl. It was nice to be tall—I often wish I were.

"That's okay. It wasn't really your fault." At least the beer hadn't gone on my wretched skirt. I was planning to gratify Drake by leaving the party early enough to get a couple of hours of the long evening twilight for my census work.

Thinking about Drake, I glanced around the room and spotted him by the back door, talking to a swarthy fellow in a loud Hawaiian shirt. The door was open, letting in the aroma of roasting meat. I rarely eat meat, but for economic reasons, not moral ones. My mouth watered.

"Listen, can I get you a drink?" The man in front of me hovered, still looking abashed. "There's beer somewhere, or I think I saw some wine—"

"Ed! Congratulations!" Emery came up and slapped the man on the shoulder in that painfully hearty way men have. "Heard about the new product."

"Thanks, Emery." Ed's face creased into a pleased smile. "We're pretty excited."

Emery turned to me. "I was hoping you'd come, Liz. This is your current employer." He flourished his hand, presenting me grandly. "Liz Sullivan, Ed Garfield, CEO of SoftWrite. Ed's got a hot new software product coming out. When is it, next week?"

"Officially, Monday." Ed held a finger to his lips. "But actually we're doing a bunch of stuff in the next couple of days to hype interest. Hard for a small company to get any ink without a major effort."

"I dunno." Emery laughed. "From what I heard, MicroMax has given you a little free publicity."

Ed's face clouded. "None of what you read is true," he protested. "I don't know where they got hold of a story like that. Our code's developed entirely in-house. It's completely original."

"Of course," Emery said soothingly. "It's just hot air from them. Every time us little guys turn around, some mega-company claims we stole from them. Shoe's on the other foot, mostly."

"Right." Ed sipped at his beer and realized it was empty. He turned another apologetic look on me. "I've poured my beer all over your guest. Liz, did you say? So you're doing some temp work for us."

"Here you go, Liz." Emery reached into a nearby drawer. "Here's a towel."

"Thanks." I blotted the beer off my arm.

Ed hovered a little. "Now you won't want to come back to SoftWrite, I guess. What do we have you doing?"

"Data entry. This morning I did spreadsheets and mailing labels."

"Fascinating." Emery wrinkled his nose. "Liz is a multi-talented person, Ed. She writes, gardens—and she's even doing the census too."

"Really?" Ed looked a little doubtful.

"I'm just temping mornings," I hastened to explain. "Your office manager said that was fine for now."

"I would never interfere in Angel's arrangements. She keeps everything running so well." Ed gave me that nice grin again. "So what are you doing for the census? I thought that was years ago."

"They miscounted." I shrugged. "Now they're counting again."

"Typical government." Emery shook his head. "If it wasn't for putting some welcome income into Liz's pocket, I'd really feel it was a waste of taxpayers' dollars."

Drake came in the back door, heading for Emery. "The chicken wings are done," he said, tenderly holding a small plate of them. "You'd better get them off the fire, Emery." He handed me the plate. "Thought you might like some."

"Thanks." I took the plate from Drake, while Ed drifted after Emery to the back door. The chicken wings were hot, almost too hot to eat, and coated with spices. "They're great."

He took one, too. "I plan to eat as many of these as I can and not bother with dinner," he announced. "Too bad your niece didn't come. Then you wouldn't have to bother either."

"How do you know she didn't come?"

"Trained eye, my dear." He plucked a bottle of mineral water from a cooler behind the kitchen door that I hadn't even seen. "Here."

"Thanks." I sampled the mineral water. "You're taking such good care of me. Why?"

"Do I need a reason?" He gave me a one-armed hug. "I'm just keeping you away from the sangria, so you don't get tipsy before you go out and mingle with the weirdos."

I took a swig of the mineral water and promptly got the hiccups. "Drake," I hicced, "you mingle with weirdos every day."

"Don't be so hard on yourself." He pounded me on the back. "I don't think of you that way at all."

I choked. "You—"

"Oh, you mean in my job." He was smiling, but it faded. "Just take care of yourself, Liz. There's a lot of madness out there. I'd hate to be taking a professional interest in you."

"It's not even going to be dark for two more hours." I cleared my throat and wiped my greasy fingers on a napkin. "Actually, I was just leaving."

"Liz—"

"See you, Drake." I shoved the plate back into his hands, then reached for the last chicken wing. "For the road," I mumbled, heading back through the living room.

I waved good-bye to Claudia and Bridget, and went to mount my rusty steed and earn.

5 _____

THE Venus's-flytrap looked a little wilted. Its tightly clenched spikes reminded me of Amy's haircut. I firmed the dirt in the small pot and give it some water from the plastic watering can that sat on Wanda Sorenski's porch wall, glancing around to make sure no one was watching. I hate feeling responsible when houseplants die. It's like not taking care of pets. I put the Venus's-flytrap in the shade; even the late evening sun was hot for a plant in shock.

Nobody answered when I knocked on Wanda's door. It was a relief. After trying twice, I could write it off. As a formality, I checked the mailbox to see if the name agreed with my register. With that information, I could call Wanda Sorenski. But if I never spoke to her again, it would be fine by me. I was starting not to care whether my work was satisfactory, as long as I was paid for doing it.

With that numb-brain attitude, I plodded up the outside stairs to apartment 3. The low sun behind me threw my shadow up the stairs, long and thin. I thought wistfully that it would be nice to be long and thin.

Someone was home in apartment 3. A man answered the door, spatula in hand, and listened impatiently while I introduced myself. "Can this wait?" He glanced back at the kitchen. A smell of frying onions drifted past my nose, reminding me that the chicken wings had been small and not very filling.

"I could come back in half an hour or so, after I've done a couple of the other apartments." I was trying to be flexible and accommodating, like we'd been told to be in training.

"Fine. Fine." He shut the door, then I heard him throw the deadbolt. Maybe he thought I was a threat to more than his privacy.

Apartment 4 still didn't answer; the drapes at the window next to the door were coming off their hooks, and the late afternoon sun illuminated a narrow slice of the living room. I peered through the window, shading the glass with my hand. It was empty, with rectangles on the walls where pictures had hung, and some good-sized stains on the dull beige carpet. I marked it vacant on the register and moved on to apartment 5.

This time I hit the jackpot. The man who answered the door invited me in, offered me a drink, went through the long form with no problem, and even told me that Wanda was divorced with a child, lived in a two-bedroom apartment and drove an '86 Honda Civic, which allowed me to fill out basic information on her. Curtis—after about ten minutes he'd asked me to call him that—was semiretired on disability. He seemed to know all about his neighbors.

"I'd rather ask you about these people than talk to them—Wanda particularly." I was only half kidding. If gossip was the only way to move on through the register, I was ready to gossip.

"I just wish for your sake they were more interesting," he said, laughing. "Wanda is only amusing when she's angry, although that's often. Bill Aronson"—the man with the spatula—"is frightened of me—thinks I'll make a pass at him, as if he was that attractive."

Curtis laughed again. He was middle-aged, medium height, skinny and graceful, punctuating his words with expressive gestures. His conversation had the pent-up air of someone who doesn't get much opportunity to talk. He told me he'd been at a back rehabilitation class that morning. His apartment was very pale, very spare, with two comfortable chairs in the living room, a wall system of expensive-looking components beside the door, and a series of huge, startling canvases on the neutral walls.

"So all the apartments are two-bedroom?" I remembered that Jenifer downstairs had said she had two bedrooms.

Curtis nodded. "All the same—two bedrooms, one bath, impossible kitchen, not enough closets. But the price is right. It's even better if you have a roommate, like Jenifer. But I can't live with anyone else."

"Is Jenifer's roommate female?" I caught myself. "Never mind. I'm gong down there after I finish Bill Aronson."

"Jenifer's a cute little thing," Curtis said fondly. "But so young. Still expects the best of everyone. Her roommate is different—into one of those strange religions, and even less fun than she used to be. I hope she doesn't really convert Jenifer." He got up when I stood. "We chat at the mailbox sometimes," he confided, his loneliness more apparent. "Nice girls, really, both of them. Catch Wanda chitchatting, or even letting her little boy talk. I invited him to play catch one day, and you'd have thought I had 'Man-Boy Love' tattooed on my forehead. Honestly!"

I got away at last, wishing I had met Curtis under other circumstances. He would make a good friend. I went back across the upstairs walkway and knocked on Bill Aronson's door. There was no answer. I could still smell the onions, but the man with the spatula was lying low. I knocked a third time. A curtain twitched in the living room. Still no answer.

When I turned away, Curtis was standing in his doorway. "What did I tell you," he crowed. "He's holed up in there, but he won't come out. Well, what do you need to know? I'll tell you about Bill, and what I don't know, I'll make up." He raised his voice on the last few words. The curtain twitched again.

"Thank you, Mr. Hall." I raised my voice a little, too. "We are supposed to ask the neighbors for information if people won't speak to us."

Bill Aronson's door banged open. "You don't speak for me, pansy."

"Speak for yourself then, Bill." Curtis winked at me and went into his own apartment, shutting the door.

"Why are you doing this?" Bill Aronson scowled at me. "I value my privacy. I don't want the government poking its nose into my personal business."

I had been trained to answer this with exquisite courtesy and a whole page full of statistics, boring the listener into acquiescence. Tactful courtesy is not my strong suit.

"If you think the government doesn't already know a lot about you, Mr. Aronson, you've got another think coming." I waved my register at him. "Your name and address are here already. The IRS knows how much money you make and where you make it. Would you like the Census Bureau to have to activate that file? The FBI probably knows if you make trouble, and Social Security and Medicare know about your health. State and local agencies have their hands out to the federal government, and the government is going to look at the census data before putting any money in those hands. Do you want more potholes because your illusory privacy is so important? Do you want fewer schoolbooks, less mass transit, longer waits in the emergency room? Fine. You've got it. If you'll excuse me, I'll go on to someone who wants to be counted."

I stomped down the stairs before Bill Aronson could do more than sputter. The trouble was, I didn't really believe what I had said. I also don't want the government to know too much about me. I don't want to be in anybody's database.

Jenifer Paston's apartment was silent, except for the puppy; I could hear it whining inside. There was no response to my knock; either both of the women were out, or else they were also refusing to answer the door. After the shouting match with Bill Aronson, everyone in the building must have known the census taker was here.

I knocked harder. The door, improperly latched, swung open a little way. The puppy's desperate clawing opened it further, and he bounced out and jumped up on me, licking at my knees, whining and writhing in a frenzy of welcome.

"Jenifer? Miss Paston?" I pushed the door open wider, but didn't enter. We were not allowed into people's homes unless specifically invited. The puppy's invitation didn't count. "Your dog's out." The puppy had run into the parking lot, then back to paw at my knees again. "You'd better come and get it."

No response. The puppy finally squatted right beside the door and let go, with an expression of mingled shame and relief.

I picked him up when he started to dash away. The wiggly body was hard to hold onto. His fur was soft and silky. After a moment he licked my face.

I tucked him under my arm and stood in the doorway. "Miss Paston?" The drapes were drawn, making it gloomy inside, not like Curtis's light, glowing room above. There was a sofa with its back to the door, facing a wall unit that held a TV and stereo equipment. The carpet was a muddy green shag. The puppy slipped out of my grasp and ran behind the sofa, and then out again, barking aggressively at me.

Hesitating, I stood in the doorway. "Miss Paston?" A car pulled into the parking area behind me, and I turned, hoping it was Jenifer or her roommate.

A woman got out—tall and nicely dressed, with shoulder-length blond hair and a tight, controlled face. It was Clarice, from SoftWrite. Of course, it made sense that she was Jenifer's roommate. The motherly way she'd pressed the aspirin on the younger woman came back to me.

Clarice strode over, clutching her keys defensively. "Can I help you?" Her voice made it clear that the only thing she wanted to help me with was leaving as soon as possible.

"Hello, Clarice." I held out my hand. She didn't take it, maintaining her grip on the keys.

"Do I know you?"

"I was at SoftWrite this morning, doing temp work."

"Oh." She peered past me at the open door. "What are you doing here?"

"I'm also a temporary census taker," I said. "Jenifer was here this afternoon when I started this section of the register. She didn't feel well, so I came back this evening to talk to you."

The puppy bounded out of the door and jumped at her.

"Down, Barker." She pushed him impatiently. "Where's Jenifer? Why is this dog out?"

I shrugged helplessly. "It was like this when I knocked. The puppy came barreling out and I tried to put him back. I didn't go in."

Clarice pushed the door all the way open and stepped inside. "Jenifer?"

"Look, the questions only take a few minutes." I moved a little closer, hoping she wouldn't shut the door in my face. "I already got most of the information from Miss Paston."

"Jenifer?" Clarice Jensen flicked on the light. "Jenifer? Are you—" Her voice ended in a strangled gulp. She leaned on both hands, propped on the sofa back. I couldn't see what she was looking at. The puppy was growling softly; it pranced around the sofa corner, carrying something in its mouth. A well-chewed terry scuff, the kind Jenifer had been wearing earlier.

"Oh, my God." Clarice's voice wavered and broke. "Oh, my God. She's dead."

6

CLARICE sobbed with abandon, draped over the sofa back. I hesitated, on the brink of just fading away, and then went around the sofa, wondering if Jenifer was really dead. She was flat on her back between the sofa and the entertainment center, as if she were just having an impromptu snooze. Her clammy arm seemed to point reproachfully at me. I noticed how peaceful she looked, still wearing the old bathrobe I'd seen her in earlier. The puppy pranced beside her, shaking her gnawed-up slipper and growling ferociously.

A brown plastic prescription medicine bottle lay on the floor next to Jenifer's flaccid hand. It appeared to be empty.

I knelt and put two fingers on that thin, pale wrist. It was cool to touch; I couldn't detect a pulse. I couldn't think well enough at the moment to calculate how long it would take to die from an overdose of prescription pills. The pill label faced the shag carpet; I didn't turn it over.

"Stop touching her!" Clarice came flying around the sofa as I stood. She pushed me and I teetered, afraid to fall over onto Jenifer.

"I've stopped, okay? I just wanted to see if there was a pulse."

"She's dead," Clarice repeated tonelessly, her eyes wide with the horror of it. "Can't you see? She's dead. Get away from her. Get away!" She wheeled and grabbed for her purse. I was thankful she'd dropped her keys; she might have raked my face with them. I tried to edge past her, but she was blocking the space at the end of the sofa.

"Excuse me," I said while Clarice rooted frantically in her purse. "I could call the police for you."

Clarice turned back, a can of Mace in her hand. "Don't move. Don't even think of—"

I ducked, putting my clunky black census briefcase up to guard my face. "Look, I got here just before you did. She's been dead for a while—she's cold."

"Cold. Cold and dead." Clarice dropped the Mace after one short blast. She sank onto the couch, crying gustily.

I looked around for the phone, my eyes burning from random Mace droplets, and called 911. I tried not to touch anything, from some befuddled idea that it would be bad. I went back into the living room and stood there, uncertain what to do. I wanted to split. Getting mixed up with dead people leads to trouble, in my experience. But there was a live woman there, too, and she was obviously incapable of handling things.

She was holding that cold, limp hand in hers now, and batting at the puppy, who tugged playfully at the sash of Jenifer's robe. I cleared my throat, and she rounded on me.

"What do you want? Can't you see—"

"I called the ambulance." I didn't intend to stay around if the only use I had was to be yelled at. "I'm very sorry."

She swallowed. "Thanks, I guess." The puppy climbed on her, and she thrust him off angrily. "Get away, Barker. You're impossible."

"He's a cute little fellow." I snapped my fingers, and Barker gamboled over to me, tongue lolling out.

"Jenifer's." Clarice teared up again. "She wanted him— said she'd take care of him. Now what will I do? Why did she do it? Why did she . . ." She was sobbing again.

"Look, I suppose it *is* suicide." As soon as the words were out of my mouth I wished I could call them back.

Clarice's thoughts weren't running on the same track as mine. "Accident, you mean? Maybe. I didn't even know she took medication." She reached for the pill bottle.

"Better leave everything just as it is." There was a sound of sirens in the distance.

"What? Oh, yes, I suppose so." She looked vaguely around. "Is that the ambulance?" She made a horrible sound. After a moment I realized it was a giggle. "What good is the ambulance? All Jenifer needs is a hearse."

The sirens came closer. I felt worse and worse about being there for the discovery of a fresh dead body, being questioned, having the events of the previous fall raked up again. Several murders had been committed then in the name of greed, and though I'd been the one to benefit, I'd lost a couple of people who were important to me. This scene was bringing it all back too freshly.

"Look," I said. "I'll show them where to come. And then I'll take off. You don't need strangers around."

She just nodded, still clutching Jenifer's hand. The puppy pawed at her skirt, and she angrily knocked him away. "Stop it, Barker."

He yelped a little. "I'll take care of the dog for a few days, if you want." The words were out of my mouth before I knew I was going to say them.

"Fine." She pushed him toward me. "It gives me the creeps, the way he licks her like that. And he'll howl all night."

I picked up the wiggly little body. The sirens were deafening now. Clutching Barker and my black briefcase, I went out into the parking lot to direct the paramedics.

The sirens had brought people out of their apartments. I waved my briefcase, and the paramedics charged past me. Curtis leaned over the railing of the upstairs walkway. "What's happened?" He had to shout over the noise.

"It's Jenifer. Clarice probably could use your help."

He bounded down the stairs. "Is Jenifer hurt? Why do you have Barker?"

I didn't want to be the one to tell the bad news. "Clarice can't take care of Barker right now. Do you want him?"

Curtis reached to pat the puppy, who growled at him. He backed away. "Heavens, no. I'm a cat person, anyway. They can tell, I guess. Take him, by all means, if Clarice doesn't want him. Do you think I should go in?"

47

"Maybe just be ready to help."

"But what happened?" He craned to look through the doorway, where paramedics were seething around.

"Overdose, it looks like."

"Oh, poor Jenifer. Poor Clarice." Curtis seemed genuinely distressed. "Now, why would she do such a thing? I'll see if Clarice needs anything." He disappeared into the apartment.

I wanted to disappear, too. Bill Aronson's curtains were drawn all the way open; I could see him standing back from the window, a dark, eager shape. The doors and windows of the apartment building across the courtyard were also full of gawkers.

Awkwardly clutching puppy and briefcase, I walked through the courtyard and onto the sidewalk. My bus was parked half a block away. I didn't know if the police were called about a suicide attempt. But if they were, I wanted to be long gone when they arrived.

I pulled away from the curb just in time. A squad car cruised up the street, lights flashing but no siren. I drove on, threading the residential streets that led to El Camino Real. Just as I turned onto El Camino, a battered Saab turned off. I pretended I didn't notice, but Drake would have seen me. He saw everything when he was really looking, and in cases of suspicious death, he really looked. I was lucky he didn't pull me over right away. But he knew where to find me later.

At least this time I wasn't a suspect. Jenifer had committed suicide, and although people might go to any lengths to avoid the census, I didn't think I had anything to do with her death.

If it was something more sinister than suicide, any suspects would have to be found closer to the crime. Clarice could perhaps provide motivation for Jenifer's actions. I pictured her in the hot seat, being grilled by the detectives. Better her than me.

But Drake, I remembered, had a kind of weakness for the females he questioned. Luckily this was suicide, not murder. Clarice wouldn't really need to arouse his chivalrous instincts. I found myself being glad of that.

The bus made that funny noise again while I drove down El Camino. This time I ignored it.

7 _____

"**WHAT** a darling puppy!" Amy picked Barker up when he bounced at her and hugged him; it was hard to say which one was more delighted. I thought about food and vet bills and how big his feet looked at the end of his cute little legs. He smiled at Amy with his engaging doggy grin; she laughed when he licked her face. "Where did you get him? I thought you were doing census stuff."

"I'm keeping him for someone for a while." I glanced over my shoulder and wondered if I could swing a temporary fence of some kind between my house and Drake's, where the hedge we perpetually planned was to go. "We'll have to watch him carefully when he goes out. There's some clothesline on the back porch to make a leash."

Amy buried her face in his soft fur. "Are you a stray, too, Barker? You've come to stay with Aunt Liz?" She was right. I was running a flophouse for the alienated and unwanted—including myself. Another set of responsibilities, for someone who'd spent the past few years ducking them. I half expected to look up the driveway and see a procession of laid-off victims of the moribund California economy coming to camp under my plum trees.

But so far it was only Amy, who ran dizzily beneath the branches in the golden twilight, with Barker chasing and leaping around her. The sight, for some reason, gave me great pleasure. Their noisy game of tag seemed necessary, the sort of amenity every house should have.

I didn't quite know how to tell Amy about what had happened that evening. I kept seeing Jenifer Paston as she had been earlier, yawning while she leaned against the door. Perhaps she had taken the overdose before I spoke to her. But in that case, why had she made an appointment for seven? Her death, the manner and unexpectedness of it, depressed and alarmed me. I just couldn't talk about it.

Instead, when Amy collapsed on the grass in front of me, breathless and smiling, I asked about her trip to Walgreen's. It was only eight by the old schoolhouse clock, though it seemed way past my bedtime. After years of going to bed near sunset, I don't often stay up late. The morning is my power time.

Amy bubbled over with the coolness of the scene in downtown Palo Alto. She'd already met some really nice kids. One of them had a lead on a job in a deli she might be able to get, and that would be cool because it was in walking distance—"I don't want you to have to drive me, Aunt Liz," she assured me, wide-eyed.

I had no intention of driving her. We are given legs to keep us from being a burden on the transportation system. When I imparted this bit of wisdom (Rule Number 27), Amy grew thoughtful.

"Dad wouldn't let me drive, after two teeny little accidents," she confided. "I didn't think it was fair." She stroked Barker, who'd settled down for a snooze in her lap. "He told me to walk if I wanted to get anywhere. So I did—right to the bus station." She giggled.

"So your dad isn't always wrong." I wasn't going to bite on this kind of blackmail. "The VW bus is only driven by me, Amy. It's cranky, and might decide not to start again after you drove it somewhere. If you don't want to walk or take the county transit bus, you could get a bike. One of the rules about staying here is that I don't have to worry about you."

"You won't," she promised, lifting Barker and kissing him on his black and pink nose. She got to her feet and stretched. I envied that careless ease and limberness—I have to struggle with yoga and swimming just to keep it all

51

from racing downhill instead of sliding gently. "One of the guys I met tonight has a car."

She didn't wait for me to absorb this before delivering the punch line. "He's picking me up tomorrow to show me the ocean."

With great difficulty I bit my tongue. The girl was sixteen, for heaven's sake. Either she had some sense, or she didn't. Either way, I couldn't chain her to my ankle all day. "Just the two of you?" I had to say it—I couldn't stop myself.

"No, a whole bunch," she said carelessly. "Don't worry. We won't drink, do drugs, or fuck in the sand."

I blinked.

"That's what you were going to warn me about, isn't it?" She grinned at me. "That's what my mom and dad would have said, anyway."

"Not in those exact words, I suspect."

"Maybe not. Are you shocked?" She sounded hopeful.

"I've been in shock since this afternoon," I said truthfully. She didn't know the half of it. "Amy, about sex—"

"Listen, Aunt Liz, I'm not going to have sex." She stared at me earnestly. "Like I said, I did it once. It was gross. And two of my girlfriends had terrible problems—one got pregnant and had an abortion and felt really bad about it, and the other one got chlamydia and had to take these awful drugs. Sex is just more trouble than it's worth," she said with a worldly air. "But when I tried to tell my mom that, she freaked. She wanted to send me to the priest for counseling, but another one of my friends had been hit on by a priest, so I said I wouldn't go, and that made big trouble, too." She heaved a sigh. "They just wouldn't listen."

"I'm listening." I was, too, fascinated by this glimpse of a girlhood so much different from mine. "Amy, if you feel like you're in trouble, I'll come and get you. Just call—" I stopped short.

"You don't have a phone, though." Amy shook her head. "I mean, on the one hand, you're right. Nobody can call you up and yell at you, like my parents or anything. But what about emergencies? It's, like, a dilemma, huh?"

"Right," I said hollowly. A dilemma that hadn't really existed before today. Drake let me give his number to the temp agencies and editors; they left messages that eventually got to me. I'd lost some temp jobs over that, which contributed to Mrs. Rainey's lack of enthusiasm for me.

It was getting dark, and the mosquitoes had found us. I followed Amy into the house. She looked tired in the bright glow of the living room light.

"Can I go to bed?" She yawned hugely and for a moment my throat caught, remembering Jenifer. "I'm really beat. And Randy is coming early tomorrow—they want to catch the surf at high tide, or something. I wasn't really listening. They have jobs in the afternoon—Randy and Eric."

"What other girls are going?" I took the cushions off the couch and yanked the bed part out of its coffin. The mattress had a lumpy look. The sheets were very old, very soft cotton, part of my inheritance from Vivien Greely, the dear lady who had left me her house and contents the year before. Amy lent a hand spreading them while she told me about the kids she'd met on the corner of University and Waverley downtown.

"Elise has a job at this deli downtown, and she's the one who said they might have an opening. And Kimberly is doing summer school, but she has tomorrow off for some reason. We're planning to be back by one or so, when the guys have to clean up for their jobs at the mall. There's a terrific mall, Kimberly said, right over there." She pointed in the direction of the Stanford Shopping Center. "That's a good place to work because you get discounts on really great stuff. But those stores don't want you to have nose rings or anything, so Elise didn't apply there."

Nose rings. "They sound like nice kids," I said faintly, digging an old quilt out of the cedar chest against the wall.

"You can meet them tomorrow morning," Amy promised blithely. "I told them we could have breakfast here." She caught my eye and giggled. "They're going to bring some

53

bagels or something. Honestly, Aunt Liz, you look just like Daddy when you have that expression on your face."

"Thanks for the compliment." I tossed her a pillow from my bed. "Have you given up on your stock exchange idea?"

"Not exactly given up," Amy said, holding the pillow under her chin while she put on a clean pillow slip. Watching her, I had a vivid flash of myself as a girl, gripping the pillow beneath my chin, both hands free to open the pillow slip and pull it halfway up, then raising my chin to free the pillow for a brisk shake the rest of the way into the case. My mother would be flapping the sheets, wearing the calm expression of one who knows exactly what her job is and how to do it. That certainty had driven me wild with rebellion, but now I understood how she could barter freedom for a narrow security.

Amy put the pillow on the Hide-A-Bed and I pulled myself out of the past. "I'm going to do some research on investment houses at the library tomorrow," she said, looking like the farthest thing from a button-down stockbroker that I could imagine. "There's a library downtown, Elise said."

I spread one more blanket on top of the bed; nights are cold even in June. "That sounds like a good idea."

She picked up her big leather bag and pulled out an immense T-shirt. "Can I take another shower? I still feel, like, positively groady."

"Sure." I looked at the Hide-A-Bed, taking up all the space in my small living room. "There's not a lot of hot water, though. The heater doesn't work too well, and I haven't saved enough for a new one yet."

"Okay," she said. "It'll be like camping."

I spread my census paperwork on the kitchen table, but I couldn't get down to it. The interruption I'd been expecting came while the water was running.

Drake knocked with his usual impatient rat-a-tat, and didn't bother waiting for me to open the door. He came in, holding a big paper bag.

"I can't believe after all that happened last year that

you'd leave the scene of a crime," he said, shoving the paper bag into my arms. Drake had been the investigating officer the previous fall, in my brush with contrived death. That's how we'd met—how he'd been on the scene to snap up a bargain when I decided to sell one of the houses Vivien had left me.

I was glad Amy was in the shower. "I didn't know there'd been a crime." Inside the paper bag was dog food, a leash, and some food bowls. "Looked like suicide to me. How did you know I was there?"

Drake shrugged impatiently. "Suicide is a crime in some states, for your information. Any dead person you discover, you're supposed to wait until the police get there. I saw you driving away, and when Miss Jensen said there'd been a sinister census taker on the doorstep when she got there, I managed to add two and two."

"I waited for the ambulance. Clarice more or less told me to leave." I took the bag to the kitchen and Drake trailed behind.

Barker rose from a brief nap and attached himself to Drake's pant leg, growling ferociously, the hair standing up on the back of his neck.

"And you removed evidence." Drake shook Barker off his leg and picked him up by the scruff, which instantly cowed him. "This dog."

"According to Clarice, he was a nuisance. I did her a favor." I filled the water bowl, and Barker immediately came to drink from it as if he were dying of thirst. "It's not like I want a puppy planted on me." I crossed my arms and returned Drake's glare with interest. "Why are you involved, anyway?"

"Suspicious death." He sat at the kitchen table, uninvited, and looked expectantly at the teakettle on the stove. I filled it with water and turned on the gas, getting out the box of ginseng tea like he likes. "I hate that kind of thing," he grumbled, waiting for the water to boil. "Everything messed up and no clear indications of what happened." He shot me a look from behind his wire-rims. "Miss Jensen said you were the first person on the scene."

"I was after her into the apartment." I gave him a brief description of how Clarice and I converged on the door. "I didn't touch anything," I concluded. "I felt her wrist and didn't find a pulse. There was an open, empty-looking prescription bottle by her hand."

"Prescription bottle?" His gaze sharpened. "I'll have to speak to Miss Jensen again."

"Did you find a note? I assumed there was always a note."

"Not always." He didn't answer further, and I didn't press him. Drake is good at getting information without giving it.

"You haven't heard the weirdest part." I said reluctantly. I'm paranoid about the police, I admit, which makes me very ambivalent about having a cop live practically on my doorstep. Nevertheless, I'd learned that the best way to deal with the police is to tell them everything, and let them sort out the important from the dreck. "The strangest thing is I met them both this morning. Jenifer and Clarice. I temped at SoftWrite, and they both work there. Worked," I corrected, thinking of Jenifer.

Drake stared at me. The sound of the shower stopped, and the sweet scent of shampoo drifted into the room. "Well. Let me get this straight. You did temp work this morning at a company, and some of those workers then showed up on your census register? And this evening, one of them is dead?"

"It's a populous area," I said defensively. "I was doing mailing labels, and I noticed a lot of SoftWrite's people live in Palo Alto. I might even have more of them on my register. People tend to ask their friends and coworkers about apartments when they need one, and that creates a cluster effect." I made that up on the spur of the moment, but it sounded authentic, and Drake nodded.

"Take you and me, for instance," he said, giving me a look that blended irony and speculation nicely.

"Right." I poured hot water into the cups on the stove. He thanked me absently when I served him, and dunked the tea bag up and down, frowning into the cup.

"So do you suspect me?" The words burst out from the nameless emotions that roiled inside of me. I saw Jenifer's pale face, and Clarice's tear-streaked one. I remembered Ed Garfield at Bridget's party, and the rumors that he was romantically involved with Jenifer. He'd be devastated, if so. And the other woman, Suzanne, whom I hadn't met yet—how would she take her rival's death?

"Suspect you of what? Posing as a census agent to make the poor girl take an overdose? Don't be ridiculous. Coincidences do happen, and that's all you are, the victim of coincidence." He lifted the tea bag out of his cup and plunked it into a saucer. "At least your being on the scene gives me a reliable account of what happened. Miss Jensen was incoherent." He looked up, curious. "Was she like that this morning? What were your impressions of them?"

I thought back, and described the scene at the table—Clarice's motherly behavior, including the two aspirin she'd given Jenifer; Jenifer's tense, stressed-out air. I repeated what Mindy had said about Jenifer's being given a lot of responsibility for someone so young. Drake made a few notes on the jumble of papers he shoves into any convenient pocket. They were more for show than anything else—he remembers like an elephant.

The sound of Amy's humming came faintly from the bedroom, and he swiveled in his chair to look at the Hide-A-Bed occupying major space in the living room.

"So your niece is staying for a while."

"Uh-huh."

"That's nice for you." He raised his eyebrows. "Isn't it?"

My turn for diplomatic silence. Barker gave up untying my shoes and went to sniff at the Hide-A-Bed. It was just too high for him to crawl up into. He began to trot around the living room, sniffing and whining.

"Clarice is going to call my number to let you know

what she decides about the puppy," Drake said, watching Barker. "Guess it'll go to the Humane Society."

Barker wasn't listening to this callous disposal of his future. He was too involved in puddling on the floor right in front of the door. I grabbed him and rushed him outside, and Drake followed.

"Great," I muttered. "Wonderful beginning to house-training."

"Let's see." Drake thumbed through his papers. "You met them both this morning. This evening you were there when Jenifer was found dead. Anything else I need to know about?"

I shook my head. "I told you I saw Jenifer before I came home at lunchtime, didn't I?"

"No, you didn't." Drake sat down on the rickety bench I keep by my front door so I can look at the roses. I finished wiping up the puddle and sat on the step to talk, watching Barker sniff his way around the tiny lawn. In the dark, his black and white spots blended in, making him a moving shadow.

I knew what Drake wanted—not just the actions, or even the words, but all the sounds and smells and impressions I'd gotten while talking to Jenifer and her neighbors that day. I obliged as fully as I could.

"You thought there was someone with her," he said when I was done.

"A person, or the radio, or some TV show she couldn't bear to miss." I snapped my fingers, and Barker came back from the driveway. "Your guess is as good as mine."

"And when you were upstairs, you heard footsteps going away. Could they have been from her apartment?"

"Look, Drake, they might have been. I just couldn't swear to any of this."

"I know." He was silent a moment. "I also know you observe very well. We're left with some unanswered questions for a suicide." He took off his glasses and rubbed his eyes. They looked naked and defenseless without those light-catching lenses blocking them. "She had a brother—that seems to be the only family. He lives in the city somewhere—Clarice give me his phone number, which was all she had. She said that he would be totally broken up. But he's not home. She offered to notify him about his sister's death—that takes guts."

"She looked as if she could be capable," I murmured, remembering the Mace. My eyes still smarted.

Drake is not my boyfriend, although certain of our mutual friends would like him to be. I've been man-shy for a while, and he's still getting over a previous relationship. We're friends; at times I've thought that our friendship might grow warmer. But I admit that something about the way he spoke of Clarice Jensen gave me a pang of heartburn. I can't compete for a man; I have no womanly little wiles. And like Amy, I'm still feeling that sex is gross.

"So you don't see her as a suspect."

He put his glasses back on. "There are no suspects in a suicide. And if it's not, then everyone's a suspect."

"Including me?"

"You're a witness. That's different." He shook his finger at me. "Just don't go sleuthing around. Even though it's suicide, people have things to hide. It's up to the police to uncover them, not a nosy civilian."

"The Census Bureau is paying me to be nosy." I picked up Barker and got to my feet. "My interest, like yours, is purely professional."

Drake put his hand on my shoulder, looking directly at me. "Be careful, Liz. Women shouldn't be going house to house, especially in the evenings. Bad things can happen."

"I'm just going to finish my register before I quit. People are too rude to census takers. Some jobs just don't pay enough for the aggravation."

"Why don't you find some nice office job?"

"Why don't you?" The words were out before I could withdraw them. "Looking into violent deaths isn't the safest thing in the world, you know."

"I know." He got up, rumpling his already wild hair.

8

AMY'S friends arrived before she was up in the morning. I had taken Barker out, just as I had in the night when he woke me up whining at my bedside. I had fed him, walked him briefly in the yard, and been at my desk for half an hour, hoping Amy would wake and take herself off so I could stop feeling like an interloper in my own living room.

She slept as innocents do, tucked primly into bed. I had looked twice to make sure it was the same girl. Her skin, washed clean of the white and black makeup, was incredibly fresh and dewy. Even the few blemishes couldn't really mar it. Covering that complexion with thick makeup should have been a crime.

The knock on the door accomplished what all my keyboarding and throat-clearing couldn't. Amy sprang out of the Hide-A-Bed, shrieked, "Ohmigod, they're here already!" and rushed into the bathroom.

I opened the door, with Barker, living up to his name, around my ankles. Eric and Randy were big, strapping fellows, I guessed around eighteen, one carrying a bulging bag of bagels, both smiling sunnily at me. "Good morning," they chorused.

Elise and Kimberly, behind them, had already put their faces on for the outing—exaggerated eye makeup, with lots of red on the lids so they looked like they hadn't slept in weeks. Elise's hair was dead black, but at least she'd left the white off her face. Kimberly's hair was an improbable cerise.

Amy emerged from the bathroom, wearing torn cutoffs and a skimpy T-shirt. Eric's and Randy's eyes lingered for one awed moment on the amount of bosom exposed, before politely retreating. I didn't blame them. She, too, had left off the dead white in favor of the sunblock she applied with a lavish hand. The bright feathers of her hair were spikily arranged.

She greeted her friends graciously. I had put a bowl of oranges on the table—there was an orange tree in Drake's backyard from which I could help myself. These were the last of the season's fruit, pithy and not too great, but the kids wolfed them down, along with the bagels and cream cheese they'd brought. I would have to get groceries. No, I thought, *we* would have to get groceries. If Amy was going to eat it, she was going to see it paid for.

The noise they made was considerable, and yet they weren't talking especially loudly. In fact, I got the idea they were trying to be subdued, although not succeeding.

"Amy told us your neighbor in front is a cop," Eric explained after shushing a burst of laughter from Elise. "We don't want to get you in trouble or anything."

"That's thoughtful." I peeled an orange myself. The young people looked very comfortable, eating and drinking around the table, but I wanted them to leave. I needed to get some of my own work done before heading off to SoftWrite for the morning. If Clarice's account of last night's trouble hadn't made them decide they didn't want me.

So I cleared my throat once more. "Where are you all going today?"

Eric was polite enough not to acknowledge this hint. "We're just going over to Davenport," he said, managing to chew and talk at the same time. "The waves aren't so great this time of year anyway, so we're just going to check it out, really."

Randy nodded. "Brought the boogie boards along for the girls," he said indulgently.

Elise smacked him on the arm. "I can surf as well as

you," she declared. She was the bossy one, despite her small size—she must have weighed less than a hundred pounds, and was shorter than I was, which is saying something. Beside her, Amy looked statuesque. It would have bothered me when I was her age. She seemed serene, however.

"I don't know anything about it," Amy announced. "Is the water nice?"

The others rolled their eyes at each other. "Yeah, nice for penguins," Randy said. "It's freezing. I brought my old wet suit—might be a little big for you, but better than nothing."

"Wet suit." That dampened Amy's enthusiasm.

In response to some signal—perhaps that the bagels were gone—they all got up. In a few minutes the clutter of breakfast was swept into the trash—including the orange peels that I meant to compost—and they were crowding out the door.

Barker thought that he, too, was invited. Eric picked him up. "Great puppy," he crooned, letting Barker wash his face. "Wanna go to the beach, puppy?"

"I've got my dog in the van," Randy said, looking at me. "And water bowls and stuff."

"Can he come?" Amy took Barker from Eric, nestling him into her cleavage. Once more that awed expression appeared on Eric's face.

"Sure, take him if you want. Here's his leash." I handed it to Amy, who tucked it under one arm and Barker under the other.

I stood on the front step to watch them leave. Eric's van was a nondescript Ford. He ran a reverent hand over my old bus.

"Fine wheels," he shouted, before remembering that he was trying to be quiet.

Amy looked proud. "My aunt fixes it herself," I heard her say before the door slammed.

The van backed slowly out of the driveway and took off. I hoped that Eric was as careful a driver as he seemed. I hoped they didn't drink a lot of beer and lose it on one of the curves along Highway 84 or Highway 9 or Highway 17, all of which are notorious.

It wasn't yet eight o'clock. The cool morning air was laden with intoxicating scents—roses, moist earth, the pleasing sharpness of redwood foliage. I left the front door open to enjoy it while I settled to my work. I had barely gotten into rewriting the lead of my *Organic Gardening* story when Drake ran up the steps.

"You're so popular these days." He tossed a yellow envelope at me. "If you're going to get more of these things, do you think they could be delivered to your front door at the crack of dawn, instead of mine?"

"Touchy, touchy." I opened the telegram—I didn't know they even existed anymore. It was from Renee and Andy, of course. I should have expected it. AMY STILL MINOR YOU ARE DETAINING HER AGAINST OUR WISHES STOP CALL IMMEDIATELY STOP. I handed it to Drake.

He shook his head as he read it. "You just get into more trouble." He handed it back to me. "I'm not a lawyer, but I'd call them if I were you. Maybe they'll send money to get her to leave."

"She won't go back, probably." I was filled with foreboding and frustration. "She'll run away somewhere we don't know about, and they'll blame me for it."

"That's about the size of it," he agreed. "If you call before eight, it's still night rates. And then you can pick up the message that came in this morning while I was showering. Your temp agency wants you."

I made a face. Mrs. Rainey must have some horrible job that no one else would do, like the place I'd been to last time, where the boss had pinched me not ten minutes after I got there. My response to that had not been too harsh, in my opinion, but it had earned me a scolding from Mrs. Rainey, who felt that no matter what the provocation, a knee to the groin was overreaction.

I saved the few feeble sentences I'd managed to write and followed him across the yard to his back door. Luckily

Information in Denver had my brother's number, because I didn't. Even luckier, I got their answering machine.

"Listen, Andy," I told the machine. "I didn't ask your daughter to land herself on me. If you want her back, I suggest you come and get her. Or send a nonrefundable plane ticket." I hesitated a moment. "It might be better, though, if you let her try her wings a little. Have you and Renee gotten any counseling? Do you have any guarantee this won't happen again? I'm not your problem, whatever it is. Fix it before you look for a scapegoat. I don't play that role anymore."

I was getting angry just thinking about it, so I hung up. I didn't leave Drake's number for them to get in touch with me. Something told me he wouldn't like that.

He came back into the kitchen, knotting a tie, an indication of hassles to come in his office that day. Usually he gets away with pretty slobby apparel on the job.

"You should get your message." He nodded at the answering machine. "Maybe she's got a client asking for a jeans-wearing, groin-kneeing, tea-drinking, stray-adopting technophobe."

"Those jobs are a dime a dozen." I rewound the tape and listened without enthusiasm to Mrs. Rainey's perky voice. Drake held up the teakettle, his eyebrows raised in a question, and I nodded. I would call Mrs. Rainey after my cup of tea.

"How is your investigation going?" I perched on a kitchen chair while he manipulated his espresso machine.

He yawned. "I went back to the office after I talked to you—we were up late with the paperwork and trying to get in touch with the brother. Parents are dead, evidently. Poor kid seems to have been pretty alone in the world."

He showed me a tea bag, and I nodded acceptance—Melrose's Queen's Tea. I would suspect him of sarcasm for keeping that around for me, if I wasn't grateful to be spared Lipton.

"So the brother wasn't home last night?"

65

"Not in his apartment, anyway." Drake looked stern. "Remember what I said, Liz. You keep out of it."

"I don't exactly find it flattering for you to treat me as if I'm butting into your case like Miss Marple," I pointed out. "I'm younger and more beautiful, for one thing."

He had to smile, but fought it back. "I just don't want to see a pattern developing here." The phone rang, and he gulped his espresso, glancing at his watch. "There's Bruno, wondering why I'm not at the office."

It wasn't Bruno Morales, Drake's partner in homicide investigations when Palo Alto has one, which isn't often. The phone call was for me. Drake handed me the receiver and carried his cup over to the sink, noticeably eavesdropping.

"Hello, Liz?" It was a woman's voice, slightly accented. "This is Angel Lopez, from SoftWrite. I spoke with you yesterday."

"Yes, Mrs. Lopez."

"Angel. You were coming in this morning to do some data entry, right?"

"That was the plan." I braced myself for the brush-off. Clarice must have told them that I'd been lurking around in an unsavory manner at the scene of Jenifer's death.

"Well, we were wondering if you could give us the whole day today, to fill in for our receptionist. She's got the flu and we're really shorthanded here." Mrs. Lopez did sound harried.

I thought for a moment. There hadn't been enough people around during the previous afternoon to make census taking worthwhile. I could do that evenings, and make more money temping all day. "That's fine, Mrs. Lopez. Angel."

"Great." She sounded relieved. "There's a lot of stomach flu or something going around—our regular temp place couldn't help us today. We can put the data entry off until next week. Sarah didn't sound like she'd be recovered until Monday."

"I'll be in soon."

"You're a lifesaver." Mrs. Lopez hung up.

I had been a temp receptionist once before. I'd learned to work those big phones that businesses all have now instead of switchboards. Most important, I'd learned how to fake it. If you don't blatantly read magazines or file your nails, no one minds whether you really try to fill the shoes of the absent person.

I just hoped my denim skirt would be adequate for my new position. At one place I worked, there was trouble when I turned up for the second day of work in blue jeans. A couple of the men had been wearing them, but receptionists are often held to a higher level of grooming than the rest of the staff. Not that they're paid well enough to afford nice clothes. It's a puzzlement.

I called Mrs. Rainey and got her answering machine, left my message of unavailability, and turned to face Drake.

"So is this the same place you were yesterday? The place Jenifer Paston worked?" Drake was drying his special little espresso cup and saucer. He likes his kitchen very tidy, unlike the rest of his house. His living room looks as if hurricanes pass through it regularly.

"Yeah. Guess they don't know yet what a dubious person I am."

He scowled at me. "You're just trying to survive, Liz. No one could possibly suspect you of any complicity in this suicide." He hung the cup carefully on its special hook. "I'll be stopping in there today to talk to people. Being under a lot of stress at work is a motive for taking your life."

"Right." I looked down at my sweatpants and the old Birkenstocks that Bridget had given me, which I wear in the garden. "Guess I'd better change."

"Hey, maybe your niece has something you could borrow." Drake grinned. "Her wardrobe looks interesting."

"Something black and tight?" I considered the suggestion. "Perhaps I could use a tablecloth as a sarong, or turn bandannas into a business suit."

"Just be careful at lunchtime," he said, breaking up at

this feeble joke. I left him chortling against the sink and went to change.

I want to be above clothes, I really do. Most of the time I am. Nothing makes you feel poorer than needing something and being totally unable to obtain it. When I first started temp work, I wore the same skirt and blouse everywhere. I noticed women who dressed as simply, but with a wave of the accessory wand, changed their adequate clothes to something special. I don't know how to do that. I tried belting my T-shirt on the outside, over my skirt. On me it just looked like dweeb city. Another trip to the thrift store was called for.

A sweater covered the wrinkles in the red shirt I'd worn the day before and washed before going to bed. The old pair of emergency panty hose I'd found in the back of a drawer had just one little run. I could pretend I didn't know about it. I brought the toe-torturers along in a tote bag so I wouldn't have to walk in them. I brought the paperwork for the census, too, and a notebook for the projects I was working on. Looking busy was usually part of the job, especially if the phones weren't heavy.

It was a brisk and pleasant walk downtown; the traffic hadn't yet begun to thicken and the sidewalks looked clean and fresh. The coffee place on the ground floor of Soft-Write was roasting beans again when I went up the front stairs; it smelled like burned toast and was as thick as fog. I was glad to get through the plate glass door at the top, but the smell was still strong inside the foyer.

Yesterday, before Angel had whisked me off to meet Mindy and my computer, I'd noticed that the reception room was bigger than my living room. Now I had time to take in the spare but tasteful furnishings. In the middle of the room was a black desk, no clutter—just computer and phone console. A huge flower arrangement, sprouting many twisty twigs and birds-of-paradise, squatted on a tansu chest against the wall. Through an archway behind the desk I glimpsed the maze of cubicles where I'd spent the previous morning. Two doors with frosted glass panels flanked the reception room. The ceiling was high, as were the windows, so there was lots of light but no real view.

Mindy was behind the desk, an example of the chicness I'd striven for. Her black shirt had silver zigzags of lightning all over it. While she talked on one phone line, another one rang. She waved at me and juggled the calls.

"Can you hold? Thanks. Can you hold? Thanks." She banged the receiver down. "Thank God you're here, Liz. Sorry to just throw you to the wolves, but we've got other people out today besides Sarah."

"Are the phones heavy?" I put down my carryall and sat in the client chair to change out of the faded red high-tops I'd gotten at Goodwill.

"Moderately. Mostly it's a question of taking messages and transferring to extensions." Mindy stood up. "Don't bother changing unless you want to—the high-tops are great. There's a list of extensions beside the phone, and a Rolodex in the drawer in case Ed asks you to get anyone for him. Ed Garfield, the big cheese," she added, pointing at the frosted glass door in the right-hand wall. "Remember, I told you about him. And Suzanne Hamner." She pointed to the glass door on the opposite side of the room. "Can you work this phone?"

The console looked intimidating, but once I'd found the hold button I knew I'd be okay. She watched while I transferred the holds to the proper extensions.

"Great work." Mindy pushed her glasses up on her nose and smiled at me in approval. "I'm snowed under at my desk, but buzz me if you get lost—I'm extension 253. Everything's upset here today," she added under her breath.

The door on the right opened—I'd been thinking of it as Door Number One—and Ed came out, his arm around a weeping woman. Ed himself looked shaken and gray.

"Now, now," Ed said. He saw me and nodded, before directing a helpless look toward Mindy.

"Come on, honey," Mindy said, taking over. "I'll get her some coffee, Ed." The woman raised her head from Ed's shoulder. It was Clarice.

"Yeah. Thanks. Thank you too, Liz. Appreciate your filling in like this." Relieved of Clarice, he vanished into his office.

Clarice didn't notice me. She was too busy trying to stop crying, and not succeeding. "I'm sorry," she wept, clinging to Mindy. "I'm sorry. I don't know why I'm crying so much. It just—I just—"

"I know," Mindy said soothingly, leading her away, deeper into the maze of office dividers. "It's the shock."

"It's the shock." I heard Clarice agree, her voice watery.

"We'll all miss her." Their voices died away.

I scanned the phone list. Employees were grouped into divisions, starting with Ed Garfield and Suzanne Hamner at the top. Clarice Jensen was listed under personnel.

Under the section marked software, I found Jenifer Paston, extension 496. But she wouldn't be needing voice mail anymore.

9

     THE phones didn't allow time to think. They rang incessantly, for marketing, for Ed Garfield. All the action was caused by the company's new product. The whole scene was much more glossy than the seat-of-the-pants way Emery Montrose did business.

Ed came out of his office several times, hurrying off into the maze of dividers. Once he went across the room to Door Number Two, where a woman's voice greeted him. That would be Suzanne Hamner, extension 132, vice-president of software development.

The phones tapered off about nine-thirty. Mindy came back with a cup of coffee, and raised her eyebrows at my polite refusal.

"Oh, that's right. You're a tea drinker. Do you remember where the hot water is?"

"I can find it, I think."

"I'll watch the phones for you, if you want. The cups are in the cabinet beneath the coffeemaker."

I carried my tea bag away, wondering if I should ignore Drake's wishes and do a little snooping about Jenifer. After all, I was in a unique position for that.

The maze of cubicles was confusing. I ran into a couple of dead ends before finding the lounge area. The labels on the two coffeepots had been changed; one said "Killer," the other "Wuss." I filled my cup and set it in the microwave for a little extra heat, punching buttons until it started and trying to eavesdrop discreetly on the knot of people who stood in the middle of the area, heads together intently, talking in low voices.

One of them noticed me anyway. "Oh, Liz. I'm so sorry I wasn't on hand to get you started this morning." It was Angel Lopez, the office supervisor. She was about fifty, plump, casually elegant in khaki pants and a sweater. Her glossy black hair, just touched with silver, framed a pleasant face. "Are you doing all right up there? Do you need help?"

"Mindy showed me the ropes. It's not too complicated. I'm just getting a cup of tea, and I'll get back to it."

"Did you find a cup all right?" Angel peered into the microwave. "There isn't always a clean one, because no one seems to wash up after themselves, but we don't have disposable cups anymore. Saving the environment, you know."

"Ha." A tall, beautiful woman tossed her head as she spoke. "Considering the amount of paper we go through, that's a joke."

Angel smiled. "That's Tess," she said. "Tech writer. She's a cynic."

"A realist," Tess corrected, nodding at me. "Hi. I heard there was a temp shortage when I asked for someone to do some word processing for me."

"Liz was already on board, catching us up with the data entry," Angel explained. "She was recommended to Ed, not from the agency."

"Ed? I see." Tess looked blank. The third member of their group nodded knowingly. He was short and overweight, with a bland, disinterested expression belied by the sharpness of his little dark eyes. He smoothed the strand of hair that bisected his shiny scalp from ear to ear.

"Ah, yes," he said, his voice a surprisingly deep baritone. "Sarah's not the only one out today. Will they be getting a temp for poor little Jenifer?"

Angel made some gesture of protest, and Tess's eyes narrowed.

"A temp programmer wouldn't be much use in Jenifer's

72

work." Tess turned her back on the man, who merely grinned annoyingly.

I cleared my throat. I'm not good at playacting, but even Drake couldn't complain if I just stuck to the truth. Not the whole truth—the convenient parts. "I met Jenifer yesterday, I think. Lovely girl."

"Didn't Mindy tell you?" Tess ignored Angel's tiny shake of the head. "Jenifer died yesterday."

"How tragic." I felt wooden and unconvincing, and soon it would be too late to contribute to the office gossip that I had extra insight into Jenifer's death. I knew enough about scuttlebutt to realize that if it came out later, I'd be sunk. "Was it an accident?"

"We don't know." Angel shook her head and frowned at Tess.

"We don't know for sure," the man said, his deep voice rolling out the words. "But the word suicide has been bandied about, hasn't it, ladies?" He looked around, complacent.

"You do all the bandying, Larry." Tess sounded disgusted. "Whatever happened, it's very sad. She was so young."

"And such a pretty thing," Angel said sadly. "Poor Clarice is devastated."

"Her roommate," Tess explained to me. "Sad for Clarice. First the divorce and that thing with—" She broke off. Angel breathed in sharply. "And then her new roommate dies," Tess went on without finishing her first sentence. "She should take some time off, get counseling."

"That's for human resources to recommend," Larry said, drawing himself up. "We will, of course, take all the circumstances into consideration. If you ladies will excuse me—"

He strolled away, and the two women looked after him, Angel with tolerant contempt, Tess with impatience. "That Larry," she burst out when he was scarcely out of earshot. "Why a clod like him would be promoted to HR manager, I don't know."

Angel glanced warningly in my direction. "He has his strengths," she murmured. "Did you find everything you need, Liz? Today would be a good time for you to talk with Larry and get your temp-employee paperwork filled out. I'll remind him to set up a time."

"Thanks." I got my cup out of the beeping microwave and tossed the tea bag into a nearby trash can. I had been dismissed very nicely. "I'll get back to the phones."

I walked around the divider that separated the coffee area from the cubicles. The first cubicle was empty; its six-foot-high walls shielded me from view. I stood next to the divider, where I could hear Tess's and Angel's low voices conferring, but I didn't catch any words until near the end of their conversation.

"All the same," Tess said, her voice carrying a stubborn note. "I still say he was harassing her. We should tell someone."

Angel sounded agitated. "No, no. It's just gossip, Tess. We have no proof. And she was not—I don't think she saw it that way at all."

"She was infatuated, you mean," Tess retorted. "If it wasn't harassment, it was definitely taking advantage of her. What about that scene yesterday morning? She must have gone straight home afterward and—and taken an overdose."

"She was over twenty-one." Angel's voice was quiet, final. "It was none of my business. None of yours, either. I've got to get back to work."

I headed for the front desk, carrying the cup of tea and chewing over what I'd heard. Rounding a corner in the maze, I nearly bumped into Larry, who was coming out of a door.

"Ah, the temp." His voice was so rich and jovial I expected it to be advertising something. "I need to talk to you. Can you come right in?"

I followed him through the cubicle to an inner office, the door of which he unlocked with great ceremony. "In here, Ms.—I didn't get your name?"

"Liz Sullivan." I stopped just inside the door. Larry went behind his desk.

"Sit down, sit down." He pointed out a chair. "I'll just get the forms—"

"I am registered with an agency. You can call them and they'll handle it."

"Open an account with them?" He didn't care for that idea. "Let me just get a little information on you first, Ms. Sullivan." He pulled a pad toward him and took up a pen in his thick fingers. "By the way, how do you know Ed?"

"I don't. Someone else I've worked for recommended me to him."

The way he smiled said he didn't believe that. "Would you just give me your address and phone number?"

Larry's oleaginous vibes made my knee positively ache for action. "I'll give you the agency's phone number, or if you like I can call Mrs. Rainey and have her call you."

"Certainly, if you wish to go through them." He put his pudgy hands together on the desk. "It costs you their percentage."

"It's better for tax purposes."

Larry shook his head. "Very well. You may have your agency call me." I could feel his eyes on my back as I left the office.

Mindy leaped to her feet when I finally got back to my desk. The phone console blazed with flashing hold lights. She stayed for a moment to see how I handled it. I was pretty smooth by this time, I have to say—only gave one person the wrong extension.

Of course, that one person was Ed Garfield, the big cheese. He barreled out of his office door after buzzing the call back to me, and stood watching while I sent it to the right destination. Mindy put her hand on my shoulder and smiled brightly.

"Still learning," she told Ed. "Liz is really doing great."

Ed leaned against the door frame, regarding me. He was a little stooped, as if hanging out with shorter people had affected his height. His blond-streaked hair fell over his forehead. A few intriguing lines crinkled around his bright blue eyes when he smiled. I remembered his smile from the previous evening—it was disarmingly shy and somehow conspiratorial, as though the two of us were bucking the world together. Today, it seemed mechanical, on the surface.

"Liz." He came forward and took my hand, his own palm dry and hard against mine. "Did I thank you yet for helping us out? We were really in a bind. It's a busy time for us, and not easy for someone to just walk into." He shrugged, self-mocking. "Certainly I've been single-minded about it lately."

"A new product, isn't it?" Out of the corner of my eye, I could see Mindy staring in frank admiration at Ed.

"That's right." He turned up the interest a little, and I felt the extra wattage. People who get ahead in business have a kind of star quality of their own, an intensity and drive that can be felt. Sharp intelligence beamed out of those blue eyes when he willed it. "Do you keep up with the software market?"

"Not really—just what I hear occasionally from Emery." I gestured at the phone. "But from the calls today, you've really got something."

Ed turned the smile on Mindy. "It's great of you to help out at the front desk, Min."

She blushed. "I'm glad to do it, Ed. We have to pull together, with Jenifer's death on our minds."

A cloud crossed his face. "Poor little Jenifer. How could something like that happen to such a nice kid?"

I looked from one to the other. "What happened?"

They were silent a moment. The answer came, surprisingly, from Door Number Two. "She killed herself." We all turned. A woman stood in the doorway—presumably Suzanne Hamner. She spoke unemotionally. "Mindy, I need the documentation on the last software update for the new product. Ed, could I talk to you for a minute?"

Mindy scurried off. Suzanne and Ed faced each other across the reception room. She was nearly as tall as he was, rangy and badly dressed in faded corduroy pants that had shrunk to reveal her ankles, which were encased in a grayish-white pair of those short athletic socks that have little pompons on their backs. Her running shoes were scuffed and dirty. Her shirt, a once-green polo, hung untucked. Abundant dark brown hair was pulled back from her intense, bony face with a rubber band.

Her face was beautiful, in the ageless way of fine sculpture. It could have belonged to a model—high cheekbones, great dark eyes, a full-lipped mouth held tight just then with irritation. She, too, looked to be in her early forties, not because of the fine wrinkles at the corners of her eyes, but from a sensation of maturity and pain that she radiated.

Between her and Ed stretched a nearly visible force field of vibrating emotions. It hurt just to be in its way.

"Can it wait?" Ed glanced at his watch. "I've got another appointment any minute."

"This won't take long." Suzanne held her office door open, politely indicating that he should precede her through it. He straightened with an impatient sigh.

Before he could cross the room, though, the plate glass doors swung violently open. The young man who stood there carried his own aura of powerful emotion. His eyes were reddened, and his hair wildly disarranged.

He advanced on Ed, though he glanced at Suzanne. "So you finally did it." His skin was pale, blotchy around his eyes. His words came with a shaky effort that was familiar, and I realized he was holding back those gusty, hysterical sobs that come—I had thought, only to adolescent girls such as I had been—after crying in the total abandonment of grief. "You finally killed my sister."

10 _____

ED stayed calm.

"You're overwrought, Jason," he said kindly, guiding the young man to the client chair in front of my desk.

Jason wouldn't sit. He bounced up, shaking off the pats Ed bestowed on his shoulder. "It's all your fault," he shouted, sounding much younger than he looked. I put his age at about twenty-five or twenty-six. "I know what you were doing."

People began to gather in the corridor between the dividers; Angel peeped curiously around the edge, along with Mindy and a couple of others I didn't recognize. In a place so open, arguments would have to take place behind Doors Number One or Two to keep from being broadcast wholesale through the office.

Ed stopped patting. He put one hand up to screen his hurt expression. "I don't know what you're talking about, Jason," he said softly. "But if you want to blame me, go ahead. Maybe there was something I could have done—said—that would have stopped her."

Jason looked uncertain for the first time. "You were working on her, pushing her all the time to have an affair. Couldn't you see she wasn't ready for that? God knows you're old enough to know better." He looked disbelievingly at Ed. "You're past forty!"

Ed winced. "Why don't we continue this conversation in my office," he suggested. "This is hardly the place—"

"I don't care who hears what I have to say," Jason declared vehemently. He glared at the audience, which by

78

now had filled the hallway and probably included everyone who worked at SoftWrite. "My sister is dead! Doesn't that matter?"

Suzanne had been hanging back in the open door of her office, glancing nervously from the employees to Ed to Jason. Now she strode forward and put her arm around Jason's shoulders. He didn't shrug her off.

"Of course it matters." Her deep voice was harsh with feeling. "It matters more than anything. But it's over, don't you see? Nothing you do can bring back the past. You just have to go on."

There was silence for a moment, and in it Suzanne seemed to recollect herself. She dropped her arm from Jason, glancing around with an air of truculence.

Jason didn't notice. He turned on Ed, his expression still accusing. "I'm going to get to the bottom of it," he said. "And when I do I'll find you there, seeking your level, you worm."

"That's an interesting point of view." It was Drake's voice. Unnoticed by those caught up in the drama, which included me, he'd pushed through the glass double doors.

Everyone turned to look at him—except me. I looked from Suzanne to Ed to Jason. I was hoping for one of those revealing moments you hear about, when people taken unaware display their emotions so nakedly you can read them like a book. But Suzanne simply looked blank. Ed was faintly puzzled, trying to recall where he'd met Drake before. And Jason plainly didn't care.

Drake looked around, taking the office in as if he was writing a description down in the messy notebook he kept. He passed over me blandly, as if I were just another anonymous receptionist. His gaze stopped on Ed and Suzanne, and the distraught young man who stood between them.

"Paul Drake. Police," he said. "I've been trying to get in touch with you, Mr. Paston."

Jason looked defiant. It occurred to me to wonder if he were an actor—all his emotions seemed so apt.

"Ed Garfield—we met last night," Drake continued,

shaking hands. "And you were at Emery's, too, Ms.—?" He looked inquiringly at Suzanne. She introduced herself, her voice dull again, with no sign of the passion that had infused it earlier. "I'll need to talk to both of you," Drake continued briskly. "And anyone else who feels they have something to add. Miss Paston's death has been classified as suspicious, and that means a lot of routine and boring questions, I'm afraid."

"As long as you find—as long as he's punished—" Jason's voice wobbled. Abruptly he sank into a chair and burst into the threatened sobs, interspersed with stuttering gulps of air.

Suzanne shooed the workers away; most of them were already evaporating on their own, with the exception of Angel, who had gotten a glass of water and offered it with genuine concern, and Larry, who had perched on a corner of the tansu chest, watching avidly.

Ed stayed in the open door of his office, and Suzanne retreated to hers, so they faced each other across the room again. Jason wept on his chair. Drake, hands stuffed into the sagging pockets of his sport coat, surveyed us all.

"I'll want to talk to you all, one at a time," he began. "I also want to look through Miss Paston's desk."

"That's what I came to do," Jason mumbled. "I don't want strangers touching her things."

"Given the circumstances of her death," Drake said, not unkindly, "the police are going to have to touch things. And do more than that, perhaps." He gave me a warning look. "We don't like having evidence messed up."

Ed caught the look, though he didn't know what it really meant. "That isn't Jenifer's desk. I'll show you her cube, if you want. Everything's just as she left it."

Jason's mouth opened, and Drake said hastily, "I'll talk to Jason first." He looked around, saw Larry. "What's your connection with Miss Paston?"

Larry jumped up and backed swiftly away, his hands behind his back. "None," he said, sounding a little less resonant. "I'll just get back to work now."

80

"If there's no room with a door to use, we can do the questioning downtown," Drake said.

"Use my office," Ed said at once. "I'll get a cup of coffee and go over some things with the marketing people." He nodded at me. "Buzz me there if I'm wanted."

Suzanne hovered for a moment before going into her office and shutting the door softly behind her. Drake looked at it.

"Wait for me in there," he told Jason, gesturing to Ed's office. Sullenly Jason walked into the other room. Drake came over to me.

"Are you keeping your nose clean? Remember what I said this morning."

"Was it only this morning? I feel ten years older." I glanced around the reception room. "There are land mines everywhere, Drake. If these people find out I was at the scene, I'm hosed. Nobody in an office ever forgives anyone who withholds juicy gossip."

"Very funny." He drove his hands through his hair. "Maybe you should get the flu, too, and get out of here."

"I need the money." I hesitated. "Look, it's wasteful for me not to snoop around a little. I'm here, they're talking— make use of it."

"No way," he said at once, before I could tell him about the intriguing bit of conversation I'd already overheard. "You're not a cop, Liz."

His voice had risen a bit on the last words. I shushed him. "This place is as private as the locker room at Rinconada Pool. You're blowing my cover, Drake."

"You have no cover," he said, biting off the words. "Answer the phone if you want, but don't nose around. I mean it, Liz. For once stay out of trouble."

He went into Ed's office, banging the door behind him. I felt sorry for Jason.

The ringing telephone called me back to work. It was the local newspaper, for Ed. I buzzed marketing.

"I'll get back to them." Ed didn't sound eager for the free publicity.

When I told the caller on line 1 that Ed was in a meeting, she gave me about six numbers where she could be reached when he was available—by phone, fax, or cellular phone. "Tell him it's about the MicroMax rumors," she added. "He would want to respond to that, I'm sure. What do you know about it?"

Her sudden attack took me by surprise. "I'm the temp. I know nothing."

She laughed. "Well, if you find out any information, give me a call. I might be able to do something for a good tip."

It sunk in that she meant money. "You pay for stuff like that?"

"Sometimes—if it's good and juicy and we can't get it any other way. Somebody at SoftWrite already knows that."

"What do you mean?"

"How do you think MicroMax got wind of the trouble? One of your guys leaked it. And I'm betting that person's bank account is fatter now."

The reporter hung up. I cradled the phone, staring at the twisty branches of the flower arrangement across the room. I had thought of SoftWrite as a simple little company like Emery's, where everyone was so busy just trying to survive that there was no time for office politics. That was obviously untrue.

Mindy came back with the files Suzanne had asked for and plopped them down on my desk. "I don't know if I want to go in there." She chewed uncertainly on her lower lip. "Things seem kinda tense today."

"I noticed."

Mindy looked up as someone else approached from the cubicles. "Clarice. How are you feeling, honey? Did you want to go home now?"

"Home?" Clarice's voice also had the wobbly quality associated with hysterics. She sank into the client chair, a tissue pressed to her eyes. "I can't go there." She used the tissue thoroughly and glanced around. "I left my purse here earlier—"

"Here? Or in Ed's office?"

"Out here, I think . . ." Clarice hadn't recognized me.

Helpfully I ducked behind my desk, rooting around. "Not here." My voice was muffled.

"I've got it." Mindy pulled a big leather bag from behind the tansu chest. "Must have slipped off."

"Thanks." Sniffling, Clarice rooted in the bag for another tissue. Then she stiffened. "Where's—wait a minute. It's gone!"

"What?" Mindy picked up the box of tissues from my desk. "Use these, Clarice."

"Not the tissues." Clarice rooted again in the bag, impatiently. "Someone's taken it."

"Taken what?" Mindy was asking the questions, so I stayed silent, keeping my low profile as intact as possible.

"The notebook." Clarice's voice got louder, shriller. "I had her notebook in here—I was going to show it to— And now it's gone!"

Mindy frowned, bewildered. "Notebook? Jenifer's notebook, you mean?"

At Jenifer's name, Clarice moaned. "I can't stand it." Her voice was thick with emotion. Mindy offered the tissues again, and Clarice helped herself liberally. When Mindy put the box back on my desk, Clarice saw me—really saw me. She sat up straighter.

"Wait a minute. Wait just a minute here." Her voice grew even shriller. "You—aren't you—?"

"I'm the temp." I tried a smile. "We met yesterday, remember?"

"You're the census taker." She jumped to her feet. "I know you are. I remember you."

Clarice wasn't as well put together this morning. Her makeup had been less than careful; there were dark smudges beneath her eyes. Her hair, too, hung limp and uncoiffed around her thin face.

She clutched her bag, staring at me with loathing. "I remember—you touched her—and now the notebook's gone—" Her voice had risen and crescendoed until her last words were a scream.

Door Number One popped open and Drake tore out. When he saw Clarice confronting me, he relaxed a little. Behind him, Jason peered curiously through the door. Suzanne reemerged.

Drake strode up to Clarice and shook her briskly. When that didn't work, he took the untouched glass of water Angel had procured for Jason, and dashed it into her face.

She broke off, sobbing and gasping.

Angel rushed into the room, concern etched on her face. "Poor Clarice," she crooned. "This has all been such a terrible shock."

Clarice, still gasping, pointed at me. "She—she—"

"I'll need to talk to you, Ms. Jensen." Drake put an arm around her and led her toward the office. "Then I'll finish with you, Mr. Paston. If you'd wait?" He swept the reassembled crowd with a resigned expression. "Your turn comes later, folks."

People drifted away. Mindy followed them, darting little looks at me. Jason plumped down in the chair. For a few minutes he gazed blankly into space, his hands rigid on the chair arms. Then the phone trilled, and he jumped. While I transferred the call to marketing, he stared at me.

"What did Clarice mean, you touched her? Were you there last night? Who are you, anyway?"

"I'm just the temp," I said, rather helplessly. "I don't think we're supposed to be talking."

"So what? He suspects me anyway." He jerked his head toward Door Number One, behind which Drake presumably grilled Clarice. "Thinks I made her do it, probably. But it wasn't me." He put his hands to his head, as if it threatened to fly apart. "What does it matter? How could any of it possibly matter? Jenny's dead. I can't really believe it. I was just talking to her Tuesday night. How can a person be alive one minute and dead the next?"

"That's the way it usually happens." This bit of comforting didn't seem to hit the mark. I told myself to shut up.

He wasn't really listening to me anyway. "We took care of each other—we had no one else. Now I'm alone."

Door Number One opened and Drake ushered Clarice out. "What's done is done, Ms. Jensen. No use worrying about it now. If you happen to see the notebook or remember anything about it, please let me know right away. Wouldn't it be better if you went home now? You're not in any shape——"

"Home?" Clarice stared at him. "You mean, the place where poor little Jenifer died? I'm not going back there." Her mouth worked. "I have no home."

Jason straightened his shoulders. "You're not the only one, Clarice."

She turned to look at him, and something passed between them, a consciousness or knowledge that needed no words. "That's true," Clarice said. "You're by yourself now." There was savage satisfaction in her voice.

Jason flinched. "Clarice——"

"Don't speak to me," she said, her voice low and intense. "Don't try to get in touch with me. You're vile, Jason. You deserve to suffer."

Drake just stood there, watching, his face intent. I felt things were getting out of hand.

I hadn't realized Suzanne was listening. Now she came into the reception area. "Clarice." Her deep voice was still harsh, but there was sympathy in it. "You don't know what you're saying. Don't take your grief out on this poor fellow."

"Poor fellow. Poor Jason." Clarice shook her head. "He fools you, doesn't he? But Jenifer remembered, Jenifer knew. Not that he would admit it—oh, no! Ask him what he told her, the last time he saw her! Why don't you?" She turned on Drake.

"You encouraged her to believe those lies." Jason stepped closer to Clarice. "You manipulated her—took advantage——"

Clarice stood her ground. "You were so angry, remember? You said she'd broken up your engagement by telling your fiancée. You said she deserved what was coming to her——"

"Officer." Suzanne took Clarice's arm, cutting off her spate. "Can't you do something?"

Drake stepped forward, reluctantly, it seemed to me. "I'll talk to you now, Mr. Paston," he said, gesturing toward Ed's office.

Jason seemed relieved. "Fine," he said, moving across the room. He turned at the door and looked back at Suzanne. "She's crazy, you know. My sister was the most important person in the world to me. I would never have hurt her. Never."

Drake ushered him inside and closed the door. Clarice's shoulders sagged.

"Where are you staying, Clarice?" Suzanne put an arm around Clarice and drew her toward her office. "Can I help you find a new place? We'll get the movers for you."

Clarice shuddered and stepped away. She obviously still had a temperament to vent. Her wild gaze alighted on me. "Is it true, what the policeman said?" She advanced toward the desk. "This is some kind of incredible coincidence?"

I nodded, aware of Suzanne's puzzled look. It was all going to come out, I could see. I would miss the paycheck, but the worst thing would be not knowing how it all ended.

"I don't believe it," Clarice declared flatly. There was a feverish glitter in her eyes. "You're plotting something. You're in this."

"Clarice." Suzanne was alarmed now. "You're not making sense here. We'll get you some counseling or therapy."

"She didn't tell you?" Clarice turned back to Suzanne. "This woman was there, last night. When I found Jenifer."

Suzanne stopped dabbing ineffectually at Clarice and looked at me. "I don't know what you're talking about."

"She was there, I tell you. She was right behind me when I found the body." Clarice put her hands over her face. "The body." Her voice was muffled. "I called Jenifer the body."

"Is there someplace for her to lie down?" I got to my feet.

Suzanne divided a suspicious look between me and

Clarice—I could see her wondering who was crazy. "In my office." This time she managed to herd Clarice through Door Number Two. "You'd better come as well. We'll put this whole thing to rest, if possible."

Suzanne got Clarice onto the shabby sofa in one corner of her office and poured her a glass of water from the fancy water-purifying carafe on her desk. Clarice gulped it, while Suzanne turned to me. "What's happening?"

"I do a lot of odd job–type stuff to earn money. One of the jobs is census taker. One of the housing units on my list is their place—her place." I jerked my head toward Clarice, who took a sobbing breath. "Last evening I'd made an appointment with Jenifer to fill out the census form. I got there just before this lady. When we went in, she was dead."

"How gruesome! Incredible." The suspicion was still in Suzanne's eyes. "That was after the party last night? I noticed you there. Ed was talking to you." Her expression gave nothing away, but I got the feeling that Suzanne would always notice who Ed was talking to.

"I'm a friend of Emery Montrose. He mentioned to Ed that I do temp work, which is why Angel called me in yesterday morning to do some data entry for you. In the afternoon, I went through my census register, and came back in the evening for people who weren't there earlier." I glanced at Clarice. "It truly is just coincidence."

"I see." Suzanne looked thoughtful. The phone rang, and she went out to the reception room to answer it herself.

Clarice blew her nose and wiped her face with one of the tissues she still clutched in her hand. "You don't expect anyone to believe that story, do you?"

"Why not? It's true. I'd barely met you and Jenifer. What reason would I have to interfere?"

"How should I know?" Clarice sank back on the couch. Though she looked spent, her voice was strong with venom. "But I think you should just get out."

The words were strongly reminiscent of something. It

took me a moment to place them as having been said by a couple of uncooperative anti-census people.

"She's not here permanently." Suzanne was back in the room. "We need someone to handle the phones. You're not up to it, Clarice."

"It's not my job." Clarice drew herself up.

"It's not Mindy's, either." Suzanne stared at me. "I don't even know your name."

I was getting angry. I didn't really blame them for their suspicions—the circumstances were bizarre. But I felt, however unreasonably, that it was unfair to victimize me because of those circumstances.

"Why should you need to know someone's name to fire them? Peons don't need names." I walked to the door. "Go ahead. Take away my livelihood. I despise office work anyway." Clarice stared at me, her mouth open as if an insignificant mosquito had suddenly become Kafka-ized in front of her. "You all just reinforce what the census has been teaching me—even the lowest opinion of human nature is too high."

"Wait," Suzanne said. "Look, this is awkward. But leaving won't make it better."

"Sure it will, for me." I jerked my head toward Clarice. "I won't have to listen to accusations of wrongdoing that are totally off the wall."

"At least think about coming back tomorrow." Suzanne followed me to the door. "Our phones are going nuts."

That was true. They were ringing again—two lines, brr-brr, brr-brr. It was maddening. I stalked to the console and put both of them on hold.

"There. See you."

"Wait—what about your check?"

I stopped at the door. "Forget the check," I said grandly, although it cost me a pang. "The morning is on me."

11 _____

AMY and Barker were still at the beach when I got home. The house was blessedly quiet, the hide-a-bed neatly folded away. I sat on the sofa for a little while, letting the silence sink into me and remembering that, not so long ago, I'd led a tranquil life.

I needed dirt. I changed skirt for jeans and drove to my garden.

The community gardens are one reason why I put up with some elitist crap to live in Palo Alto. I tended a plot behind the main library. The city will probably build on the garden site someday—open space is just too valuable for vegetables to use. I picture it, all our wonderful dirt trapped under buildings and asphalt. But for now it's a fecund, burgeoning place where gardeners weed and mulch and water amid towering tomatoes, vast walls of raspberries, tracts of corn.

There was no corn in my ten-by-twenty-foot space—it took up too much room. I did have beans and tomatoes, peppers and herbs, eggplant and artichokes. Gardening is a tranquilizer—the smell of dirt and compost and crushed herbs, the satisfaction of winning, for a brief space, the ongoing Bermuda grass war. I like the feel of that loamy earth I've helped create against my bare fingers.

This bright June day there was a lot of weeding to do. I worked gradually through the beds, uprooting the evil Bermuda grass, pulling out mallow and lamb's-quarters and purslane, adding mulch around the tomatoes and peppers, pinching back the basil and inhaling its wonderful fragrance. I saved the little flowering tips I pinched off; they were fabulous in salads and omelettes.

After twenty minutes of this I was able to regain perspective, and admit that, although it bothered me to leave SoftWrite before finishing the job, I was most upset by Jenifer's death and my own unwilling involvement in it.

Something about the alert way Drake had looked around that morning made me doubt that Jenifer had taken an overdose of her own volition. Strangely, that was a comforting thought. I had found her youth and niceness appealing. Suicide tarnished her in a way murder didn't. It was a gruesome distinction, but somehow comforting.

Silicon Valley is a hotbed of nervous businesses. Evidently SoftWrite was one. There was a kind of Greek city-state air about it—intertribal warfare that closed ranks against outsiders. A few months before, I'd temped at a design firm; there are hundreds of them around here, all staffed with incredibly creative people who are always on edge about keeping their jobs in the face of the incredibly creative unemployed designers who constantly buzz around. Three times in the course of the two days I'd spent at their switchboard I had heard raised voices, and I'd witnessed an episode of arm-waving, stomping-out temperament and a couple of shoving matches. However, at 4:30 P.M. on the second day, a Friday, they'd all gathered in the foyer and headed for the bar down the street. When I'd walked past half an hour later, they were still in a big, laughing clump. Go figure.

Some of the unpleasant vibes at SoftWrite could be attributed to the new product. That's a tense time for a company, large or small. But the two founders, facing off from their opposing doors, signaled that something more was amiss.

I finished digging out Bermuda grass. The carrot seedlings raised their feathery plumes, uncrowded by weeds. The sun was hot on my shoulders; the scents of herbs and tomato foliage surrounded me. A few other people were working around me. The peaceful, humming quiet was composed of wind in the tops of the plum trees that surround the garden, and traffic swishing by on Embarcadero Road and in the library parking lot. It was so quiet that I was surprised when I picked up a pile of weeds to carry to the Dumpster and saw Bridget in her garden plot, two over and three down.

Not that it surprises me to see Bridget. It was just that the air of peace hadn't been shattered by the shrill noises of her numerous offspring.

She waved a dirty hand at me and set out another cucumber. She was late for that, of course, but Bridget's garden is always a haphazard, last-minute thing that somehow manages to produce vegetables at an astonishing rate. Sleeping near her in a small Barcalounger-type seat was a baby—Moira, the fourth and last Montrose child.

"Hey, Liz. I thought you were working at that temp job." Bridget firmed the dirt around the cucumber plant and stood up, stretching. She was nothing extraordinary to look at—a bit matronly as to figure, a couple of years older than me, with flyaway hair and warm brown eyes, as clear and dancing as dark amber. Her beauty is inside, for the most part, shining out through those eyes and her bright, infectious smile. She was my only friend in Palo Alto for a while, and a great help to me in getting my freelance career off the ground. Because of her, I got to teach a writing workshop at the Senior Center from September through May that paid enough to take care of my postage bill.

"I did temp, yesterday morning and for a couple of hours today." I clutched my weeds gloomily. "I'm off now because of the body."

She laughed, then looked closer. "You're not joking."

"Nope."

"Oh, no. Not again!" She turned a bushel basket over beside the baby chair and sat. Moira slept on, shaded by an awning thing on the chair. "What happened?"

I dropped my pile of weeds. "Maybe you can fill me in. Remember that guy at your party last night, the one who poured the beer on my arm? Ed Garfield."

"Yeah. He's the one Emery told about you, when he was complaining about the temp shortage last week."

"What do you know about his company?"

"SoftWrite? That's not just Ed, it's both of them, Ed and Suzanne." Bridget peeked beneath the sunshade to check the baby. "Suzanne is so quiet, she's often overlooked. But Emery thinks she's the brains behind that screen saver—their first product, you know."

"Aren't they competitors of Emery's?"

Bridget squinted against the sun. "Not directly." She put her hand over her forehead to look at me. I moved around so my shadow shaded her and she smiled gratefully. "Emery is doing custom applications, real-time analysis."

"Is there some other kind of time?"

She laughed. "For the techies there is, evidently. Emery's got his own niche. He's not too worried about the other small companies. They tend to respect each other's territories. But if the big guys sound like they're getting into the same field, then he worries." She wrinkled her forehead. "SoftWrite, now—their new product is something to do with personal assistants. A lot of big companies like Apple and Oracle are jumping into that. It's risky—those big guys like to squash the little players."

"A newspaper reporter asked about MicroMax today. Some rumor or other."

"Really?" Bridget looked interested. "I'll have to ask Emery about it. There's more gossip in Silicon Valley than in the Valley of the Dolls." Moira made a little noise in her sleep, and Bridget smoothed a lock of fine red hair away from the baby's face. When she looked up, her smile faded. "Now what about this body?"

I told her about Jenifer, getting myself worked up again while I went through it. Suicide or murder—whatever it was, it was wasteful. Young people should be getting on with the business of saving the world. It's their main job. Knocking themselves off or being killed doesn't do a thing for the universe.

"So SoftWrite has employees whose address is on your

census sheet." Bridget looked thoughtful. "What are the odds of that happening, I wonder?"

"Not as weird as it sounds, probably. I had several people on my register in different apartment buildings in that same neighborhood who worked for the same law firm at Palo Alto Square, a place where I also temped a few months ago. Of course, it's a big law firm."

"And the temp job really grew out of our connection with you." Bridget brightened up a little. "The jungle drums thing. It's really pretty powerful, isn't it? Emery may need some help if you're free."

"It's nice of Emery to think of me, but he can't afford to make up jobs for me, and you know it."

Bridget looked abashed. "I know. But he always does need help."

"I'll spend full time on the census. And Saturday I have Claudia's garden work. Don't worry about me."

"That's the ticket. Maybe you'll get the whole register done this weekend and be through with it." Bridget's nice face was worried. "I don't like you going around to houses where homicidal lunatics might be living. You need some quiet temp jobs where you have time to edit your manuscripts."

"First I have to write some." I thought of my pile of projects. "And with Amy around, that's going to be difficult."

"Amy? Oh, yes, your niece. Poor Liz. It never rains but it pours." Bridget tossed her trowel into the rickety bucket that held a rusty collection of garden tools. Moira stirred in her chair. "Just be sorry for me. School's out next week."

No wonder it had been so quiet. Second-grade Corky, kindergartner Sam, and preschooler Mick were safely incarcerated in their various learning situations. After only twenty-four hours of surrogate motherhood, I had a new appreciation for what Bridget went through. "Boy, that is a shattering thought. Will they go to camp?"

"Maybe a couple of the recreation programs, but we're having a financial crisis right now, so they'll mostly be home." Bridget clutched her flyaway hair. "I'll be up to my ears in children!"

"Okay, you have it the worst." I grinned at her. "Amy's going to get a job as a stockbroker or investment banker or something, so I'll probably never see her."

"You'll have fun with her. It sounds like you enjoy her, actually." Bridget picked up the chair with Moira in it and tucked it under one arm. She reached for the bucket of tools, but I took it and led the way to the parking lot. Bridget's old Suburban was parked beside my VW bus. She went through the ritual of putting Moira's chair thing in and strapping it to the car several different ways. Moira still hadn't opened her eyes. She was a cute baby, nine months old, with plump, rosy cheeks and a halo of curly red hair like her father's.

Bridget finished securing Moira. "I wish I'd met Amy last night." She shut the car door carefully and took the bucket of tools from me. "Maybe you should bring her over for dessert tonight. Claudia's thinking of looking in again. Your niece might have fun." She thought, then she shook her head. "Boy, that makes me feel old—realizing that my friends and I would be boring to a teenager."

"I'll come, anyway," I said. "Amy can do as she likes." I felt a little qualm when I said this. Amy was probably counting on my inattention so she could go off and act like a teenaged jackass.

"Around eight," Bridget said, climbing into the driver's seat. "I'm going to try to have the kids in bed by then."

I watched her drive away and then went back to carry my weeds to the Dumpster. My gardening equipment is not much better than Bridget's, though I clean it carefully to make it last. I loaded up the bus with the tender lettuces, basil tips, the last of my potatoes, some beets, carrots, and scallions, and headed for home.

It was a little past noon. I figured Amy and Barker would be home, expecting me to produce lunch out of my hat. She was there, sitting on the front porch while Barker slept in a nearby patch of sunlight.

There was someone sitting with Amy. At first I thought it might be Eric or Randy. They were chatting comfortably as I drove up; I was glad she had sense enough not to let one of the boys into the house when she was there alone.

Then I recognized the man. It was Ed Garfield.

12 _____

AMY bounced off the step when I parked the bus. She was reddened by the sun, her hair sticking up all over her head in a wild, wind-styled disarray. "Aunt Liz!" She hung on the bus's open door while I collected my produce. "You locked the door! I couldn't get in!" She lowered her voice, glancing mischievously over her shoulder. "Your friend couldn't get in either. He's pretty eager to talk to you."

Ed stood by the porch steps, glancing at his watch.

"He's hunky." Amy whispered while we approached. I nodded stiffly to Ed and unlocked the door. Amy swooped down on Barker and danced inside, carrying him. Ed hung back.

"You must be wondering why I'm here," he said.

His presence on my doorstep didn't exactly rank with the mysteries of the universe, but I was curious.

"I have to put my vegetables away." I said. "Do you want a glass of water or anything?"

He followed me into the kitchen. Amy was already there, rooting through the refrigerator. "We don't have any food," she announced.

"*We* haven't gone shopping." I poured the veggies out of my garden basket into the sink, and scrubbed the beets and carrots and potatoes.

Amy got herself a glass of ice water and offered one to Ed. "Aunt Liz doesn't do sodas and things," she said, gulping thirstily. "She's, like, into healthy stuff." She snatched a radish and crunched into it. "This is good." She sounded surprised.

I scrubbed and trimmed the rest of the radishes and put them in a little bowl, with some salt in another little bowl.

"See," Amy told Ed, who perched uncomfortably on a kitchen chair, "this is lunch, for my aunt."

Ed made a strangled sound, and I gave Amy a look that evidently she recognized.

"I'm going to take a shower," she said hastily. "Nice to meet you, Mr. Garfield." She flounced out of the room.

I was hungry, but damned if I was going to offer to feed Ed. There wasn't much to eat, anyway, as Amy had noticed—it would be a choice between couscous and scrambled egg. One egg. I added some tiny carrots to the dish of radishes and joined him at the table with my own glass of water.

"I guess you really needed the work." He looked at the kitchen, his shifting weight making the elderly chair creak. "I'm sorry you decided to leave."

Pity is worse than suspicion. "Nobody does temp work except for money," I pointed out, crunching another radish.

"Suzanne said you were doing census stuff, too—is that how you—found Jenifer?"

"I was there, yes."

Ed shook his head. "I had no idea—look, Liz. Ms. Sullivan." He leaned forward, gazing at me earnestly. "Let's let bygones be bygones. Clarice is going to be gone the rest of the day. We still need someone to answer the phone. I hate for callers to get just the voice mail, especially with our new release coming up." He passed a hand over his hair, pushing it out of his eyes. "How about your coming in just for today and tomorrow? That finishes the week, and Monday our receptionist should be well again. You were doing a great job. In fact, I think we could throw in a little bonus, since the phones are so heavy."

It made me feel strange to be offered extra money, as if I was a commodity, easily purchased. And yet, the person answering phones does work just as stressful as the person making decisions. More, because the phone answerer is often treated like nothing by the people who use her services. So I deserved more money, of course; most of my pink-collar sisters do. I just didn't care for the context in which it was offered.

"Why did you come over? Why didn't you just call?" I knew he hadn't wanted to scope out my degree of poverty. Bosses never think about that stuff until it looks them in the eye.

"I did, but I kept getting someone's answering machine." He picked up a radish, turning it in his fingers as if it came from the alien Vegetable Planet. "And—well, there were things I wanted to ask you face-to-face. About Jenifer."

"I don't know anything."

"Clarice wasn't able to be coherent at all after you left. I want to know—how Jenifer looked, and all. You see, I had a special feeling for her." He looked up with the ghost of a smile on his face. "Despite what Jason said today, I'm not that old." The smile faded. "I can't help but wonder—can't help but blame myself."

He fell silent. I didn't know what to say, so I said nothing. The water hissed and banged in the pipes. Through the half-glass door that led to the little back porch, I could hear the ancient water heater light up with a whoosh.

Ed spoke again. "Was she—did she look—peaceful?"

I still didn't know what to say. Was I supposed to tell people about the scene of the death? If I didn't tell, would Clarice? "She looked very peaceful," I hedged. "No trauma."

He turned away, but not before I saw the glint of moisture in his eyes. "Stupid," he muttered. "It's just been one hell of a day, that's all."

I cleared my throat. "It would be uncomfortable to work at SoftWrite after what Clarice said this morning."

Ed touched my arm briefly. "Listen, she wasn't making any sense at all. We're so busy right now, nobody has time to think. And the phones are going crazy." His jaw was rigid, his hands tense. When I looked closely, I could see the strain in his face.

It was rather satisfying to be begged to come back to a job. That had never happened to me before. "Can't you just get another temp?"

"We did manage to find one girl. She couldn't hack the phones. She left after twenty minutes and said she wasn't coming back."

So this was the secret of my attractiveness. He added, "I wangled your home address out of Emery's secretary and came up to ask you back." He looked at his watch again and stood up. "Whatever it takes. Double what you usually get from temp work. Look, I don't have much time. I'm in the middle of important negotiations. I can't put them on hold, I can't even take time to realize that Jenifer—" His voice broke. He turned away.

I could hear the sullen groans of the water heater from the back porch. It wouldn't last much longer.

"Okay. I'll be there in half an hour or so." Life was taking on a hectic tone. Office work for the next two days. That evening was Bridget's hen party. Then there was grocery shopping, laundry to do, puppy training, and garden tasks.

"Thanks, Liz. Ms. Sullivan." Ed had his face under control again. "We're all too busy to gossip right now. Probably no one will even notice you."

That sounded like famous last words.

Barker roused as we came into the living room. He stretched and scratched, and I added flea patrol to my list of tasks.

Ed stared at him. "Isn't that—" His expression was ghastly.

"It's Jenifer's puppy, yes." Barker came prancing over, his tail waving. I moved quickly to open the door. "He's still being trained."

"Why do you—" Ed broke off, backing away.

Barker started growling. He certainly didn't like men— first Curtis, then Drake, now Ed.

"Clarice didn't want him—at least for now. Don't you like dogs?"

"I like them," Ed said, breathing deeply. "But I'm allergic to them. They sense that, don't they?"

I picked Barker up and shook him by the scruff. "Stop it." He stopped, but he didn't put down the fur on the back of his neck.

"Well, I'll see you at the office later." Ed was out the door. "Tell your niece I enjoyed meeting her."

"Okay." I held Barker until Ed was out of sight at the end of the drive.

Amy came into the living room, toweling her hair. She wore a torn T-shirt and leggings.

"Your friend didn't stay long." She sat cross-legged on the couch.

"He's not my friend. He's my employer."

Amy looked roguish. "If you say so, Aunt Liz." Barker ran over to her, wriggling and licking until she picked him up. "Yes," she said, snuggling her face into his soft fur, "we had a fun time at the beach, didn't we, boy?" She gave him a squeeze, and he settled down on the couch next to her, sighing the deeply satisfied sigh of a dog on a piece of forbidden furniture.

"He was such a sweetie, Aunt Liz." Amy stroked the silky fur of Barker's ears. "You should have seen him biting the waves, and running into them after the stick—what a smart boy!" Barker put his head on her lap, raising his eyes to her face adoringly.

"I'm glad you both had fun." I headed for my bedroom. "But I don't want him on the furniture, Amy."

"I know." She put him on the floor and made him sit. "No, boy. You can't be up here. I'll sit with you." She slid down to the floor, combing her hair with a kind of *über*-comb that had the most immense teeth I'd ever seen.

Her voice filtered through the door of my bedroom, filling me in on her morning. "The ocean is, like, incredible. I had no idea. It goes forever, you know? I was, like, totally overwhelmed by it, and it went up and down, and pretty

100

soon I thought I was going to hurl, but Elise and Kimberly and me climbed up a cliff and from up there it was okay, and the guys were so radical surfing, I mean, they were like sea gods or something, only Eric kept wiping out and once the surfboard hit him on the head and Randy had to kind of drag him in, but he was okay. They said they only go with buddies because of that. It was awesome, and I'm going to learn how, Aunt Liz, only maybe I'll start with a boogie board or something, or maybe just bodysurf, Eric said. . . ."

I stopped listening. Her voice was soothing, somehow, like incomprehensible radio waves from a distant galaxy, and I had a lot on my mind, not just whether I could get the pantyhose on again without starting another run. When I came back in the living room, dressed for what passed for success in my life, Amy stopped talking.

"I'm going back to work," I said, taking advantage of the silence. "What are your plans for the afternoon?"

"Well, I guess I'll have some yogurt for lunch and hang," Amy said after a moment.

I fished around in my wallet and handed her my library card. "There's a library downtown; they have *Barron's* and those stock market rags as well as books." I pulled out a five-dollar bill and tried not to look too reluctant when I gave it to her. "There's a grocery store a few blocks from the library, on Emerson. Maybe you could get us something inexpensive for dinner."

She took the money, looking troubled. "Aunt Liz, five dollars—well, thanks, I'll try, but you know that's really nothing these days. I mean it's like a nickel in the olden days."

"I know it's a challenge, Amy." I shouldered my tote bag. "But think of it as a game—how much food can you buy for just five dollars? Remember, we have fresh vegetables, so lentils or beans or some grain could be the protein."

She clutched the money. "Yeah," she said, unconvinced.

13

I could hear the phones ringing from the other side of SoftWrite's plate glass doors. Angel got up from the desk when she saw me. "Long lunch." Her voice was tinged with accusation.

"You could say that." I slid into the chair and put someone on hold. "Everything under control?"

"No." She didn't sound like the soft-spoken woman I'd met before. "Everything's horrible. Suzanne's holed up in her office, acting really weird; Clarice was taken away in hysterics; that policeman and his partner were here for almost an hour, upsetting everyone; and Ed is just beside himself with grief and worry."

I sat there, listening to her tirade and wondering what it had to do with me. By the end of it, she was glaring at me as if I personally had caused it all. I would have replied, but she just took a breath and went on.

"I don't care about the stories. People are saying you're some kind of bad-luck Jonah. Someone even said you were Ed's new girlfriend, and you went and told Jenifer, and that made her commit suicide." She was disbelieving. "As if Ed would—well . . ."

"Take up with me when he had a cute young thing like Jenifer around?" I touched Angel's shoulder. "I'm just a bystander, really. Just trying to make a living."

Angel sniffed. "What I care about is that if you say you're going to do a job, you show up to do it. The phones are driving us crazy. The reporters are getting past this desk and hassling people. Do you know, one of the programmers said he'd been offered money to spy around?" She stopped, breathing heavily, glaring even more because I was giggling. True, it was nervous laughter.

"I believe you. I was offered money, too."

"Well!" Angel calmed down a little. "Luckily you don't know anything. But this has to stop. Can you screen the calls, Liz?"

"I'll try."

"Thanks." The lines of stress smoothed away from her forehead. "I'm sorry to yell at you," she said gruffly. "Honestly, I don't know what this place is coming to. It was better when we were just starting—just Ed and Suzanne and Tess and Clarice and me. There was a spirit then—we had such confidence." She walked away, shaking her head.

I fielded some more calls, wondering how I was supposed to screen. Would anyone identify themselves on the phone as a reporter looking for corruptible employees? Most of the calls were for marketing anyway, and they must have known how to handle the situation.

When a call came in for human resources, I did ask who was calling—Larry was just the type to enjoy the role of corporate mole. A few minutes after the call went through, Larry's shiny dome peered around the partition.

"So you're back." He sauntered into the room, smiling benevolently.

"Finishing my day," I said, hunting in the center desk drawer for a new pad of sticky message forms.

"I'm surprised, after the scene Clarice made. Does Ed know?" His nose quivered like a truffle-hunting pig's.

I nodded, responding to the flashing light on the phone console. It was for Suzanne; the phone kept ringing while I transferred the call, and for a few minutes I was busy putting people on hold and then trying to retrieve them, a task not made easier by Larry's hovering presence. As soon as there was a lull, he was at me again.

"Clarice seemed to think you were involved in Jenifer's death. Is that true?"

"I see no possible reason to answer that question."

"Really?" He came a little closer. "She told Angel you were at the door when she got home, probably coming out after suffocating Jenifer. And you'd only met the poor girl once. Don't you think it sounds fishy?"

"So Clarice told Angel all this guff in front of you? Or did you just make it up?" I stood up, trying to be imposing. "Ask the police if you want to know more about Jenifer's death. Don't bug me."

Larry inflated his chest. It did wonders for his waistline. "I am head of human resources here. It's my responsibility to know about employees' backgrounds."

"I'm not your employee." I put another call on hold and glared at him. "I'm a temp. I don't have to answer any of your questions. Stop bothering me, or I'll walk out and leave you to answer the phones."

Larry looked outraged. He started to reply, but someone else spoke first.

"She's got a point," Suzanne said from her office door. Larry turned, his face going red. Suzanne's lips were twisted in a wry smile. "You don't have to take responsibility for the temps, Larry. You probably have enough to do without worrying about that."

Larry smoothed the strands of hair across his scalp. "It's the welfare of the company I'm concerned with, Suzanne. Morale—"

"Morale is low, I'm sure." Suzanne waved him away irritably. "If your only solution to that is to hassle the temp, perhaps we need to take a closer look at how you do your job."

His eyes narrowed. "You do that. We'll have a good, long talk. And afterward, I'm sure you'll want to keep me on as long as SoftWrite is around."

He strutted away. Suzanne stared after him speculatively.

I thanked her for her intervention and finished transferring my calls. She was still standing there at the next lull.

"Would you go into my office, please, and wait for me?" Despite her worn jeans and straggly hair, Suzanne had authority.

I did as she asked. Behind me, she punched Mindy's extension and asked her to take the front desk for a little while. I settled into a scuffed wooden chair by Suzanne's desk and waited for the third degree. It had definitely been a mistake to return. If you can't go home again, it follows that you can't go back to the office once you've left after a glorious scene.

She came in, closing the door, and took her seat behind the old metal desk. I was struck again by how much her office differed from the sleek, designer-based atmosphere everywhere else at SoftWrite. She stared at me for a moment, then sighed and looked away. "Why did you come back?" Her voice was soft now, not demanding.

"Ed said he couldn't get anyone else, that you were all too busy to care about any gossip." I looked at my hands, noticing a line of dirt under one fingernail. It's an occupational hazard of gardeners. "And I need the money." I could say that to Suzanne, with her shabby office and non-power clothes.

Her hands were steepled in front of her; the nails were chewed down to the quick. "Did you know Ed and Clarice were lovers?"

I was taken aback. "How would I know that?"

She gazed straight at me for a long moment. "Perhaps I was mistaken. I heard—" Her voice trailed off, then strengthened. "It's true this hassle over our new product has unnerved us all. Certainly I'm not thinking clearly. Rumor has it that you were Ed's latest lover."

"That's what Angel said, but she realized it wasn't true." I didn't know whether to laugh or yell. "Look, I only met people here yesterday. I didn't even meet Ed until Emery's party last night."

Suzanne listened to me wearily. "Of course you'd say that. And maybe it's true. I don't really know why I called you in here, except to warn you."

"Warn me?" I was getting the whirlies from all the mental reorganization I had to go through.

"Yes. Admittedly, you don't look like someone Ed would

106

come on to, because he's into that male renewal thing right now where he likes younger women."

I let that unflattering assessment of my charms pass—after all, it was what Angel had said.

"But I thought he was taking an interest in you," she went on. "That's how it starts, you see. I should know." She turned a pain-filled face to me. "We were lovers, too, a few years ago. We started SoftWrite together. My brain and his marketing savvy, he said." She laughed a little. "He still loves my brain, I guess, although Jenifer . . ." She stared down at her hands for a moment. "Poor Jenifer . . ."

All this revelation made me uncomfortable. I stayed in my chair, fingering the edge of the seat nervously, wondering when I could go back to the phones, or if I should just walk right on down the stairs and back home, where at least I could control the amount of garbage I had to endure from the outside world.

"I don't know why I'm telling you this," Suzanne said, echoing my thoughts. "I don't talk about it. Ed said we should keep our relationship quiet, though people guessed. That sure left him with a clear field."

"Sexual harassment?" I offered the phrase tentatively; it was getting a lot of press in Silicon Valley lately.

Suzanne shook her head in sad tolerance. "Haven't you been paying attention? It's not harassment. Women come on to Ed. He resists for a while. If they're really determined, they can get him into bed. He can't help himself—he's not really mature." She sounded like his mother instead of his ex-honey.

"And Jenifer . . . ?" I asked the question delicately.

Pain crossed her face again. "She was different—she resisted him, although it was clear to see that she idolized him. She scared me—she was smart and good with computers, just like I was, only pretty—prettier than I ever was. And she was too young to see the pattern—maybe too much in love." Suzanne turned away; her voice was so low and choked I almost didn't understand her. "I thought he would marry her. I thought she was the one he'd marry."

She was silent. I wanted desperately to get out of Suzanne's office. The shabby furniture, the shelves of books and disk holders, all seemed oppressive now. The air was thick with emotion.

"Sorry to lay it all on you." Suzanne turned back to face me. The twisted smile was in place again on her lips. She was a beautiful woman who'd given up trying to be beautiful, but it was still there for those with eyes to see. "What do they say—we unload on strangers before we talk to our friends. I didn't know all that was going to come out."

"I won't tell anyone," I said, answering the subtext of her remark. "I won't stay either, if it makes you uncomfortable. I still have some census work to do, and with the flu going around like it is, there'll be other temp jobs through the agency."

"And what about our phones?" She smiled more genuinely this time. "You appear to have some integrity, Liz Sullivan. Stay for today. We'll see how it goes." Beeping sounded behind her, and she whirled her desk chair to face the intimidating bank of computer equipment grouped around her desk.

"So it finished that," she mumbled, keyboarding like mad. "Gotta start compiling the rest of the data."

Fascinated, I lingered, watching her fingers fly over the keyboard, her eyes fixed intently on the screen.

"Do you ever lose stuff? Do you know a good way to get it back again?" Computers were such a mystery to me. I pictured all the files I'd ever lost, digesting in the digital craw of my elderly computer. Maybe Suzanne had a quick fix that would help me.

"I don't usually lose anything unless there's a power failure." She spoke absently, her attention still on the screen in front of her. "And I'm careful to back everything up. That's the one important rule."

It sounded like a good one; I added it to my own list of rules. Suzanne's computer produced a series of beeps, whirls, and trumpeting noises. Mine didn't make sounds like that. I kind of liked it.

She typed some more, the computer brayed triumphantly, and she leaned back in her chair and looked at me. "Was there anything else?"

"No. I'll get back to the phones now."

"Great. That's what we need." I thought I detected a note of condescension in her voice. "I'm sure things will work out now that we understand each other."

I left her office, thinking crossly that all these people seemed to regard the job of answering their phones as some kind of plum for me. I hated the panty hose and the need to be polite to people like Larry, whom in reality I despised. I didn't care to be cooped up in the viewless office on a beautiful June day. I didn't like the way Mindy scurried off when I came back to the reception desk, eyeing me as if I were going to produce a big knife and start carving.

Obviously office gossip was at a fever pitch about me; I figured Larry must have accomplished that. Ed was still out to lunch; his stack of messages had gotten pretty tall, and with the addition of the bone I had to pick with him, would be heavy as well. I wanted a drink of water or a cup of tea, but had no desire to brave the walk through the partitions and the inevitable group of whisperers at the coffeepot. And Suzanne's confidences sat uncomfortably on me.

The phone was the only thing that kept me in my chair. It rang constantly. I started to enjoy my power—putting people on hold, routing them here and there, taking messages and figuring out whether the caller really needed to speak with anyone or could be fobbed off with a stock answer. I realized that Larry's extension was only one digit different from the office manager's, and after that I "accidentally" gave him all the salespeople who called wanting to talk about copier supplies and fax paper and antiglare computer screens.

As the afternoon wore on, I started thinking about Bridget's dessert gathering that evening. It was a conflict between going out with the census register or enjoying myself. An enjoyable evening for me is often as simple as finding a recently published book at the library before someone else does, and reading it until the wee hours in the morning. Sitting in my own cottage, with electric light and, if it's cold, a fire in the fireplace, reading something I've looked forward to since seeing it mentioned in Drake's copy of *The New York Times Book Review*, is a pleasure that's only been available to me for a short time. I will never get tired of it.

But now my living room was Amy's bedroom, the fireplace was unneeded until fall, and I had the opportunity to visit with the small circle of friends I'd found in Palo Alto.

The register would have to wait. In fact, it could wait until Saturday, after my work in Claudia's garden was done, as far as I was concerned. Then maybe I could finish it and put it behind me.

Just before five, Ed breezed in. "Liz. How's it going?" He was with a couple of guys in dark suits, white shirts, and exquisite ties. "Right in there, fellows." The suits marched obediently into Ed's office. I smelled venture capital. "Liz, do you think you could arrange for coffee?" Ed beamed at me.

"No. It's five. I'm leaving. I suggest you go ahead and turn on the voice mail." I stood up as I spoke.

Ed's jaw tightened. "What's the problem here? Are you holding me up for more money?"

I shook my head. "This afternoon has not been easy, Ed. You were wrong about the gossip. My presence is just stirring things up instead of quieting them down."

His face relaxed a little. "Look, I know that's a drag, but we need you to finish the week. I'll make it worth your while. We can't afford to loose momentum now."

Suzanne's office door opened, and he swung around to look at her. She seemed tired; her hair was coming out of the rubber band to curl around her face.

"So how are the money guys?" There was a touch of acerbity in her question.

"Just fine," Ed said steadily. "Very interested. Do you want to join us? We'll be going out for dinner in an hour or so."

She glanced down at herself. "Like this?" When she looked up, she caught the expression on his face and smiled that tight smile. "Don't worry, Ed. I don't want to go out with you. I don't want to have anything to do with it."

I picked up my tote bag; I didn't wish to be in the middle of their fight. "See you."

"Tomorrow?" Ed aimed the force of his personality at me. "You'll be here tomorrow?"

"I guess. Let me know if you find someone else."

The phone rang, and Suzanne crossed to the console, pushing a couple of buttons. "Now it gives voice mail," she said, barely glancing at me. "Good-bye, Liz."

"Good-bye." I walked out, leaving them confronting each other.

14

I hadn't gone half a block when Jason Paston fell into step beside me.

"You're the one who was there with Clarice," he said, grabbing my arm. "When my sister died."

I pulled away and kept walking. "For five minutes or so, yes."

"Clarice won't talk to me at all." The light at University and Bryant turned red. He stopped beside me at the curb. "She's got a lot to answer for, if you ask me. That crazy religion of hers! It just made Jenifer's problems worse."

This was a new angle. I nobly resisted the temptation to pump him myself. "Did you tell Drake, the detective, about it?"

"Oh, the cop." The light turned green, and I started on up University. Jason kept pace with me, walking with his hands behind him and his head down, almost talking to himself. I had to strain to hear him over the traffic noise. "Yeah, I mentioned something about it to him. I don't know just what I did tell him." He shook his head and glanced at me. He seemed very young then. "Just can't make it real," he said, blinking, before looking back down at the sidewalk.

My nobility wore off. "So what religion? Baptist?"

"No." The idea seemed to startle him. "Some goofy thing with chanting and stuff. I didn't recognize the name, and now I've forgotten it. You get clear by shedding the burdens of your old life." His lip curled when he said that—probably something he'd heard Jenifer say. "You know—telling people what you really thought of them and stuff. Clarice had done it—guess that's when she got divorced." For a moment he smiled.

We crossed Waverley with the light. I didn't really want him to tag after me all the way home, but I didn't want to go out of my way, either. I turned down Waverley toward San Francisquito Creek. "So you think that might have had a bearing on your sister's suicide? The religion thing?"

"I don't know."

The Waving Guy was bicycling slowly down the street, heading for his usual place at the corner of University. He wore spotless white tennis shorts, a white sweater with red, white, and blue stripes around the neck, and a jaunty white yachtsman's cap. He rose no-hands, his body arched, arms extended above his head, holding up two fingers on each hand in the V-for-Victory sign. When he saw me, he waved, smiling his usual broad, triumphant smile. I waved back. Jason paid no attention. Living in San Francisco, he probably saw weirder things than the Waving Guy every day.

"Look," he said, "can I buy you a cup of coffee? I—I just need to talk to you."

One more person unloading on me would be three too many. I am not sympathetic; I am not like Bridget, to whom people tell the most extraordinary things. But so far that day, people had been spilling their guts to me as if I were Oprah.

"Please?" It was hard to resist when a good-looking young fellow begged for my company.

"Okay." I nodded at the sidewalk tables of a little coffee place on the corner of Waverley and Lytton. There are more coffee places around here than you can shake a stick at; the Seattle area may have started the mondo coffee trend, but the Bay Area was not slow to embrace it. Constant quaffing of high-octane caffeine has a lot to do with the sad shape of our society, if you ask me.

It was nice, though, to sit at a table on the sidewalk and watch people, and have someone else pay for the refreshments. Since it was a hot afternoon, I asked for one of those fizzy drinks they make with syrup and soda water. Jason disappeared inside, and I turned my face to the sun, relaxing.

Around the corner on Lytton, traffic roared by, but on the Waverley side of the building it was quieter. The fragrance of herbs and small trees planted in pots competed successfully with car exhaust. Farther down the street were picket-fenced gardens fronting turn-of-the-century bungalows and cottages. It was as good a place as any to talk about a young girl ending her life.

Jason brought back my soda and slumped in the plastic chair across the table. He sipped his iced mocha, or whatever it was, gazing unseeingly down the street. I sipped too, making it last. I rarely get such treats for myself.

"I don't really know why I'm bugging you," Jason admitted finally. "It's just—I just feel so alone. Jenifer and me—we didn't have anyone else."

"You were orphans?"

"Our folks died when I was twelve and she was ten." He set his cup down, still gazing into the distance. "We lived with grandparents for a while, but they were old and didn't really want us around. When I went to college I got an apartment in Santa Clara and she moved in." He brought his gaze back to mine. "I don't know why I'm going on like this. I just—miss her so much."

"You weren't living together anymore." The comment slipped out. I didn't really want to poke around, but Clarice's accusation that morning recurred to me.

Jason reddened. "That's right." He didn't say anything for a while. "I moved to the city after I graduated, and she stayed in Santa Clara to finish her computer science degree. She was so smart." He looked at me proudly. "She got a job right away with MicroMax in Seattle. Then, when she came back down here, she found a place to live, close to her new job." He hesitated. "My apartment in the city is small, and she didn't really want to live so far from work. I was just glad to have her back in the Bay Area. Clarice seemed nice, too." He gripped his cup but didn't lift it. His eyes lost focus while he cruised Memory Lane. "But she had changed already. People she met in Seattle—they claimed—she said she remembered—"

"Look, this is too painful for you." And for me.

Jason wasn't listening. "I took care of her. I would never have done the things she said she remembered." His voice was little more than a whisper, but even over the traffic noise I could hear the agony in every word. "She was wrong. I tried to tell her, but she didn't believe me. Then she told Francine. Now Francine wants to break our engagement."

Mercifully, he stopped talking. I didn't know what to say. I let the silence lie there. He stared into his cup as if it held the answer to all questions.

After a while I cleared my throat. "I've got to be going soon." I had Amy to worry about, after all. I sucked up the last of my soda. There was a loud, embarrassing gurgle at the end.

Jason was beyond noticing. "I just wanted to know—did she suffer? Was she—"

"She looked very peaceful." I felt like a parrot, repeating this over and over.

"Can you tell me more about it?"

I hesitated. "Look, I told Ed Garfield to ask the police about that. They were there, too. They'll tell you about it."

"Ed Garfield?" Jason shoved his chair back. "What did he want?"

"Search me."

"That womanizing snake. He was seducing Jenifer. He told her lies, tried to get her into bed."

"How do you know?" I shouldn't have been asking questions. As soon as the words left my mouth I wanted to call them back.

Jason, caught up in his grievance, didn't seem to care that I had no need to know. "She told me about him. She was falling in love with him. A man almost twice her age! I told her—but she wouldn't listen." His voice was a monotone. "Guys like that think they can have any woman. I told her not to get involved, I told her she needed help, but she said—"

A motorcycle started on Lytton with a roar. Jason blinked. "Sorry."

"It's okay." I was turning into quite a gossipmonger, a new role for me.

"If you can't tell me any more, I guess I will go to the police." Jason stood and so did I, feeling that I had gotten the best of our encounter—a nice drink in a sunny spot. I thanked him for the drink, and by the time I'd picked up my tote bag he was striding back toward downtown.

I went on down Waverley, past the picket fences and rosebushes, through the park where children played. It took a conscious effort to shake off the emotional burden of the confidences that had been laid on me. I visualized the breeze blowing them away.

Strolling past the other community gardens just beyond the swings, I compared the state of my tomatoes to everyone else's. I wondered what Amy had found for dinner, and whether I could get any writing done that weekend with her around. It felt good to be free of SoftWrite for the day; by the next evening I would be done with them forever.

Amy was in the kitchen when I got home, bustling distractedly around. Every cupboard door stood open and every pot and pan I owned, admittedly not many, had been pressed into use.

"Making dinner?" I stifled any other comments about the condition of the kitchen.

Amy beamed at me as she stirred something on the stove. "It was gnarly, Aunt Liz. I almost bagged it. I mean, five dollars! And that wasn't a cheap store you sent me to—everything costs a lot more than at home."

True, Whole Foods is not known for bargains. "What did you get?"

Amy opened the oven and peered inside. "Well, they had lots of grains, so I got a bag full of some soup mix, like you suggested." She stirred the pot on the stove again. "Lentils and split peas and like that, with some other stuff.

116

Hope it's not too gross. I saw this great-looking bread, so I got some. I'm heating it up. And I thought you would make a salad?"

"Sure." I changed quickly, washed my hands, and started putting together the salad.

Amy pointed to a dollar and some change laying on the tabletop. "Money left over," she said proudly. "And I got some apricots for dessert—they were on sale."

"Good work." I finished the salad and added oil and vinegar to it—I have a taste for good vinegars, and Bridget had given me some herb vinegars she'd made the previous Christmas, so I felt very luxurious. "You'll soon be as good a skinflint as I am."

Amy thought about this. "You have to be careful when you don't have much bread," she said, as if this was an original thought—and to her, it must have been. "My mom is always saying how we don't have much and my dad should make more. But there always seemed to be plenty of food."

I set the table, and Amy dished up her soup. "This is plenty of food." I took a slice of the bread and tasted the soup. "It's good."

"So it is." She sounded surprised. "I cooked in school, but I've never spent much time in the kitchen, you know? I'm a better cook than I thought."

I kept quiet, spooning up the soup, and she smiled at me. "Actually, it was easy," she confessed. "I put some water in a pot, but it was the wrong size, so I got a bigger one, and put in more water, and put in the weird things, and added some bouillon cubes, and some bits of stuff from your little jars—" She pointed to the jars of home-grown herbs on the shelf by the stove. "And some celery that didn't look too good. It was fun."

"You are hereby dubbed chief cook," I said, raising my water glass to hers in a toast. I tried not to see the chaos in the kitchen. Cooking is a lot of trouble; often I just eat yogurt and fruit and a salad. "After dinner we can drive to

117

the regular supermarket and get some supplies. You can tell me what you like."

"I like anything," Amy assured me, her mouth full. "At home I eat a lot of chips and things, but I noticed in the store that those are pretty expensive. Maybe I'll wait until I have a job before we get any of that."

It was actually enjoyable cleaning up the kitchen together. Amy found a lot of my comments wildly humorous, which was certainly endearing of her. It wasn't quite so much fun in the Co-op later, when we clashed over the groceries.

"Frosted Flakes—I love them!" She held up a box emblazoned with the '90s version of Tony the Tiger—wearing a bandanna that looked gang-inspired.

"Shredded wheat is cheaper per ounce," I pointed out.

Amy's lower lip made an appearance. "Shredded wheat is old-lady food. That's what Gramma eats."

"Oh, well, that does it. We couldn't eat it as well."

Amy giggled. "How about this granola stuff? Isn't that what you like?"

"How about some oats, and we'll make our own granola?" This compromise was acceptable. She shoveled oats out of the bulk grain bin, and I got some raisins. We went through the whole store like that, battling over just about everything—flavored yogurt versus a big tub of plain, whole wheat bread versus air bread, and the ice cream Amy wanted. We got the wheat bread—but also the flavored yogurt and ice cream. I'm human, after all.

"We can have some ice cream when we get home," Amy said dreamily on the drive back.

"Oh, I forgot to tell you, we're invited to Bridget's for dessert."

Amy wasn't enthusiastic. I told her about Bridget's first book, due to come out soon. It was a novel, although Bridget got a little vague when anyone asked what it was about. I told Amy about Claudia, too—her biographies of women whose lives she considers important, the latest being Juana Briones, an early settler in our area. My niece was not really impressed.

"I guess I'll go with you," she said. Barker, who was along for the ride, jumped into her lap. "Can we bring the puppy?"

"Better not." I pulled into the driveway. "We'll fence him into the kitchen. He's got to learn to stay by himself sometime."

A chair across the kitchen door was enough to keep Barker in during this, his small stage of life. As we walked away, we could hear him whining. Amy felt sorry for him, but his howling made me shiver a little. It reminded me of the previous day, when I'd heard him whine while on my census rounds.

I hoped it wasn't a portent.

15 _____

"NICE to meet you, Amy." Bridget opened the door. "Come on in!" She gave me a hug and shook Amy's hand. "We're just hunkering down in the kitchen while Emery puts the kids to bed."

The boys' room opened off the living room, not too uncommon in these old houses. Corky popped out. "Hi, Aunt Liz. Say, is this your niece?" His eyes widened when he saw Amy's hair. Sam wedged his way in beside his brother.

"Hi." Amy shook their hands as if they were grown-ups. "I'm Amy. What are your names?"

"I'm Corky. He's Sam." Corky indicated his brother with a careless wave. "Your hair is radical!"

Emery came up behind them. "Boys, we're trying to read here." He greeted us, his finger holding a place in the pages of *The Sailor Dog*. "Nice to meet you, Amy. Glad you could make it, Liz. I'll come get acquainted after I put these brats to bed."

"Not a brat!" Sam was indignant. "I want her to read to us." He pointed at Amy with the hand that wasn't holding his blanket.

Behind Emery, Mick began to howl. Bridget shook her head at her boys.

"Amy is a guest," she said sternly. "Your dad loves to read to you. Get back in there and let him."

Sullenly they retreated, and Emery shut the door. "I don't mind reading to them," Amy offered, following me into the kitchen.

"That's nice of you, Amy." Bridget pulled out a chair for

her. "They sure took to you. Maybe if you have free time some evening you would babysit for us."

Claudia and Melanie Dixon were gathered at the round table. Bridget poured cups of mint tea from the big teapot and passed a plate of still-warm brownies.

"That was some party you had last night," Claudia said. "You're brave to invite us over again."

Bridget laughed. "It was so hectic I felt cheated out of talking to the people I really wanted to see." She lifted her own mug of tea. "To the ladies who write!"

We clinked mugs. The brownies were heavenly—gooey and so chocolatey I knew they would keep me up late. I ate one anyway. Amy deliberated carefully before choosing the largest one.

"Those computer types." Melanie Dixon sounded disparaging. "A lot of them act like they never see food unless it's at a party." She was a dainty little woman, always well put together. She could afford to be a poet; her husband was with a hot venture capital firm, and she herself came from an old and well-connected Palo Alto family.

"Hugh must entertain a lot of techies in his line of business." Bridget passed the brownies again.

"Some of them seemed quite presentable." Claudia took another brownie. "The one who spilled his beer on you, for instance, Liz. He was very attractive."

"Ed Garfield?" Bridget set the plate down beside Amy. "He's not usually so clumsy. A few years ago he and Emery thought of going into business together, but Ed and Suzanne decided to do their own thing."

"He's pretty dreamy, for an old guy," Amy said, making a contribution to the conversation. "Does he own a company?" She turned big eyes on me. "I didn't know you were hanging with VIPs, Aunt Liz."

"I'm not. I'm temping, that's all."

Emery came into the kitchen in time to hear that. "Do you ladies mind if I join you?" He reached for a brownie but turned down the herb tea. "I need something stronger after getting the monsters to bed." He took a beer out of the refrigerator, raising his eyebrows in invitation. Claudia accepted a beer; the rest of us stuck to tea.

"We were just gossiping about your cohorts," Claudia told Emery. "They're even louder than writers in a social setting."

"And they eat more." He pulled up a chair between Bridget and Melanie. "Biddy was a little steamed at me for taking over her get-together." He gave her an affectionate bonk on the arm. "That's why I'm stuck with bedtime for the rest of the week."

"Nonsense, dear. You love bedtime." Bridget smiled sweetly at him. "Just because your buddies ate all the hors d'oeuvres before they'd even defrosted, let alone been served around—"

"Okay, okay, the young guys are a little rambunctious. But don't forget about the time one of your writer friends got tanked up and demonstrated his pitching arm by knocking all the flowerpots off the porch railing."

She laughed and ruffled his flaming red hair. "Evidently we have the friends we deserve."

Emery turned to Melanie. "Speaking of Ed Garfield, as I heard you doing, is it true SoftWrite is going after more venture funding?"

Melanie wrinkled her forehead. "Not from Hugh's group—that name doesn't sound familiar."

"They're talking to money people," I put in, and immediately felt indiscreet.

Amy spoke up. "SoftWrite?" She glanced around the table. "I read an article in *Barron's* today about small companies that were, like, going public. There was a company from Palo Alto mentioned—I think it might have been SoftWrite. Something like that, anyway."

Emery started to laugh, but Bridget's elbow in his ribs changed it to a cough. "You follow the stock market?" Bridget looked at Amy with respect. "That must be interesting."

"I'm looking for a job in a brokerage house," Amy confided. "The market is so deep, you know? In a school project we picked different stocks, and I did really well. I'm, like, just a beginner, but I want to learn about it."

Melanie regarded her thoughtfully. "I know someone at Fidelity," she said, breaking her brownie into pieces.

Bridget and Claudia exchanged smothered smiles; the scuttlebutt in the local poets' group, of which Melanie was a founding member, was that she knew everyone, and had something on half of them.

Emery finished his brownie. "So you saw SoftWrite mentioned as on the verge of going public?" He took a swig of his beer, his eyebrows drawn together in thought. "That surprises me. Someone mentioned a public offering to Suzanne last night, and she squashed the idea." He grinned at Bridget. "Of course, I would too."

"Yes, we have lots of stock in Emery's company." Bridget borrowed Emery's bottle for a swallow. "We just don't have any money."

"Going public gives you money?" I asked.

"Hopefully." Emery stole the beer back. "Kind of embarrassing if you have a stock offering and nobody buys."

"Is that what you're afraid of?" Bridget patted his hand. "Poor unpopular baby."

"It's a concern." Emery shrugged. "And of course, it really does dilute your stake in your own flesh and blood, so to speak. That's how I feel—not that I'm in any position to go public."

"But if SoftWrite is talking to venture capitalists, why would they go public, too? I mean, they'd get money from the venture capitalists, right?" Amy's forehead wrinkled. She appeared to find all this financial talk interesting.

"Guess Ed really wants to cash out," Emery said. "Maybe he's afraid this MicroMax stuff will affect his sales, and wants to weather a slump with some capital. Dunno."

"A reporter mentioned MicroMax today," I said. "What's the story, anyway?"

Emery took another brownie from the platter and broke it in half. "Like a lot of the big companies, MicroMax sues

123

anyone it thinks might be using its proprietary software to accomplish a task. Sometimes it's a whole program they object to, sometimes it's just look-and-feel, which means the software acts like theirs does."

"I didn't know that was against the law." Amy's eyes were round. "You mean, like when you use Windows it's the same as MacWord? I thought that's the way they were supposed to be."

"It's complicated. But the big guys often reach agreements with each other about stuff they can use. Any small company that hasn't got an agreement or paid a royalty is in trouble if MicroMax brings them to court. The legal fees are huge and the outcome's uncertain. Sometimes the little guy wins, but not too often, and even then it's expensive." Emery got to his feet and stretched. "Well, it's been real, ladies. But I'm one of the little guys, and I hear some proposals calling my name."

After he left, the conversation switched to writing. I listened more than I talked, since I hadn't been writing that much lately. That made me feel worthless and guilty, and my brain was stuffed so full with food for thought that I had mental indigestion.

Melanie got up. "Well, I have an early day tomorrow, so I'd better get going." She glanced at Bridget. "It's my Food Closet day. Didn't you say you had some fruit or something?"

"Oh, yeah." Bridget hauled a cardboard box in from her back porch. "We got all our peaches at once this year, and I can't possibly deal with them. Do you need help out to the car?"

"I can handle it." Melanie turned her gimlet gaze on me. "We could use some volunteers at the Food Closet, Liz. I thought you'd be interested."

"I don't really have the time right now," I said politely. The suggestion made me writhe inside. I would feel hopelessly condescending in the role of Lady Bountiful handing out food to the unfortunate. Last year I was on their side of the counter. Considering my income, I probably still was.

I'm not knocking what the Junior League types do to help the street people and homeless families. I just can't see myself as one of the haves. Handing a bag of food to a vagrant like Old Mackie with a gracious smile would make both of us feel too weird.

Melanie accepted my excuse, but something about the set of her jaw let me know the topic wasn't dead forever. Amy sprang up to carry the box for her, and I stood as well.

"Going already?" Bridget looked disappointed.

"I have paperwork to do."

Amy nodded at Claudia and Bridget. "It was so nice to meet you all," she said brightly. "And thanks for the idea about the job," she told Melanie.

Melanie took a card out of her Coach bag and wrote on the back. "Take this to the Fidelity office downtown tomorrow. I've written my friend's name there. Tell him I sent you, and he might be able to find an internship or something."

Bridget wrapped a couple of brownies in foil and pressed them on me—I didn't refuse. Amy carried the box of peaches, and we left.

The air outside was cool and felt a little damp against my face. Amy put the peaches in Melanie's BMW, but I turned down the lift she offered us, much to Amy's disappointment. After Melanie drove off, Amy said wistfully, "I've never ridden in a Beamer. Elise was talking about her dad's today. Does everyone in California have them?"

"Obviously not." Amy shivered in her tank top and shorts. "Let's get going and we'll warm up."

We strode down the street. "They were nice women," Amy said after a moment. "Do you think that cute one's friend will have a job for me?"

"Melanie—make sure you remember who's recommending you. Anyway, you've got nothing to lose." I cleared my throat, wondering how to bring up the traumatic subject of work clothes. "Uh, Amy?"

"Hmm?" She was clearly preoccupied. "Aunt Liz, I was wondering—could I borrow a skirt or something from you?

I didn't bring anything like that with me. And if I get a job, do you know any thrift stores around here? Do they have them?"

"Do they have thrift stores!" I put one arm around her shoulders for a brief hug. "Amy, you've come to the right place."

16 _____

BARKER was glad to see us and escape from his prison. I took him out for a sniff around the deepening twilight, then spread my census paperwork out on the kitchen table, determined to polish off all the odds and ends so I could start Saturday afternoon with a clean slate. Amy wandered off to the living room to work on her nails, my ancient radio right next to her on the couch, turned to some monotonous, pounding music that I was glad I could barely hear. It made me feel old and fuddy-duddy to find the music of the young so objectionable.

It had totally slipped my mind that I hadn't let her know about Jenifer's death. After all, how could it concern her?

The knock at the door was Drake's familiar pattern. I went to let him in; Amy, wet polish gleaming as she started another toe, was in no condition to get off the couch.

"Have you been out doing census stuff?" Drake wasn't even in the door before he was grilling me. His hair was wild, a sure sign he'd been clutching his head over some problem for a while.

"Not today." I gestured him into the kitchen. Amy twinkled her talons at Drake in greeting and went back to her painting. Barker growled a little, but when Amy spoke to him, he flopped back down beside her.

"Just where have you been, then?" He tossed a sheet of notepaper on the kitchen table; it was covered with his own scrawl. "This message was on the answering machine for you."

"Farwell's Rhododendrons—holding a plant for me?" I shook my head. "I don't know anything about it."

"Farwell's is up on Skyline. Did you go up there today?"

"No." I stacked some of my papers together. "I don't buy expensive shrubs like rhododendrons. And I didn't have time to drive up to Skyline today. They must have gotten the wrong number."

"The message said your name." Drake sat down. The way he slumped, it must have been a long day for him. "What did you do today?"

"I went to the garden after I left SoftWrite. When I got back at noon, Ed Garfield was waiting. He wanted me to come back and keep working till they could find another temp, so I did. On my way home, I ran into Jason Paston, who bent my ear for half an hour. Amy was here when I got home—must have been about a quarter to six. We ate, and after dinner we went grocery shopping, then to Bridget's for writer talk and brownies." I unwrapped the foil package Bridget had given me and put it on the table. He didn't take one. That meant we were having a serious conversation. "Now I'm talking to you."

"Your bus has been here all afternoon?"

"I drove to the garden before lunch and to the market after dinner. That's all." His questions were making me uneasy. I trust Drake not to be a jerk, and usually he isn't. "What's happened?"

"You probably remember Bill Aronson, one of the people in the apartment building where Jenifer lived."

"The paranoid one." I got up to fill the teakettle. "He doesn't want to talk to me—maybe to anyone."

"He can't talk now." Drake made the statement baldly. "He's dead."

The burner whooshed into life. I turned and stared at Drake.

"He died today sometime." Drake's voice was precise. He returned my stare, his granny glasses winking in the light. "In his car, parked in a scenic overlook on Skyline a little way south of Farwell's Nursery. Carbon monoxide poisoning."

I realized I was still holding the kettle. I set it on the burner.

"Suicide?"

Drake blew out a tired breath. "We don't know yet. But Bruno's wondering about suicide as a motif here. He wants to know what all the other people in this case were doing today."

It's always unnerving to find someone you've thought of as a friend treating you as business instead. "And I'm in the case? How flattering."

Drake stood, catching my arm as I took cups from the shelf. "Don't be ridiculous," he said gruffly. "Of course I have to check you out, just like I do Jenifer's brother and all of Aronson's neighbors and associates and anyone else he dealt with in the past few days. It's a formality—or it was, until I got this message from Farwell's." He shook his head. "I know you didn't go up there if you say so, but you have to admit it's weird, like someone was trying to put you at the scene. Only the scene of what? A suicide? That doesn't make sense." He tore at his hair again. "I'm confused," he complained.

"You're not the only one." I set the cups on the table with a thump. "I resent anyone implying that I would be so effete as to buy a rhododendron when I've got my eye on a nice free one in the yard of that old place on Embarcadero where they're going to build condos."

Drake got distracted. "You wouldn't just boost it, would you?"

"Rustle it, you mean?" I had to laugh. "No, Drake. I've already talked to the contractor. He's checking with the developer."

I found the jar of mint. When I came back to the table, Drake was deep in his troubles again. "I don't like this," he fretted while I spooned mint leaves into a little bamboo strainer. "This whole thing stinks. If Jenifer's death was suicide, then Aronson's looks funny beside it. If her suicide was faked, then maybe his was too. Two suspicious deaths—two too many."

I didn't get to reply. Amy stood in the kitchen door, perfect as to finger- and toenails, ashen in the face. "Suspicious deaths? Aunt Liz? What's going on?"

Drake glanced at her. "Your aunt found a body yesterday. Didn't she tell you? It's kind of a hobby of hers," he added.

I pulled the foil-wrapped package away. "Just for that crack, no brownies."

Amy looked worried. "What is this about, Aunt Liz? Should I call you a lawyer?"

"Okay, I'm a lawyer," I said. Drake snickered. "Don't go ballistic, Amy. Drake's just jerking your chain. I'm not in any trouble, except maybe for selling a house to an over-imaginative cop."

Drake laughed outright at that, and pulled the foil toward him.

"There's nothing to laugh about." Amy was indignant. "Who are these dead people?"

"Nobody you know, and no one I knew very well."

"That doesn't make it any better." She looked sternly from me to Drake, who was digging into a brownie. "You should show respect."

"You're absolutely right." I had a nervous desire to break into helpless giggles. Reprimanded by my niece for inappropriate behavior! Drake would never let me live this down. "Look, Amy," I said desperately, "Drake and I have some stuff to talk about here. Why don't you clean the bathroom? Take the radio with you if you want."

"Just don't get in any bathtubs with it." Drake found his remark pretty funny.

Amy didn't. She gave both of us a Look and stomped away. I realized that the last thing anyone would want to do with twenty perfectly painted finger- and toenails was to clean the bathroom, but at least she had disappeared.

Drake finished chuckling. I poured hot water over the mint into his cup, swirling the bamboo strainer. The clean, fresh aroma was soothing.

"Bill Aronson wasn't connected with SoftWrite in any way, was he?" I knew Drake was thinking that these two deaths were related—and not because they were suicides.

"Nothing's turned up so far to link him that way." Drake picked up his cup; I poured more water over the mint into my cup. "He was a clerk at an auto parts store."

I put the kettle back on the stove and pulled a chair up to the table. My census paperwork was spread out every-where—Drake was dropping brownie crumbs on it. I shook them off and tucked everything away in the clunky brief-case. "Wonder how I should list him now that he's dead? Does it count that he was alive when I started the register?"

"Look, forget about the stupid census for a while." Drake reached for a napkin from the basket on the table, and plunked the second half of his brownie onto it. "Look at the trouble it's already caused you."

"My other job's not much better." I broke off a piece of his brownie, disregarding his mumbled protest. "SoftWrite is just teeming with angst and intrigue." I glanced at him slyly. "I didn't snoop, Drake, but I couldn't help picking up some stuff. Don't you want to hear it?"

"We've already established that SoftWrite has nothing to do with Bill Aronson." He eyed the other brownie hungrily. "Those are good, aren't they? Why didn't Bridget invite me tonight?"

"Ladies' night." I pulled the foil away from him again. "That's Amy's if she wants it, and judging by the way she's eaten everything else around here, she wants it."

His face fell. "She gets it all? It'll just go to her hips."

I gave in, broke the brownie in half, and wrapped Amy's portion to avoid temptation. Drake munched thoughtfully.

"Bill Aronson was very nosy." I remembered what Curtis had said. "He had a rep for offering to sell his silence on sensitive issues."

"I talked to that neighbor," Drake said impatiently. "The guy who lives above Jenifer's apartment."

"Curtis Hall. Nice guy."

"I'm not asking you to speculate, Sully. Go ahead, tell me what you heard. You know you're dying to."

He seemed very skeptical of my stories of jealousy and rivalry at SoftWrite. Ed's peccadilloes, Suzanne's anguish, Clarice's jealousy, and Jason's troubles finally got an airing. When I talked about them in the flat, emotionless way Drake preferred, I had to admit it all sounded pretty nebulous.

Finally he couldn't think of any more questions, and I couldn't think of any more bits of gossip to feed him.

"You didn't have your tape recorder on." I finished my lukewarm tea.

"That's all you know." He pulled a tiny little tape recorder out of his breast pocket.

"You didn't ask my permission," I said, shocked.

He drained his cup. "So sue me. You know my notes are illegible if I write them."

"You need a little computer." I shaped it with my hands. "About like so. You can just type in everything the witness says while they're saying it."

"Maybe you can." He held up his two index fingers. "I'm a hunt-and-peck man. I'd get one word of every sentence." He put the little tape recorder back in his pocket. "Bruno may want to talk to you, too."

"My friends, the police."

Drake shook his head over my flippancy. "Because I am your friend, I'm going to say that it makes me uneasy to see you getting tangled up with this stuff, Liz. Maybe you'd better blow off the SoftWrite thing. That phone message about the rhododendron bothers me."

"Simple wrong number." I carried our cups to the sink. Drake followed me.

"I'll check it out tomorrow. Think about it, Sully. Take your niece to the redwoods for a few days or something. Let me get this straightened out without you cluttering up my landscape."

"Poor Drake. I didn't realize I was in your way."

He touched my shoulder, briefly. "Don't be ridiculous."

I shrugged, uneasy. Drake removed his hand and headed for the front door. "I guess we're stuck, anyway," I babbled, following him. I couldn't stop talking, trying to erase any potential tenderness before it led to something I couldn't handle. "You don't have enough equity to move, and I am never going to move again."

He turned at the door and took my face between his hands. His hands were small for a man's, faintly calloused and warm. "I don't like the way things are shaping up here, Liz. Take care of yourself." He pressed a light kiss on my forehead, and stepped back. "Don't do anything stupid, for once." He cleared his throat and stomped away.

I shut the door and leaned my forehead against the cool glass for a moment.

"Is he gone?" Amy peered around the bedroom door. "Oh, Aunt Liz. Are you in terrible trouble? What happened?"

I was tired of the whole wretched story, but Amy wouldn't be put off. She would have been right at home in the Inquisition. Even the brownie I'd saved for her didn't distract her. I kept it as brief as possible.

"Well," she said when I was done, "it's pretty interesting, but I don't see what it has to do with you."

"Not much." I yawned, wishing I were snuggled into my bed, watching the moon and stars through my tall window and trying to figure out what was happening to the friendship between me and Drake that I tried so hard to keep casual.

"I guess the cop isn't your lover after all." Amy sounded disappointed. "He didn't offer to protect you or anything."

"I told you he wasn't." I felt heat in my face again, and turned away. "And I don't need protection. Aren't you tired? You've had a big day—the beach, the cooking, the brownies, the excitement. Bedtime, I think."

Amy trailed after me as I took Barker out for his evening sniff. "In the movies the police never find out anything. They just shoot people and take bribes."

"In real life the police work hard and sometimes are successful, just like anybody else."

Barker pawed at the bone meal–flavored dirt around a rosebush; I pulled him away.

"Aunt Liz, do you think he really does suspect you and is just setting a trap? He looked at you weird."

I paused on the front porch while Barker strained to get free and chase a cat at the end of the driveway. Drake's kitchen window was still lit.

"He looks at everyone like that." I was touched by the anxious way Amy clutched my arm as we went back inside. "What bothers him about me is that I'm so marginal."

Amy's brow wrinkled. "Marginal?"

"You know—on the edge. No real job. No secure income, health insurance, all that stuff. No safety net." We went inside, and I locked up. "He's not as stuffy as that sounds, but I bring out the conservative in him, just like he brings out the rebel in me."

Amy nodded slowly. "That's how I relate to my parents, actually."

"It can get in the way of a friendship." I felt some gratitude toward Amy. For a couple of months, I'd been struggling with my reluctance to give Drake a few signals. We're friends; he's acted as if it wouldn't be a hardship for him to know me better, in the Old Testament sense.

But I had retreated instinctively, and he didn't go far enough to risk rejection. Now that Amy had forced me to verbalize it, I saw the unhealthy dynamic at work. Drake didn't accept me as the insecure, responsibility-shy person I am. I didn't trust the controlling vibes he gave off when he lectured me about my lifestyle—or lack of it.

Amy headed for the bathroom. I gave my computer a wistful pat. It had been far too long since we'd been able to spend time together. I wanted its uncritical acceptance of whatever I told it, its low, comforting hum, and the way using it took me to a different place of my own making. And seeing it reminded me that in all the turmoil, I hadn't checked my post office box for the last couple of days.

There could be an acceptance, even a check, even a favorable reply to a query, and I wouldn't know. That was no way to run a freelance business.

I felt rebellious, coerced by my house into doing work that was not my sphere in the world. I would help out SoftWrite the next day, unless they managed to find another temp. Saturday I had Claudia Kaplan's garden maintenance to do. I would work that afternoon to finish my census register, and Sunday, too. Monday I would be back at my computer, doing the work that was mine to do, that only *I* could do. Perhaps it didn't involve a Pulitzer Prize or a fancy office with an imminent stock offering, but one good sale to *Ladies' Home Journal* or *Smithsonian* would replace my hot water heater and keep me in lentils for a while.

Amy came back into the living room, wearing her oversized nightshirt, her eyelids drooping. The sun had colored her a little; her nose glowed, as did her shoulders where the T-shirt slipped off. She unfolded the bed. Barker didn't even wait for her to get into it before he'd scrambled up onto the pillow.

"Down," I said sternly, heading for my bedroom. "You're not sleeping on beds in this house, dog." But I knew when I closed my door that he was right back up there, curled beside Amy.

I envied them their easy slide into dreamland. The moon had time to climb all the way past my window before I could stop wondering who thought I needed a rhododendron from Farwell's on the same day Bill Aronson was dying not three miles away.

17 ———————————

I was up with the dawn next day, though I didn't feel well rested. I got my swimming stuff together and crept out of the house, Barker panting at my feet and me shushing him. It would have taken a lot more than the noise we made to wake up Amy.

That gray, early morning light always makes me want to tiptoe—and not just because the grass is wet. Birds were going crazy, calling from the redwood trees to the plums, hollering their good mornings and staking out their territories for the day. The air was still and cool, holding the scents of stock and evening primroses that release their fragrance at night. Nobody else in the whole world was awake to breathe that air—no one but me and the little black and white dog that pounced exuberantly through the grass.

I left the tote bag with my towel, swimsuit, and clean underwear on the front porch while Barker and I watered shrubs and flowers. I used the hose. He didn't. We killed some snails and sprayed liquid kelp on the seedlings; it's best to do this early so the sun won't burn the leaves. I worked quietly, under the spell of the fresh newness of the day.

I was coiling the hose beside the front porch when the quiet ended. Barker started growling. At the end of the driveway a taxi paused, disgorging a woman and a big suitcase. The cabdriver didn't even bother helping her; obviously he'd written off the tip. The woman plopped the bag down and turned to stare at Drake's house.

She didn't see me at first; that gave me some time to get

my breath back and arrange my face. By the time she moved her laserlike glare around to the driveway, I had my gut reaction of dismay and foreboding well concealed. It had been many years, but I recognized my sister-in-law.

I waved feebly, and Renee, her face wearing a welcoming snarl, stomped down the driveway toward me. At least she hadn't pounded on Drake's door and made him decide to curtail my phone privileges.

Her eyes looked red, and her face was creased with sleep—or lack of it. The big shirt that matched her stirrup pants was rumpled and sported a fresh coffee stain.

"So." She wasn't going to indulge in any polite small talk. Her voice was the same strident bray. "I have to come all the way out here to get to talk to my daughter." She kicked at Barker, who was writhing at her feet in the mistaken belief that she would find him adorable. "Where is she?"

The sun still wasn't past the redwood trees that block the northeast corner of my garden. "It's not even six-thirty, Renee. She's sleeping." I looked past her up the driveway. "If you leave your suitcase on the sidewalk, it may not be there when you want it."

"I want to see Amy!" The words came out from between her teeth. Grinding them like that wasn't good for her dental health, but this didn't seem to be the right moment to share that information.

"See her all you want." I picked up my tote bag from the porch. "I'm going for a swim." Scooping up Barker in my free arm, I headed for my bus.

Renee no sooner saw me leaving than she wanted me to stay. "Wait! I've got some things to say to you."

"I'll be back after a while. Enjoy yourself." I swung myself up into the driver's seat.

Renee gaped at me. "You can't just leave!"

I rolled the window down. "Look, you said you wanted to see Amy. She's the reason you're here, not me. I trust you'll have everything settled when I'm back from my swim."

I backed up the drive. Her suitcase was right at the edge of the sidewalk; I could have run over it "accidentally," but I didn't. She was jogging up the drive to rescue it when I sped away.

I don't usually like swimming early in the morning. But during the summer, that's when the lap-swim hours are—mornings, or noon, a very crowded time. I prefer the spring and fall afternoons, with the sun warm on my back when I get out of the water.

This morning the pool in Rinconada Park had never felt so much like a refuge. I did my twenty-five laps, and some dead man's float at the end for total relaxation. I would have floated longer, but the pool got crowded with the pre-work swimmers, carrying their garment bags and all the rest of the paraphernalia—blow-driers, shoe bags, makeup kits for the women; they practically move in to go swimming. I showered and washed my hair, not enjoying the punishing hardness of the spray, but reflecting that it saved wear and tear on my frail water heater. Then I pulled on my comfortable sweats, combed the hair off my face and walked out of the dressing room.

Drake was coming out of the men's locker room, suited up for swimming. I had wondered if I'd run into him, since he was one of the before-work crowd. He usually went home afterward to shower and dress and have a big breakfast. He was lucky that his house, his work, and his exercise were all within a couple of miles of each other.

"You're up early, Liz." He put out a hand to stop me. It was disquieting to stand next to his nearly naked body. I didn't want to think about why that should be. He wore the skimpy kind of racing suit that reveals any figure flaws, like his love handles and a bit of tummy overhang. Still, his stocky body had lots of muscles; he had gotten a rowing machine for his spare bedroom a few months before.

"I'm always up early."

"I was, too, today." He smiled. "Lots of gravel crunching in the driveway. Who's your charming visitor? I saw her with a suitcase that said at least five days' stay."

"Need you ask? I thought you were a detective."

"Amy's mom. Maybe she'll take Amy away."

"Maybe." This idea didn't thrill me as it would have a couple of days ago. Amy was not as frightening as I had expected a teenager to be.

Drake got serious. "You going to that place today?"

"I'll finish the week. This weekend, finish the census. Then I'm just going to write for a while. Dead bodies don't turn up at my computer."

"Well, I'll probably be seeing you at SoftWrite today. Unless you decide not to go back there."

"They may have found someone else, but if not, I'll be there. Unless my sister-in-law loses her cool and dots me one."

"But Monday you won't go back to SoftWrite?" He put his hand on my arm. "I'm not just pushing you for no reason, Liz." He looked at me warmly, without his glasses in the way, so I got the full impact. "That message—you know as well as I do that someone might be setting you up to take the heat if this turns into a murder case. I don't want you put in danger." He hesitated. "Try to keep a low profile."

"I am keeping a low profile. You're just concentrating on the ground too much."

I walked away, leaving him there in his skimpy suit and his goose bumps. The swim hadn't altogether suppressed a panicky feeling that someone was out to get me. I'd gone to sleep with that feeling the night before, and it had still been there when I'd awakened.

"Hey," Drake called. I looked around. "Don't forget we're planting a hedge Sunday."

"Sure we are. But not rhododendrons." I walked on, my anxiety lessened. Drake didn't act as if I were on the suspect list. He had me firmly in the role of victim—not much better, but since I had no intention of being one, I could handle it. Whether or not we put in the hedge Sunday—and I would bet we didn't—at least we could still be friends.

18

BARKER had been good in the bus. He hadn't even chewed on the book I'd left out. I drove home slowly, regretting that my swim had produced so little relaxation. An unpleasant scene with Renee was practically guaranteed at some point that day, unless she had managed to collect Amy and leave before I got back. And that, too, would be unpleasant.

The house was quiet when I pulled up. Barker wouldn't jump down from the bus door so I carried him in one arm, my swimming things in the other. We pushed the front door open cautiously.

Amy still slept on the Hide-A-Bed. Stretched out beside her was Renee, who hadn't changed from the wrinkled clothes she'd worn at her arrival. She snored softly, her mouth open as she slept—the better to let the words out when she woke up. I kept a grip on Barker while I tiptoed into my bedroom; with any luck I could get away before the Sleeping Beauties woke.

I was past the point of caring what I wore to SoftWrite, and Amy had dibs on my skirt for her interview. I pulled on blue jeans and a T-shirt I'd actually bought new at a North Face irregulars sale. I laced the high-tops and crept into the kitchen. Barker followed me to the back porch to hang my towel and suit in the sun. I carried the tote bag to the refrigerator and shoved an apple and a carton of the flavored yogurt I'd bought for Amy into it. A kitchen chair laid sideways in the doorway penned up Barker. Then I slipped past the muttering water heater and left by the back door, hoping Barker wouldn't do anything horrible while my guests slept.

The sun was warm, but the air still held the cool freshness of morning. Walking toward University, the forebodings I'd felt earlier were replaced by an exhilarating sense of escape and freedom—and hunger caused by skipping my usual crunchy granola breakfast to avoid waking Renee. Under the circumstances, it seemed only right to splurge and have breakfast downtown, a frivolity that's not often allowed in my budget.

I went to the Plantation because their sidewalk gets the morning sun, and they know how to do tea there. Some of these coffee places have no idea beyond a tea bag you can find in any supermarket. Apricot breakfast tea and a poppyseed muffin cost almost as much as a whole day's rice and beans, but I didn't begrudge it. Avoiding Renee was worth every dollar.

Sitting at a little table in the sun, I watched the parade of businesspeople who thronged downtown in their expensive suits and fancy haircuts. They congregated around the tables, carrying newspapers and notebook computers; they streamed across the plaza toward City Hall and flocked into the banks and boardrooms. That morning I was one of them, with an office to go to. But I was better off than they were, because I didn't have to come back to do it all again on Monday.

Finally I gave up my table and crossed the street to the post office. The lobby was unlocked, though the garage doors were still down along the counter where, during business hours, they make you wait and wait. I had several pieces of mail in my box. The big manila envelope addressed to me by a familiar-looking typeface—my own—went on the bottom of the stack. My fabulous proposal and clips had failed to impress the editors at *Sunset* magazine. However, there was a thin envelope from *Smithsonian* that I ripped open right then and there. They wanted to see the complete article I'd pitched in my query. The terms they discussed were princely. I tucked the letter tenderly into my tote bag, visions of a new water heater dancing in my head, and noticed that the last letter in my hand was from my mother.

Even after fifteen years, I recognized her handwriting. For a minute I just stood there, looking at it—the loopy way she made her capital Es and Ss, the cramped numbers. She'd meant to send it to my house, but had transposed the street number, and some genius at the post office had redirected it to my box instead of returning it to sender.

Finally I stuck the letter in my tote bag, where it took some of the luster off the go-ahead from *Smithsonian*. During the block-and-a-half walk to SoftWrite I debated opening it. On the one hand, my mother's keeping track of my address was a good sign. On the other hand, Renee was even then snoring in my living room. She'd worked herself up, and probably my whole family as well. I didn't particularly want to read a blast of abuse from dear old Mom, who'd cast me off quite thoroughly the last time I'd heard from her.

By the time I reached the stairs to SoftWrite's office, I had decided to wait until after work to open the letter. Then its contents wouldn't throw me so much—and might even give me an edge in the Renee war.

Suzanne was unlocking the plate glass doors when I came up the stairs. She was wearing either the same clothes as the previous day or others much like them. The lines around her eyes were more prominent.

"Morning," I said.

She jumped a little and swung around, staring at me. "I—didn't think you'd be back."

"Wore out my welcome, did I?" I didn't follow her through the door. "If you've found someone else—"

"No, no." She gestured me into the room, but didn't immediately head for Door Number Two. "If you don't mind the drama, it's fine with me." She came a step closer, peering at me, with the strangest expression on her face.

"I'm finishing out the week." I walked over to the reception desk and slung my tote bag under it. "Then I'm out of here."

She unlocked Door Number Two and then said, without turning, "Someone else has died." Her back was rigid, her hand clenching the doorknob.

"How do you know?"

"A policeman came by last evening to ask about my movements. He said one of Jenifer's neighbors had been found in his car on Skyline. Carbon monoxide poisoning." She turned, slowly. "You knew about it, too, I see."

"I was questioned, same as you. But I don't know anything about it. It's nothing to do with me."

Suzanne's mouth was twisted in that funny little smile. "That's not how it looks. And given all the gossip and rumors floating around this office, you're not going to be too comfortable here today. Why don't you see if you can find a temp to replace you? A temp temp. We'll just finesse the whole situation."

She closed her office door. It was five after eight. I needed more caffeine to decide what to do. Carrying my tea bag, I went to the coffee area, and found the pots unplugged and empty. I filled a cup with water and put it in the microwave.

While waiting for the water to heat, I rummaged in the little refrigerator, looking for some milk to add to my tea. There was no milk, although there were a dozen or so strange bottles with unintelligible Chinese labels. Crammed in behind the bottles was a cloth lunch bag with the initials J.P. embroidered on it.

It gave me a little jolt to realize that it was probably Jenifer's lunch bag, brought to work on the day she died and forgotten after her well-publicized bust-up with Ed. Drake might be interested in knowing about it.

I used a couple of forks from the cutlery tray to grab the bag and set it on the counter. The Velcro fastener rasped apart when I pried the top open with my tools. Inside was a container of yogurt, still sealed with foil, and an apple. It looked just like my lunch.

Disappointed, I opened the bag wider, peering inside like a dental hygienist searching for plaque. Something rustled, but it wasn't a napkin. Under the apple was a wad of paper, crumpled very small.

I stared at the paper, wondering if this really was Jenifer's lunch bag, if the paper had anything to do with her death, if I could satisfy my curiosity without enraging Drake.

The answer to that last question was, regrettably, no.

A key scratched in the lock of the back door beside the coffee area, and Mindy came in, looking crisp and efficient in a red-and-white-striped shirt belted over a long, narrow black skirt.

"Hello." There was something guarded in her voice. She looked past me at the lunch bag.

"Hi." I put down the two forks I was holding. "Is this Jenifer's lunch bag?"

"Yes." Mindy stared at the forks, fascinated, and then at me. "Yes, it is. Why do you have it?"

"I was looking for milk when I noticed it in the refrigerator."

Mindy backed away a step. "I see."

"No, you don't." Her suspicious expression made me impatient. "Come and look."

Reluctantly she came closer. "Looks like lunch." She shuddered a little. "God, it's so—ghoulish! A dead woman's lunch."

"A dead woman's note, too." I used the forks to press the Velcro back together. "Is there a plastic sack or something I could put it in?"

Mindy rummaged beneath the table, and held a shopping bag open while I used the forks to maneuver the lunch bag into it. Her expression was lighter. "Are you going to give that to the police?"

"Right. I'm putting it in the file drawer in my desk and calling Drake right away to come and get it. I don't know what's in that note, but it might be important."

The microwave dinged. I dunked my tea bag up and

down in the cup. Mindy put her own lunch away in the refrigerator.

"Listen," she said when I fished out the tea bag. "I
wanted to tell you that Larry was going around after you
left last night saying you were mixed up with those tran-
sients' murders last year, and that you had something to do
with Jenifer's death, and a lot of guff like that. Mostly we
don't pay attention to Larry's bizarre stories, but a couple
of the software engineers got pretty giddy about it at the
Rose and Crown after work, and they made up this poem
and practiced it and everything."

"Poem?"

"Doggerel, really. They're always doing these really
tasteless parodies and stuff. Just pay them no heed if you
hear anything."

"What would I hear?"

"Really, I don't remember it all." Mindy looked uncomfortable.

"Come on. I want to hear it." I leaned against the table
and crossed my arms, and at last, reluctantly, Mindy went
on.

"Something about Larry coming on to Jenifer. It was
gross, really. One look at Larry's hide drove Jenifer to
suicide—that kind of thing. Then you turn Larry down, and
he throws his weight around. They're like children, really."
Mindy sounded indulgent. "We just ignore them."

"You've had more practice at that than I have. Sounds
like Larry's problem more than mine."

"Right." Mindy said this so fervently that I felt sure at
least one verse of the doggerel must be dreadfully insulting
to me, probably raking up my dubious past. However Larry
had garbled the events he was gossiping about, the truth
had been printed in the papers at the time, and it didn't involve me except as the victim of a frame-up. True, a murdered bum had been found under my VW bus—and I had
been sleeping in it at the time. True, a friend of his, also a
bum, had been murdered—as had Vivien Greely, who'd left
me her property. I still missed Vivien, still had a lot of am-

145

bivalence over profiting from her death as I had—but I didn't cause any of those events. It was my being set up to take the rap for them that gave Drake the notion I made a good victim. But that was then, this was now. Now I didn't give a rat's ass about what a bunch of computer jockeys thought of me. Let them act like adolescents.

I carried the paper bag and my tea up to the front, leaving Mindy with the coffeepots.

Drake wasn't in his office. I left a message on his office answering machine and put the paper bag in my file drawer

Then I phoned Mrs. Rainey, my usual temp wrangler. I didn't say who I was, and she, poor dear, didn't recognize my voice when I asked for a temp.

"Would you need someone who speaks English?"

"The phones are heavy," I said, taken aback.

"Sorry, then. There's a terrible flu going through the offices. I'm shorthanded myself."

Two other temp agencies said the same thing. I was stuck, unless I wanted to leave the phones to fend for themselves. Gradually, I began to smile. If I was stuck, so was SoftWrite.

The phone started ringing, and I didn't get more than five minutes after that to think about anything except that while I answered the phone, I didn't have to be harangued by my sister-in-law.

That alone was enough to make me stay.

19

ED Garfield breezed in around ten that morning, accompanied by a positive United Nations of suits—a couple speaking German to each other, an impatient Frenchman who kept asking for "ze pissoir," two Asians who bowed to me, to Suzanne when she came out of her office, to anyone who moved. If Ed had been grilled by detectives the previous evening, he didn't show it. He herded his companions into his office, although the Frenchman looked positively agonized. Before closing the door, Ed stuck his head out and looked at me.

"Could you manage coffee? There's a vacuum carafe back there, and a lot of cups. Sweet rolls if we have them. I should have thought about this, but I didn't."

Suzanne had avoided being herded. She still looked nervy, and not all glossed up like the veep for software development probably should look. "Potential investors," she said, meeting my inquiring gaze, her lips drawn down in disapproval. The phone rang, again. "Don't worry about the coffee. I'll ask Mindy to bring it up."

I nodded my thanks to Suzanne and answered another call. Judging from the phones, SoftWrite had really stirred things up with their new product. When Mindy dashed in with a tray of coffee and cups, and a box of hastily purchased doughnuts from the Golden Crescent, I asked her about it.

"David and Goliath stuff," she said breathlessly. "Our personal assistant software puts together a lot of features that were only available on spreadsheets before, to let people use their computers with these little carry-around things." She pulled one out of her jacket pocket—a small black case about the size of a calculator that flipped open to reveal a tiny screen and tinier keyboard. She punched some of the keys to demonstrate its uses to me. It was the high-tech version of those daily planner notebooks. "We've got an interface that connects them, so you can dump things back and forth between your computer and this little manager. One of the big software companies is coming out with something like this—we've scooped them." She took the tray off my desk, where she'd put it. "I'll take this in, if you want."

"Thanks." I went back to the phones.

Mindy came out of Ed's office empty-handed and picked up the stack of messages I'd written for callers who didn't want to use the voice mail. "My, we're busy." She sorted through them. "I'll deliver these if you want. Are they all for marketing?"

"A couple of them are for personnel—human relations, whatever. People wondering if you need to hire someone here, now that you're big and successful."

Mindy separated the messages and stuck them together in destination-oriented clumps. "Software engineers—right." She grimaced. "We've already got too many of those, if you ask me. Most of the real work is done by Suzanne and Jenifer—" She gulped a little. "Actually, maybe we'll need someone after all. Jenifer was really involved in this new product."

Once more the console lighted up. Mindy hustled off and I adjusted the headset I'd been wearing that day, to avoid the hand cramps I'd gotten from gripping the receiver the day before.

Time flew by. I never even got my notebook out of my tote bag, because I spent all my time answering the phone and shuttling messages.

Around eleven-thirty Angel and Clarice came out to the front, their purses slung across their shoulders. "We're out to lunch," Angel said. Clarice didn't speak, just stared with a look that would have curdled milk. She kept a safe distance away, as if I might throw vitriol or something.

"Great. Have fun." My own head was ringing from the phones, and I realized I was ravenous. No one had offered to spell me while I ate, so I took out my yogurt and spooned it up between calls.

Drake caught me slurping a particularly gooey spoonful. "Hey," he said, pushing through the doors. "Are you eating the evidence?"

"That's a horrible thought." I opened my file drawer and took out the shopping bag. "Her lunch is in here, untouched by human hands—or at least my hands."

He put on a pair of thin plastic gloves from his pocket and pulled the Velcro apart. "Hmm."

"See the note?"

"How do you know it's a note?"

"I don't know, because of course I didn't touch it or look at it, as Mindy will tell you. It's a wadded-up piece of paper."

"What's it doing in her lunch bag?" Drake pulled the wad out gingerly. "Don't want to smear any fingerprints," he said under his breath. "I'll just give this to the crime lab folks."

"Can't we have a peek at it?" I felt proprietary about evidence I'd found. "I'm dying of curiosity."

Drake shook his head and opened the case he'd brought. It was big and clunky, more like a salesman's sample case than a briefcase. He took out a plastic bag and stuck the crumpled paper into it. "If someone put this in her lunch bag, it was probably done on the day she died—she wouldn't have left trash in there from a previous day. Anything that has a bearing on her death has to be treated carefully."

He put her lunch bag into the case as well and shut it. "I'm going to go back to Jenifer's cube and give her desk a thorough going-over. We didn't really do that yesterday, but now—" He didn't finish. I knew he was thinking that

149

Jenifer's death looked less and less like a suicide. "It'll take a while. See you later."

Mindy came up to the front while I was still eating my apple. "That policeman is here again," she said, keeping her voice low as if Drake could hear her. "Did you give him—you know?"

"Yes, he's got it. He's searching Jenifer's desk."

She looked troubled. "What's he looking for? I don't like this."

The double doors flew open, and Jason Paston strode in.

"I've come to clean out Jenifer's desk," he announced.

Mindy and I exchanged looks. "Um, Jason," she said. "Would you—like a sandwich?" She was talking fast. "I've got extra. We can sit on the back porch in the sun and have a bite before you have to tackle that job."

"Thanks." Jason passed a hand over his head. "I haven't had lunch yet." He looked tired. "That sounds nice."

Mindy led him away.

They were hardly gone when Ed looked out of his office. From behind him came multinational chatter and laughing. Ed crossed the room, nodding absently at me, and stuck his head in Suzanne's office.

"We're leaving for lunch soon." He made the announcement baldly.

I couldn't hear Suzanne's reply, but Ed's face tightened. "Well, as soon as you can, then." He shut her door with a snap and went back into his office, saying something that brought on a gust of laughter before he closed the door.

A moment later he popped out of his office again, holding the coffeepot. "Would you bring us some more coffee? Sorry to ask you, but there's no one else."

There was him. He could get his own damned coffee. "Sure," I said, manufacturing a smile. He didn't even stick around to see it.

The pots were empty when I got back to the coffee area. Mindy was taking her lunch out of the little refrigerator. I looked thirstily at the bottles that crowded it, wondering what they were—exotic cola? Tea? Prune juice?

"That's Ed's tonic," Mindy said, noticing what I was staring at. "Some kind of foul Chinese stuff he swears by. There's some soda in there somewhere, though, if you want one."

"I'll stick with tea." The back door was open, leading out to the sunny landing. I could see Jason through the open door, sitting at a table wearily holding his head in his hands.

"I'll do the coffee," Mindy said, after watching me fumble with the filters and spill the grounds. She darted an anxious look at Jason's back. "He could use a little time alone. It's rough on him, coming here. He's really broken up."

"Thanks for the help." The phone was doing its buzz-buzz. I ran up to the front to put a series of callers on hold. When I ran back, Mindy was filling the vacuum bottle. Jason stood next to her, fiddling moodily with a saltshaker. I thanked her again, seized the carafe, and dashed back to my desk.

Suzanne came out of her office just as I got there. Gone were the faded corduroys and baggy T-shirts. She wore a perfectly fitted linen suit in a pearly gray-green with a teal silk blouse. Her hair was still pulled back from her face, but she'd put on some eye makeup and clipped a bow to her ponytail. She was even wearing stockings and expensive-looking heels. The clothes looked as comfortable on her long, lean body as the grubbies she usually wore.

She pulled a face for me while I stared at her. "Behold the corporate honcho."

"You look the part. Watch out—he's got a Frenchman in there."

"I know." She took a deep breath.

I followed her into Ed's office, carrying the coffee carafe. His room was very different from Suzanne's. The decorator had been all over it, from the beautiful Oriental rug on the floor to the softly draped valance at the window. His furniture was heavy, dark wood. A door in one corner opened into a white-tiled bathroom. I was glad, for the Frenchman's sake.

The same Frenchman had seized Suzanne's hand, bowing and grinning. I set the carafe on Ed's desk. He was watching Suzanne, but he noticed the coffee.

"More java, anyone?"

One of the Germans glanced at his watch. "Is it not lunchtime?"

I turned to leave, and they started crowding after me. First the Frenchman, leading Suzanne, with the Asians and Germans on their heels. Ed brought up the rear.

After they left, the phones took a lunch break, too. I got out a rough draft and did some editing while I finished my yogurt. It was quiet behind me, where people crouched in their cubicles eating sack lunches, or faded out the back door to get something downtown. I had time to go to the bathroom and get myself some more hot water. There was no sign of Drake. Mindy and Jason still sat on the back landing, talking earnestly.

The phones started up again around one, but less heavily. At one-thirty Ed and Suzanne came back, without all the other suits. They went into Ed's office and shut the door. A few minutes later, after the intercom light had flashed, Larry ambled past, leered at me, and went into the office.

Jason Paston came out to the front, escorted by Mindy, whose eyes were soft behind her big-lensed glasses. "I guess I'll come back Monday to get Jenifer's stuff," he told her, taking her hand. "Thanks so much for listening. I—I'd better get going now."

They were still standing there when the door to Ed's office burst open.

Suzanne ran out, awkward in her high heels. From the office behind her came a terrible sound of retching and gagging, accompanied by thumps and crashes.

"Get the paramedics, quick!" Suzanne's face was white. "Get Poison Control. Get help!"

I dialed 911 while Mindy ran for the phone in Suzanne's office. Jason sank into the client chair, looking pale. Suzanne rooted around in the lower drawers of my desk, finally finding the first-aid kit she wanted. The 911 operator was asking me questions I couldn't answer. I shoved the phone at Suzanne, but she was no help. "Get someone here right away," she yelled. "They're dying!" She flung the receiver back at me and ran back into Ed's office.

"Some kind of poison, she thinks," I told the operator. "All I know is someone's retching like his guts are coming out." I could hear that much.

Sirens sounded outside—University Avenue is close to Stanford Hospital and a fire station, but the traffic often makes the ambulances slow in the streets. This one sounded like it was pulling up on the sidewalk right under the windows. If they hadn't been so high, we probably could have seen flashing lights.

Mindy came back as the paramedics charged up the stairs. Drake ran into the room, his big case banging against his leg. He dropped it beside my desk and disappeared into Ed's office without a word. I held the glass doors open, pointing the paramedics' way.

Jason grabbed Mindy's hand. "What happened?" His skin glistened pallidly. "Who's ill?"

"Ed and Larry, I guess." Mindy nibbled at her lower lip. She took off her glasses to wipe her eyes. "I don't know what's going on." She turned to me, but I shook my head.

There was a lot of seething action in Ed's office. Suzanne stood against the wall just outside the door, her hands clutched tightly in front of her, the tendons standing out like a weightlifter's. Her eyes were closed, her whole face tight with agony.

EMTs rushed in and out; the sounds of frenetic activity came from the office. The retching noises had been succeeded by groaning. Then the paramedics charged into the reception room with their burdens.

Larry was strapped onto a stretcher, his pudgy body arched despite the restraint around his chest. His eyes looked glazed and dull; his face was fixed in a horrible kind of grin. Ed was also strapped on; he quivered with convulsions and his mouth, too, was open in a wide grimace. Only his eyes looked human, and they were horribly frightened. Suzanne ran beside the stretcher, but she got left behind at the glass doors. As the stretcher passed, Ed saw me, and his eyes changed. His tongue pawed desperately at the air, trying to make contact with his widely stretched lips, trying to say something.

Then the glass doors swung shut, and Suzanne collapsed onto the edge of my desk, weeping into her hands. "He's going to die," she moaned. "I know he's going to die."

20 _____

THE reception area was crowded with exclaiming, anxious people. Suzanne made an effort to pull herself together. "We have to do something—tell someone. The police."

A few of the engineers melted discreetly away when they heard that.

"Yes, we should." Jason glanced at me and looked away.

Suzanne looked at me, too. "Can you—"

"The police are here." I nodded at Ed's office. Drake stood there; his face was blank, but I could see that his mouth was held tight.

Everyone stopped milling around and looked at Drake. He came over to my desk and picked up his case. "Call Bruno," he said.

I started dialing.

"We'll be taking statements from everyone. It may take a while. If you were in here when it happened, stay. If not, go back to your desks. Nobody leaves." He sized up Suzanne, whose white face was streaked with tears, and turned to Mindy. "Lock the back door. Nobody goes in or out."

"Here's Detective Morales." I held the receiver out to Drake.

"I'll take it in the other office." He put his case under my desk. "Keep an eye on that for me, will you? And Liz? The same thing up here, okay? Nobody gets past you, in or out."

People left to go back to their cubicles, except for Angel

and a few others who clustered around Suzanne. Jason stood uneasily beside the double door.

Drake came back out of Suzanne's office just as a crew of people bustled in through the entrance doors. Bruno Morales was in front.

He greeted me gravely. "So, Miss Sully. Another death you're involved in."

"Not really, Detective Morales. I'm just answering the phone here."

He lifted an eyebrow at Drake. "You'll get Paolo all worked up."

Drake snorted at that, but let it pass. He turned to Suzanne. "We're going to be busy in Ed's office for a while, and when we're done it will be sealed. The other fellow's office, too—what's his name?"

"Larry Dortmunder." Suzanne's voice was dull. "What do you want me to do?"

Morales gestured to one of the people who'd followed him up the stairs. "Ms. Horton will be interviewing everyone who was in the office at the time of the occurrence. If it's convenient, we'd like them to leave after their interview. Can you close down early?"

"I guess so." Suzanne looked at the policewoman without interest. "You can start with the programmers if you want. I'll take you back."

They went out together. The rest of the police team vanished into Ed's office. Angel followed Suzanne.

Jason shifted awkwardly from one foot to the other. "What about me?" He looked from Morales to Drake. "I was here, but I spent the whole time with Mindy."

"Why were you here?" Drake fired the question briskly.

Jason reddened. "Well, I—I really came to get Jenifer's stuff, but—Mindy had an extra sandwich and we got talking—"

Morales and Drake looked at each other in the kind of silent communion married people sometimes have. "You can go, then," Bruno said in his gentle voice. "We shall call you if we want to talk to you, Mr. Paston."

Jason left. Bruno disappeared into Ed's office. Drake and I were alone in the room.

He stood where he was, staring into nothing. I took a couple of calls. One of them asked for Ed. I said he was out of the office.

"I can't get over it." Drake perched on the edge of my desk. He rubbed his eyes and put his glasses back on. "Right under my nose. I was right here, and someone slips two people a mickey."

"Whoever did it probably didn't even know you were here." I switched the phones onto the automatic answerer and took off my headset. "Did anyone see you back there in Jenifer's cube?"

He waved his hand impatiently. "One or two programmers, maybe."

"Even Jason didn't know. Mindy was keeping him away from Jenifer's cube until you were done."

Drake stood up. "Well, looks like I won't be done for a while. Can you show me this Larry's office?"

I took Drake through the maze. "He's got a door," Drake remarked. "Guy must have really rated."

"He had a good opinion of himself, certainly."

"You didn't like him." Drake tried the doorknob. It turned, and he let himself in.

"No. He had an unattractive personality—always snooping and eavesdropping. Tried to weasel my phone number even though he didn't need it." I remembered something. "He was strange when Suzanne raked him down. Said he was sure he'd have a job here as long as SoftWrite existed, or something like that. It sounded threatening."

Wearing his plastic gloves, Drake opened Larry's desk drawers. A couple of them were locked, as was the briefcase sitting on a side table. Drake didn't bother with the drawers, but he did something to the briefcase locks that popped them right open.

"How did you do that?"

"You don't need to know." He rifled the papers, flipped

157

through a pocket diary. Then his hands stilled. "Eureka." He lifted a small leather-bound book.

"What's that?"

"Hmm? Oh, Jenifer's notebook, looks like." Drake turned the pages delicately, hardly touching them. "Clarice found it under the sofa, near Jenifer's hand. She noticed some juicy bits in it about Jason, and was going to use it to 'prove' that Jenifer's allegations of abuse were true."

"Some proof." Jason's denial the day before had rung true to me. A young girl whose parents suddenly died might eventually turn her own repressed guilt and anger against her brother, and there are some therapists around eager to cash in on vulnerable people's confusion. "So Larry's the one who took it out of her bag when she made such a scene. He was sitting near where Mindy found it for her. Did he just want to snoop in it, or what?"

Drake sealed the notebook in a plastic bag. "Probably." His voice was the noncommittal one that says he won't tell.

"You're taking it away?" I watched him put the notebook in his big case. "Can you do that?"

"As it happens," Drake said, his wire-rims flashing at me, "I have a search warrant. Why don't you tell me everything you did after I went back to Jenifer's cube."

Already it was hard to remember. I tried to get things in the right order—Jason's arrival, Ed's request for coffee, Suzanne's change in appearance, the exodus of the suits and the return of Suzanne and Ed, Larry's summons. Drake had his little tape recorder on to listen for him while he sifted papers from Larry's in-box, but he listened, too, and asked questions.

"Jason was standing right there when you went back for the coffee?"

"Yes." I pictured the scene. "So I guess Mindy, Jason, or I could have poisoned it."

"You took it up front. Did you take it right into the office?"

"I followed Suzanne in."

"Were you alone in Ed's office at any time?"

"No." We exchanged looks. "But it was probably unlocked all during lunch, and I was alone at my desk a good part of the time. I could have done it then."

This made Drake more cheerful. "That's what I like, willing suspects. I'm expecting a phone call, Liz. Can you route it to me here? Or if I'm back cruising the cubicles, give it to Bruno."

I left him at Larry's desk and went back to mine. Muted thumps came from Ed's office, and voices talking. A couple of times I saw his line light up when Detective Morales or one of his team made phone calls. It gave me the creeps. I wondered if Ed and Larry were okay. I kept seeing that look in Ed's eyes, that terrified look. Had anyone else noticed that he seemed to be looking at me? Did Ed have something special to say to me?

After twenty minutes Suzanne came back, followed by Drake. "I'm letting everyone go home," Suzanne told me, her eyes not really meeting mine. She kept fingering the jade beads she wore around her neck. "You can go, too, Liz. Let the callers get a recording." She laughed; it wasn't a lighthearted sound. "What does it matter?"

Drake shook his head at me very slightly. "I'll just get things wrapped up then," I said.

Suzanne turned around, glaring at Drake. "And you don't need to follow me everywhere."

"I'm not." Drake looked surprised. "I just want to talk to you."

"I've already been talked to by that woman. I told her all about the coffee and why I didn't have any. Just because I didn't want coffee that's been sitting around in a pot for a while doesn't make me a poisoner!"

Drake listened calmly to this. "I didn't say you were. I wanted to ask you about Jenifer."

Suzanne stepped back. "Jenifer?"

"What was there about her that would make someone want to murder her?"

Suzanne's shoulders slumped. "I wondered if it was that way. I wondered if she'd been killed."

"That's what we're all doing, wondering." Drake rubbed the bridge of his nose, then shoved his glasses back up. "So give me some reasons."

She glanced at me. "Here?"

"We'll go into your office." Drake opened the door, but Suzanne hung back.

"Do we know—" She looked at me helplessly. "Has anyone found out—how they are?"

"There's no word yet." Drake took her arm. This time she followed him without further protest.

In a few minutes Morales came out of Ed's office. "Where is Paolo?"

I pointed to Suzanne's office, and he went inside. All was quiet behind the dividers. I took a couple more phone calls before the one Drake was waiting for came through.

I gave it to Suzanne's extension, and then I listened in.

It was brief. A policeman had been stationed at the hospital. He reported that Ed was holding his own, expected to pull through. Larry had been dead on arrival. Strychnine had been found in the blood and stomach contents of both men.

Suzanne came out soon afterward. She carried her briefcase; in her nice clothes she looked like just another high-powered Silicon Valley woman. But her eyes were as red as if she'd been swimming without goggles.

"The police are going to lock up when they're finished," she said. "Most of the staff is already gone. Just put the phones on auto when you go, Liz." She hesitated. "Thanks for helping us."

"You're welcome. I hope everything turns out okay."

She tightened her grip on her briefcase. "Nothing will ever be okay again." She went through the double doors. I could hear her high heels going down the steps.

I put my tote bag on the desk, but for some reason I was reluctant to leave. After a few minutes, Drake came out of Suzanne's office. He parked himself in the client chair and opened up his little tape recorder. The tape he removed was the size of a matchbox. He wrote a tiny label for it and put a fresh tape in. "There," he said. "And don't tell me how outmoded my technology is. If I have to hear that one more time I'll scream."

"Speaking of screaming, I didn't see Clarice this afternoon. Where's she been?"

He pulled out his notebook and thumbed through it. "Ah. Angel, the office manager, says that she and Clarice lunched together, then Clarice took the afternoon off to get an outfit for the funeral." He raised his eyebrows. "Funerals, now."

I shivered. "Don't."

"So you heard. Larry's dead."

"I heard."

He looked tired. "Have you got anything else to tell me? Because if not, you can go on home. We're going over this place with a fine-tooth comb."

"Don't forget the tonic in the refrigerator. Mindy said it was Ed's special stuff. Maybe it's been poisoned, too."

He made a note. "Anything else?"

"Nothing I can think of now." The fancy clock on the wall said it was just past three. That surprised me; it seemed like much longer than an hour and a half since those terrible noises had come out of Ed's office. "At least Ed's alive. Suzanne couldn't seem to take it in."

"She didn't look overjoyed." Drake's voice was flat, without inflection. "She's in charge now, isn't she?"

"I guess so." I picked up my tote bag and stood. "I guess she can cancel the stock offering and postpone the new product if she feels like it. Ed's probably not going to be up to much for a while."

Drake looked at me steadily. "I want you to be careful, Liz. Someone's really playing hardball now, and I have this uneasy feeling that you're featured prominently in the lineup."

"I didn't even make the coffee—"

"But you were there." He picked up his case. "Suzanne saw you with the coffee. Jason was on the scene. Clarice says she was shopping, but she could have slipped in while you were in the bathroom. All those people have reasons to want Ed and even Larry out of the way. And one of them may see you as a dandy red herring. Just be careful."

"Thanks. You make me feel real good." I took my tote bag and walked out the door.

There was a beautiful Friday afternoon waiting on the sidewalk, but I couldn't enjoy it, not with Drake's warning hanging over my head and my sister-in-law waiting to pounce on me when I got home.

21 _____

RENEE sprawled on the Hide-A-Bed, which still hadn't been turned back into a couch. Her suitcase was open on the floor, disgorging a quantity of underwear and clothes that covered the small amount of floor space not occupied by the bed. She'd changed from her wrinkled traveling outfit into leggings and an oversized T-shirt. She didn't look all that different from fifteen years ago, although her face was seamed with lines of discontent. She flicked through the pages of the *Utne Reader*. Amy was nowhere to be seen.

"So you're off work already?" Renee sat up on the bed. "Short days you work around here."

"Yep." I hung my tote bag on the hook beside the door. The whining sound of her voice followed me into the kitchen. She'd penned Barker up in there; he was pitifully happy to see me.

"I'm appalled at the conditions here," she began. I turned on the water to get a drink, which mercifully blocked the sound of her voice. When I turned the water off, she was still talking. ". . . impressionable young mind. I feel it's so important—"

I carried my glass of water to the living room. "Look, Renee," I said, interrupting her. "I don't have room for a lot of visitors, and my budget doesn't allow for much entertaining. When do you plan to leave?"

Her nostrils flared. "You are the rudest person I have ever known," she declared, her voice shaking. "After all you've put me through, I can't believe—"

"I didn't arrive uninvited at your house and insult you," I said gently, interrupting again. "I believe you take first place in the rude stakes, Renee."

"You lured my daughter here." Her voice was venomous. "You have some nefarious plan in mind, I know. My lawyer—"

"Will tell you to take a hike." I wasn't confident of this. Lawyers will usually accept anybody's money, no matter how thin the case. I felt a pang of nostalgia for the old days, when the threat of legal action would have meant nothing to me, because I had nothing anyone would want to take away. Now I had a house—run-down, true, and small, but on a more than buildable lot. That made it worth something in Palo Alto.

"Why won't she come home?" Renee's eyes suddenly filled with tears. "It's hurt me deeply," she sobbed, dabbing with a tissue. "She just refused, and after breakfast she stormed out. I don't know where she is or what she's doing or what awful things have happened to her—"

I sat down in my desk chair and waited for her to stop weeping. It's much harder to throw out a weeping woman than one who's merely scolding and nagging.

When Renee was somewhat in control, I got her a glass of water. "Amy's probably gone to interview for a job." I said, draining my own glass. All this melodrama was making me hungry. I went back in the kitchen to forage.

Renee followed me. "What do you mean, job?"

Half the bread was gone, all the sliced turkey had been eaten, and most of the grapes as well.

"She's got a lead on an internship at Fidelity Investments downtown." I nabbed the last bunch of grapes, just as Renee stretched her hand out to them.

"She's going to work?" Renee watched absently as I gobbled down the grapes. "What is this investment place?"

"Stockbrokers." I tossed the denuded stems into the trash and opened the refrigerator again. "I know there was some turkey in here—got it last night as a special treat for Amy—"

"She made a lunch before she left," Renee remembered, blushing guiltily. "Guess she took it all."

"Oh, well, beans again." I took the bean jar out of the cupboard, rinsed some, and started cooking them.

"Stockbrokers." Renee looked thoughtful. "I wanted her to get a job at the beginning of the summer, but no. Miss High and Mighty was too good for that." She eyed me with hostility. "Why did she change her mind here?"

I shrugged. "I can't afford to support her, and I made that clear. She's going to chip in."

Renee glanced around scornfully. "I should hardly think anyone would want to live here when they could live at home, with every comfort—why, I even do her laundry! She doesn't have to lift a finger!"

I was still hungry. At least, eating was a way to keep from thinking. I didn't want to think. I made a piece of toast and got out my last jar of blackberry jam. It wouldn't be long before the blackberries were ripe again in my secret picking spots along San Francisquito Creek, and I would replenish my jam supply then.

"Maybe that's the problem." Renee was waiting for me to answer her. "Maybe you make it too easy for her."

"Nonsense." She watched me spread the jam and put her own slice of bread in the toaster. She was a bit fatter than she had been fifteen years ago—puffy around the waist, her face round and blotchy from all the emotional upset she was putting herself through. "She's my daughter, isn't she? My own flesh and blood! And you're trying to alienate her affections. My lawyer—"

"Look, Renee." I put the toast down on the counter and turned on her, exasperated. "I'm doing nothing. I didn't ask her to come out here—or you, either. All I did was offer her a place to stay instead of driving her out on the streets. I lived there for a while, Renee. It's not a good place for a pretty, well-developed teenager to spend time. I suppose it's too much to expect decent gratitude, but you could at least cease threatening me with lawsuits."

"I—I'm not threatening," she stammered, backing away from me.

I realized I was waving the butter knife around to make a point. I put it down. "Yes, you are. You're being totally obnoxious. So okay, suppose I say you both have to get out—scram, vamoose, right now!"

"Right now?" She glanced uneasily over her shoulder.

"Yeah, right now. Find some way to the airport—I don't care where you go or how you get there. What's going to happen then?"

"I don't know." Her eyes got rounder and rounder.

"You might succeed in dragging Amy back to Colorado with you." I picked up my toast and went over to the table. Renee was poised in the kitchen door as if ready to run when necessary. "But she'll just run away again, because you haven't dealt with the problems. And next time she won't come here, because she knows I'll throw her out. Where will she go?"

"I—don't be silly." Renee was getting a grip on herself. "She wouldn't run away again. For one thing, I'd make sure she didn't have the means."

I shook my head. "Honey, she's got the bit between her teeth now. She's ready for some responsibility and freedom. The more you take it away, the more she'll look for it somewhere else—by having sex or doing drugs or finding some way to defy you."

"You don't know anything about raising teenagers! Where do you get off giving me all this advice?"

"I was a teenager." My appetite deserted me. "I made stupid choices. I did dumb things. I just wanted to help Amy not do that." I stared at Renee. "What about you? Are you proud of the choices you made? Amy's a great kid, really, but are you glad you got knocked up in the back of my brother's old Pontiac? Is that what you want for Amy?"

Renee started crying again. "That's the cruelest thing you could say," she wailed. "It was all Andy's fault, anyway. He told me he was using a rubber, but he'd been carrying it around so long it just didn't work, that's all! And I had to pay—"

"So now you're going to make Amy pay?" Wearily I pushed away the plate that held the toast. "Oh, what's the point of talking, anyway. Go home, Renee."

"What?"

"I said, go home. I don't want you here. Pack your bag and leave. Amy's probably downtown—you can go to the brokerage house and embarrass her and drag her away, if you want. I won't be in the middle of your family quarrels."

"This is—it's incredible! I would never have believed you could treat family this way—"

I pushed past her in the doorway and went into my room, shutting the door behind me.

She'd been in there, I could tell at once. The closet door was ajar, and one of the dresser drawers was pushed in crooked. There's a trick to pushing it in straight; I always do it because I hate for things to be disarranged. It comes from years of living in the confined quarters of my bus.

What Renee got out of going through my sparse possessions I didn't know. Maybe she was looking for skeletons in my closet. Certainly after the events of the past couple of days, I wouldn't have been surprised to find some there myself. I didn't hear any sounds of packing from the living room. Renee would just ignore me, camping in my house and complaining until I went mad. At least Amy would be home soon. Maybe she could talk sense into her mother and the nightmare would end. I would almost rather have been back at SoftWrite, coping with murder, than hounded in my own house by maternal lunacy.

I looked out the window at my backyard, which needed mowing. The flowers wanted deadheading. There might be green beans on the vines that grew up poles I'd made from plum tree suckers. I had writing to do and a living to hustle. And I was hiding in my bedroom from the invading harpy. It was satisfying to present all her crimes to some imaginary tribunal—"And she didn't even make the bed, Your

Honor!"—which would dish out imaginary punishments—
"She is sentenced to carry her bulging suitcase all the way
back to Denver with her teeth!"—but that didn't get me
anywhere.

There was a knock at the bedroom door. "Liz?" Renee
sounded tentative. "I need to use the bathroom."

Definitely an anticlimax. I thought about telling her to go
find a bush somewhere, but I figured that would just get me
more hysterics.

When I opened the door, she swept past me into the
bathroom with quite a regal air, slamming the door behind
her. A moment later there was the faint snick of the bolt being shot. Renee had found a hole in my defenses. She
didn't seem to have grown up much from that sulky
nineteen-year-old who'd married my equally sulky brother.

It would be interesting to see how long she could stay in
there, and what the rest of us would do if she decided not
to come out. Driven from my bedroom by her proximity, I
went into the living room, only to flee from the disorder everywhere. Even the kitchen didn't seem free of contamina-
tion.

I opened the front door to escape. Drake was coming up
the steps. "Please," I said, tottering toward him. "Arrest
me. No, on second thought, I don't want to go back to jail.
Arrest Renee instead."

22 _____

BARKER followed me out. I shut the front door and sat on the porch steps. The air in my house was too full of Renee's musky cologne to be breathable.

"What's up?" Drake glanced past me at the shut door. "Your sister-in-law getting on your nerves?"

"You could say that." I cuffed Barker, who stopped growling at Drake and licked his hand. "Isn't there a law against that? Entering and inducing mental breakdown?"

Drake dropped down on the porch step beside me. He gave his hair a thorough plowing. I couldn't stand it anymore.

"Someday it'll fall out, and then where'll you be?"

"Huh?"

I pointed to his fingers, writhing in the graying frizz that exploded out of his head. "You're a hair abuser, Drake."

He snatched his hands away. "Look, Liz. Bruno and I think you can help. Will you go through it all again, from the beginning? This starts with Jenifer. Maybe something you saw or heard will confirm—" He sighed. "I just need to hear it once more."

"I want to help, of course. But—"

"Everybody wants to help, but nobody really does." His hands reached skyward again before he pulled them back. "I'm sorry, Liz. You're tired of talking about it."

"Not tired, exactly." I didn't know how to describe what I felt. "It just scares me to be classed as a participant when I'm nothing but an observer."

He looked at me. "Observers also have to take a part

sometimes." His voice was gentle. "But no matter how you see yourself, Liz, you're not passive. You care about things too much for that."

I didn't say anything. His insight was scary. I didn't want him to be figuring me out, watching, analyzing—judging.

"So." He took out his tape recorder. "Let's talk."

"Can we go to your place?" I jerked my head backward. "Renee probably has her ear to the door right now."

Drake's kitchen caught the afternoon sun; the light reflected off shiny copper and stainless steel pots and gizmos everywhere. There wasn't much left in it that recalled Vivien, my dear friend who'd lived there for decades until her untimely death the previous fall. I didn't like feeling that mysterious death was companioning me, gobbling up people whose lives intersected with mine. And yet what was I to think? What did Drake think—that I was the Typhoid Mary of the murder crowd, carrying it with me wherever I went?

We went through my movements on the day of Jenifer's death, once again examining both my short conversations with her to find hidden meanings, missed clues. There was nothing there that hadn't already been scrutinized—the tension she'd been under at SoftWrite, her yawns at her apartment, the voice I thought I'd heard, the footsteps leaving.

Drake had his notebook open on the kitchen table, as well as the tape recorder. "I think of the facts like those little round wooden things—what were they called? I had a set of them when I was a kid. You connect them to each other with sticks."

"Tinkertoys."

"That's right. Well, I've got the round things, but I don't have the sticks. Something that connects all this stuff into one coherent picture." He glanced up at me. "I can't help but feel that you're in the middle of it, Sully. You connect Jenifer to SoftWrite."

"Drake, be reasonable. She worked there, she was already connected."

"That, too. Different Tinkertoy." He turned a page in his

notebook. "Let's go over your association with those people. You met Ed at Bridget's party."

"You did, too," I reminded him. "Suzanne was there. I didn't meet her, but later she mentioned she'd noticed me talking to Ed."

Drake stared into space and hummed a few bars of "It's a Small World."

"Yeah," I said. "Emery knows Ed and Suzanne from way back. Clarice has worked there since the beginning. Jenifer was only there since she came back from Seattle. Jason hates Ed, Clarice hates Jason, Suzanne maybe hated Jenifer, Bill Aronson seemed to hate everybody, and Larry was probably blackmailing them all about something." I shrugged. "This is hopeless."

Drake chewed his pen and stared at the undecipherable chicken tracks of his writing. He pulled the phone toward him and dialed, banging it down a few moments later. "Answering machine," he grumbled. "Maybe I can reach Emery at work—I've got his number somewhere in my office." He glanced over his notes, frowning. "Let's finish this up. After the party, you and Clarice found the body."

"She looked so—untouched, natural. Lying there." I could see it all too well. "Are you sure it's murder?"

He hesitated. "I'm taking you into my confidence to some extent, Liz. Bruno would probably kill me if he heard. But the more you know, maybe the more careful you'll be."

"Nobody can get to me without going through the layers of my relatives." I couldn't stop the shiver that ran through me. "In fact, if I die, it'll be from aggravation."

Drake saw through the bravado. His arm came around my shoulders in a friendly, comforting hug.

"Jenifer might have taken those pills of her own volition," he said after a moment. "They were Clarice's prescription— that's why she hid the bottle you saw beside Jenifer. Clarice said she'd given Jenifer one a month or so ago when she couldn't sleep. Clarice thought that might make her responsible for Jenifer's suicide. Then she found Jenifer's notebook under the sofa, and she looked through it to make sure Jenifer hadn't written a note that said she was taking Clarice's pills." Drake smiled cynically. "She says she was going to give it to me, and I imagine she hoped it would get Jason into trouble. But before she could, it was stolen."

"By Larry."

"Right." He got up and opened his freezer. "I'm going to have some decaf espresso. Want anything?"

"Uh-uh. Did you find anything else about Larry? Was he the one selling information to MicroMax?"

"There's no proof." Drake spoke over the roar of his coffee grinder. "It's certainly possible. I'm going over his bank records tonight, if the bank coughs them up." He fiddled with the espresso machine for a moment, then came back to the table. "Where was I? Oh, right. What we think happened was that someone drugged Jenifer—gave her a couple of pills in a drink before you arrived on the scene. After you'd left, when she was groggy, she was given more of them."

"And left to die." I shivered again. "And Bill Aronson?"

"There's a bruise on his head that's unaccounted for. He could have been knocked out and left in his car with the motor running." Drake hesitated. "My guess is he was suffocated, though the forensics guys are being cagey about it."

"Suffocated—then left with the motor running to make it look like carbon monoxide poisoning?"

"Right. Two could-be suicides. Maybe we would think Aronson caused Jenifer's death, if we weren't satisfied with her suicide. And maybe if we weren't satisfied with Aronson's suicide, we'd wonder why you were up on Skyline buying expensive shrubs." He grinned at me. "That was a hoax, by the way. Farwell's didn't have anyone on their order list with a phone number remotely like this one. I'd guess it was a spur-of-the-minute thing to call here and see if you couldn't be lured up there to confuse things.

Whoever planned this had a lot of backup protection built in."

"It wasn't me."

"Didn't I just say it must have been a well-organized person?" Drake patted my hand. "Nobody suspects you. Your time yesterday was pretty well accounted for. It would have been tough for you to get up to Skyline and put Bill Aronson out. However, this last poisoning—" He took his little cup and saucer out of the cabinet, and stripped some peel off a lemon that was already half-naked. "One of my esteemed colleagues swears that poison is always a woman's weapon—like it was last fall."

"Yeah, but that wasn't strychnine."

Drake froze. "How did you know what the poison was?"

"I listened in when you talked to the hospital, but it was obvious to anyone who reads mysteries." I waved at the shelf of books in his living room. "Classic, in fact."

"Right." Drake looked sour. "Well, whoever did it didn't do it right. Larry got the lethal dose, but Garfield won't die, though he's gonna feel like shit for a few days."

"So you're looking for someone who had reason to want Jenifer dead, who knows something, but not much, about poison, and who is pretty ruthless," I said, trying to sum things up. "But why would anyone want Jenifer dead?"

"That's the question, isn't it?" Drake brought his cup and saucer to the table and tasted his coffee. "That note you found in her lunch bag. There was no name on it, but it threatened to reveal that she had connived at using MicroMax's proprietary software code to beef up Soft-Write's new product. The author wanted money to keep his or her mouth shut."

"His, at a guess."

"Yeah, sounds like something Larry Dortmunder would do, based on what we've been told about him."

"That makes Jenifer's motive for committing suicide better," I said slowly.

"Could be." Drake picked up his pencil. "You told me

your impressions of Larry earlier. Now tell me about Ed and Suzanne. What are they like?"

I felt flattered. "Well, Ed's a real go-getter. But he's very nice, too—takes time to talk to the peons and wants the people around him to enjoy their work. I gather he's irresistible to women—some women. I found him charming. Suzanne seems to be carrying the torch for him still." I thought for a minute. "He listens to NPR," I offered. "Has it on in his office all the time, sort of droning away. He has a bunch of health-food kind of snacks in the coffee room, and you saw his tonic. I saw a box of that ginseng tea you like in his office. Maybe that's what kept him from dying."

Drake grunted skeptically. "What about Suzanne?"

"She's difficult to analyze." I shook my head. "Guarded, sort of. But I got the feeling that she holds herself to a pretty high standard. I'd say she has integrity, but not much business sense. She's pretty smart. She's the brains behind the software there."

"I thought Jenifer was the software person."

"One of them. Mindy said—something about Jenifer doing most of the stuff on this new product. She must have been pretty good, too."

"And Larry—the guy everyone loved to hate." Drake flipped through his notes. "One of those programmers told me Larry cheated on the football pool. He was quite indignant about it."

"Does that constitute a motive?"

"Maybe." Drake spent a minute hunting through his scrawls.

I felt almost a kind of nostalgia for SoftWrite. I wasn't going back there. But in just two days I'd developed a sense of loyalty to the place. There were nice people working there. I hoped no one else was in danger.

Drake slapped his notebook shut. "Thanks for the info, Liz. I don't know that it points one way or another, but it helps to paint the picture." He stretched and rubbed his forehead. "I'm going back to the office."

"I'm going back to hell, relatively speaking," I muttered. Amy would return soon. She and her mother and I could have a three-way knock-down-drag-out catfight. I could hardly wait.

23 _____

CLAUDIA'S backyard was a barely tamed jungle of roses and the last of the wisteria. Tall and massive, she presided over it like the goddess of gardens. I had a standing gig every Saturday morning to help her.

" 'What is so rare as a day in June?' " Claudia spoke the words in her best invocation voice, rolling them out sonorously while we snipped deadheads off the climbing American Beauty rose. It was a standard feature of our Saturday morning garden sessions that we would trade bits of poetry. "Hackneyed choice, really," she said, after the part where you see life glisten. "I don't remember the rest."

I hadn't gotten anything ready, which I usually did Friday evenings at the library. So I fell back on Browning, trying to say the song from *Pippa Passes* with the same impressive diction Claudia used. " 'The year's at the spring, And day's at the morn—' "

"It's not spring, it's summer," Claudia objected.

"And all's certainly not right with the world." Though that was hard to believe, enclosed in that bright space, with roses providing their perfume free of charge and bees making their monotonous music.

"What's the matter?" Claudia pushed her glasses up and settled her shady hat more firmly on iron-gray curls. "Is surrogate parenthood getting you down? Or is it this other stuff? Biddy mentioned after you left Thursday night that you were having some kind of trouble with the census."

"Trouble, yes." I snipped off a couple more faded flowers, and bent to pull up a mat of scraggly forget-me-nots that were sticking their seed pods onto my socks. "Nothing but trouble, lately."

Claudia stopped snipping and stared at me. "The Browning Society might have your poetic license revoked for inappropriate quoting, but otherwise your life seems as chaste and pure as that of any novice nun."

I shook my head. "Not so. Death is dogging me."

"It dogs us all."

"Not quite so near at hand. People are dying right in my face lately. It's—unnerving to have bodies turn up so regularly." My bucket was full of flower parts. I carried it to the big trash can to dump it.

Claudia holstered her Felco shears in one pocket of the faded overalls that had, years ago, belonged to her husband. "I want to hear all about it," she said, plunking herself down on the garden bench.

I didn't want to sit. I kept snipping while I told her the story. It took so long I nearly finished weeding her vegetable plot, too. She followed me around with a chair, firing questions while I talked. Claudia's queries were easier to answer than Drake's interrogation the previous day. She didn't judge every word I spoke. She just wanted the facts, and she wanted them in the right order. Biography writing had made her as nosy as all get-out about other people's lives—not everyone, just those she was interested in.

"So how does your niece feel about finding herself in the middle of this?"

"She's resilient. It's like a murder mystery to her. She doesn't know any of these people." I shivered, despite the warm sunshine. "She doesn't realize I went through something similar last fall." The rows of corn and melons were neat and weed-free, freshly hilled up. The dark earth had its own fragrance, and I enjoyed it while I could; the next step was to hoe in a little fish meal.

Claudia frowned. "Why haven't you told her?"

"It's not that I'm sheltering her or anything. It's just that she and her mother go at it hammer and tongs to the point where ordinary conversation is impossible." I got up, stretched the kinks out of my back, and headed for the greenhouse at the rear of Claudia's big yard.

She followed me. "Nevertheless, Liz, it's a mistake to assume teenagers aren't tuned in to what's going on."

"If I tell her, I have to tell her mom, and I can't face it." I filled Claudia in on the invasion of Renee. "Last night she and Amy fought and fought. I can't even go in my room and close the door, because the bathroom opens from my bedroom and they were storming back and forth from there. I didn't realize before that the bathroom was so heavily used by middle-class women and their offspring."

"Bathroom and kitchen, women's traditional territory." Claudia spoke absently, watching as I rooted through the coffee cans and paper bags stored under the potting shelf in the greenhouse. Last week we had started flats of lettuce; the seedlings were just peeking above the soil. That was one bright spot in my dull and ever more endangered existence.

"And parlor—don't forget the parlor." I found the coffee can of fish meal.

"And the kitchen garden, of course." Claudia wrinkled her nose at the sight of the fish meal. "Think I'll get some iced tea. You want a glass, Liz?"

"Sure." I wished I could escape the fish meal, but someone had to fertilize the corn and melons. It didn't take long. I raked in the meal, spread some compost on top to keep the neighborhood cats out, and joined Claudia in the kitchen.

"I called Bridget," Claudia said. "For once she was home on a Saturday morning. She's coming over."

I took the glass of tea she handed me. "That's nice. Why?"

"Because you have to be proactive, Liz. People take advantage of women who don't stand up for themselves. That meathead Drake could very well decide to make you the scapegoat, like he tried to last time."

"Boy, don't you hate when that happens?"

"Stop it." Claudia looked at me over her bifocals.

"Clowning around won't make this go away. This last poisoning could be pinned on you—you had opportunity. We have to plan your strategy."

I opened the refrigerator so I could stick my hot face in its cool interior. "Have you got any lemons?"

"Liz. Why can't you see that somebody at that company may want you to take the blame?"

"Claudia, it's just possible that Jenifer's death was suicide—the most the police will say is that the evidence is ambiguous, and maybe someone fed her a bunch of pills when she was groggy from a doctored drink. Why? Why would anyone want to kill a nice young girl like her? What could she have that anyone would want to kill her for?"

"Was she raped? Hurt?" Claudia leaned against the kitchen counter. From the open kitchen door came the deep, thundering roar that is Bridget's elderly Suburban coasting to a stop.

"No." I watched the door. "Nothing like that. Just dead. Very neatly, peacefully dead." I thought about Jenifer lying there in front of the sofa. "She was wearing a bathrobe— looked like she'd had a shower, gotten her nightie on ready for bed. The same way she looked that noon."

Bridget came up the steps. Her arms were empty—no baby, no little boy clinging to her hand. "Now, what's this, Liz? Why didn't you tell me things were getting worse?"

"They're not—not for me. Nobody's trying to kill me." I took another sip of iced tea while Claudia poured Bridget a glass. "But Claudia thinks I need saving anyway."

"Your party the other night." Claudia ignored my chaffing. "Ed Garfield was there, Liz says. Who else from his company?"

Bridged thought. "I don't really know any of them but Ed and Suzanne—we meet them sometimes at industry whizbangs. Let's see, Suzanne was at the party, wasn't she? Yes, I spoke to her. She spent most of the time standing in the corner with a beer."

Claudia set a bag of pretzels and half a box of Girl Scout cookies on the table. "Who did she talk to?"

"All I noticed was that she watched Ed." Bridget took a pretzel out of the bag. "They lived together for years and years. I remember one night a few years ago we saw them in St. Michael's Alley. It was soon after we'd seen Steve Jobs there, and Emery pointed out Ed and Suzanne and said they were starting a new company, and maybe one of them was the next Steve Jobs."

"A great honor, I'm sure." Claudia selected a pretzel after much careful scrutiny. "Who, pray tell, is Steve Jobs?"

Bridget rolled her eyes. "Never mind. Anyway, I thought that was interesting, because she's the programming brains of the two. Emery said Ed is better at the marketing stuff."

Claudia looked up from her pad. With paper and pencil, she's at her most formidable. "Just a minute. I thought this dead girl was Garfield's girlfriend."

"That was what I heard at the office, that he was romancing her and she was up for it." The iced tea glass was cold and as wet as Barker's nose in my hand. "But before that, he was supposed to have been Clarice's boyfriend. Jenifer's roommate."

"Probably he was," Bridget said, nodding. "Emery said there was a lot of gossip about SoftWrite when they broke up—about whether they'd split the company like Solomon's baby or keep on. And Ed started playing the field like a maniac—he had a lot of status dates. Rumor had it that Suzanne was pretty depressed about it all."

"So there." Claudia looked at me triumphantly. "We've only been at it for less than an hour, and we've already got a great suspect to take your place, Liz—this Suzanne. She had motive, opportunity, and she's a smart woman, which means nothing is beyond her. You're safe."

"Yeah, but I don't think Suzanne would do things like this." I shoved my glass away. "She's not matey, exactly, but she wouldn't kill someone out of jealousy. I don't think so. And she wouldn't poison Ed, would she? Not if she killed Jenifer to get him back?"

"Ed was poisoned?" Bridget put down her glass and stared at me. "I didn't know about this."

"Yesterday afternoon. He survived. But another guy died—the HR manager."

Before Bridget could answer, Claudia cocked her head toward the front of the house, and then we all heard it—the faint sound of the front door knocker.

"Salesman, probably." Claudia looked at me. "Liz, do you mind? Your legs are younger."

I didn't mind, especially when I opened the front door and found Amy there. "Amy! How did you know Claudia's address?"

"I looked it up in your Mr. Drake's phone book." Amy was all but wringing her hands. "Aunt Liz, while I was watering the flowers you told me to, he came out, and asked me all these questions about what we did last Thursday. I said my mom would be out pretty soon, and he told me to come to his house, so I did, even though I thought it might be the wrong thing, but he made me write down what we did—you know, when we went to the grocery store and then to your friend's, and when we came home, and what times and everything!"

I led Amy back through the hall as she spoke. When we got to the kitchen, mercifully, she'd reached the end of her story. "Hello, Mrs. Montrose," she said dutifully to Bridget. "Hello, Mrs. Kaplan. Sorry to barge in on you."

Claudia looked gracious at this scanty evidence of manners still existing in the young. "It's quite all right," she said, gesturing to the refreshments. "Have a cookie or a pretzel. Did you say Detective Drake was asking you about Liz's movements?"

Amy sat down in my chair and reached for the pretzels. "Yes, he was! Why, Aunt Liz? Is this about that girl who died? I thought she died the day before."

"The police are checking into another death they think might be related."

Amy's eyes grew round. "Do they think you killed the body? I mean—"

"No, they don't." I was speaking more to Claudia. "They

181

talk to everyone who ever saw or spoke to the person. It doesn't mean they suspect me."

"You have to protect yourself." Claudia sounded determined. "You should go back and tell him this Suzanne is at least as good a suspect as you."

"Who's Suzanne?" Amy crunched her pretzel. "Oh, I know. Suzanne Hamner from SoftWrite. They mentioned her in that *Barron's* article I told you about Thursday night. I went back to the library and looked it up again yesterday. It *was* SoftWrite—the Palo Alto firm that's going public."

"Suzanne was in *Barron's*?"

"No, mostly they talked about that guy who came to the house Thursday—the hunky one." Amy glanced at me slyly. "I told Aunt Liz he liked her. *Barron's* said he was one of Silicon Valley's brilliant young executives. Their initial offering is expected to go like hotcakes."

I somehow couldn't tell Amy that the brilliant young executive was recovering from strychnine poisoning. "The phones were sure busy yesterday. I thought it was because of their new release."

"Yeah, that, too." Amy took a Thin Mint and sniffed it suspiciously. "Is this one of those Girl Scout cookies? Oh." She put it on the napkin in front of her and had another pretzel. "The article said they would really cash in big."

"There! You see?" Claudia was triumphant. "Suzanne wants her cash that she's been working for and putting up with all this humiliation for. But somehow Jenifer stands in the way, so she has to kill her."

"Shaky." I got to my feet. "Don't worry, Claudia. I won't let them bully me. Thanks for the help, Biddy. Amy, you can ride back with me if you want."

Amy stood up, too, and politely thanked Claudia. Her manners when her mother wasn't in the room were really very good. "I need to go downtown, Aunt Liz. I have to get some things for Monday." Fidelity had come through with the internship, and Amy was already anticipating her tiny salary. "I can walk if you don't want to drop me off."

"I'll take you. I've got to work on my census register."

I had the paperwork and a clean T-shirt in the bus. But the register wasn't the only reason I was going back to Jenifer's neighborhood. There was someone there I wanted to talk to, someone who maybe could tell me what anyone had to gain from killing her.

24

CURTIS Hall opened his front door as far as the chain would allow. He was surprised to see me.

"It's Ms.—Sullivan, isn't it? You know, the police have been around here asking about you."

I noticed he wasn't taking the chain off the door. "Have they? That doesn't surprise me. Didn't they ask about everyone else, too?"

"Well, yes." He looked a trifle friendlier. "They made me feel incredibly guilty, and I didn't do anything."

"It's their way." I glanced at the bench beside the door. "Can we sit out here and talk for a moment? I admit, I'm just here for the gossip. It's so strange to know that people are dead, maybe murdered, and not have the details."

He hesitated. "Actually, ghoulish as it seems, I'd like to talk it over, too." The door closed briefly, then opened without the chain. "Come on in. I was just about to have a cup of coffee. Care to join me?"

"No thanks." I followed him into the living room I remembered from last time, its white walls and bold artwork like an oasis in a sea of suburban mediocrity. "I will take a glass of water, though."

"Pellegrino or Perrier?" Curtis was in the kitchen. I didn't follow him; plainly he was a little spooked by me, and I didn't want to make it worse.

"Wet is all I care about." His laugh floated into the room, and then he came in, carrying a tinkling glass and a cup for himself.

"So." He sat in the other chair and looked at me expectantly. "I'll be glad to gossip for you—I know practically nothing anyway. But you'll have to shake loose, too."

"What did they tell you?" I sipped the water. It tasted like fizzy tap water, as far as my untutored palate could tell.

"The detective that came—the same guy who was here the night you found Jenifer—"

"Drake, that would be."

"Yes, that's him. Well, he said they were just trying to eliminate extraneous people. He asked me about several others I didn't know and had never seen, and then he asked about you—if you'd been hanging around after Jenifer's death, if I'd seen you with Bill, if I'd seen Bill—you know the kind of stuff."

"And had you?"

"Seen you?" He laughed again, a little uneasily. "Of course not. I told the detective I hadn't seen anything at all."

"Do they think Bill saw something, and that's why he died?"

Curtis fidgeted with the tassel on the broad arm of the sofa. "Well," he said in a burst of candor. "Bill had a tendency to want to cash in. He was always spying, you saw that." I nodded. "Once he told me that he knew I was a faggot, and what was it worth to me for him to keep quiet." Curtis giggled. "I had to tell him, absolutely nothing! I came out of the closet a long time ago. Now that I'm on disability, I don't even have coworkers to shock. Bill was a little disappointed, I think. People like him really flourish in a closed society."

"So he might have seen something, offered someone the same kind of deal, and ended up dead." I shook my head. "I'm confused. I still can't figure out what a girl like Jenifer Paston could know that would make her a murder victim."

"Oh, any number of things," Curtis said, surprisingly. "I've been thinking about this. Jenifer was going through a religious conversion, you know. I asked Clarice about it yesterday when she was here moving out, and she told me

185

a little. Clarice is deeply into it. She got divorced, and had some kind of affair, and was pretty unhappy for a while, until she started seeing this guru-type guy. Sounded like a mixture of AA and TM to me. Anyway, she had to go around for a while telling everyone how they had wronged her and that she forgave them, and the bad things she'd done that they were supposed to forgive her for. It was boring, believe me." Curtis sighed. "It turned out that I had wronged her by planting calla lilies in the planter box downstairs when she'd wanted to plant dahlias but hadn't gotten around to it yet. And she'd had evil thoughts about my perversity."

"How—daunting." I drained my glass, but didn't put it down anywhere. All the horizontal surfaces seemed too beautiful for a water glass to mar.

"So anyway, Jenifer was getting into this, too. We had a long talk at the mailbox a couple of weeks ago, and she told me how it was making such a difference to her, and she was really going to clear the negative things out of her life. She looked a little grim when she said that. I made some remark like you just did—that such a nice young girl couldn't have that much to clear away, and she said, 'You'd be surprised, Curtis. You'd be surprised.' Just like that." He shook his head. "Guess someone didn't like whatever it was she was going to clear away."

This seemed to me a much more nebulous motive than the jealousy propounded by Claudia.

"So what could Bill Aronson have seen?" I was really speaking to myself but Curtis answered.

"Oh, the car, I should think."

"What car?" I gaped at him.

"The car of whoever killed Jenifer." Curtis spoke simply, as if it must be self-evident. "Bill was kind of a crank about parking spaces. They're assigned, you know. If anyone transgressed—if visitors parked in someone else's space, he was livid. He didn't even like it when people parked at the curb, because he used his assigned space for this old truck he was working on, so he wanted the curb space for his Chevette. He took pictures of any unfamiliar license plates. Once he even went so far as to find out from the DMV who was visiting me—hoping, I guess, to uncover some raging fag romance." He grinned at me lopsidedly. "He was very frustrated to learn it was just my physical therapist. I would have told him if he'd asked, but he was so secretive. I figure he got the goods on Jenifer's killer and applied some pressure."

"The car." I shook my head. "I was here that day, knocking on doors. He didn't answer. How could he have seen any car if he wasn't here?"

"Was that Wednesday?" Curtis leaned forward. "He was here, more than likely. He's off—he was off on Wednesdays. Probably just didn't answer the door. Also, he had some kind of camera rigged up to take pictures automatically—his bedroom overlooked the street, you know. The police took the camera away after I told them about it. Of course, Bill probably developed the film as soon as he heard about Jenifer's death. He'd be tickled to think he could profit from something like that."

"He wouldn't have committed suicide?"

Curtis looked thoughtful. "I didn't know him that well," he said apologetically, as if this were a fault. "But I would have said no. A person like that doesn't blame himself when things go wrong. And that's what suicide is—taking it out on yourself instead of on other people. If something had been bad enough for Bill to want to kill himself over it, he probably wouldn't have kept it a secret. Really," Curtis said mildly, swirling the coffee in his cup, "it's surprising he lived as long as he did, given his little hobby."

I left Curtis's place, kicking myself a little for coming. I had hoped to uncover something that wouldn't mean anything to the police—something Curtis wouldn't have thought of telling them. But Drake was good at getting that stuff out of people, and he'd obviously squeezed Curtis dry—plus getting actual physical evidence, if Bill Aronson had taken pictures. Sleuthing wasn't my strength. All I could see was that if the "suicides" were actually murders, anyone could have done them—Jason, for instance, because he was enraged by what Jenifer had told his fiancée she'd "remembered." I wondered if she could have been similarly influenced in some other direction. Perhaps she had "remembered" another episode—a rape, a crime—that would discredit someone else.

It wasn't likely. I just couldn't see anything compelling enough in Jenifer's life to cause it to be snuffed out like that.

I had gotten through a few pages of the register before talking to Curtis; there was just one more block to go, and then I'd be finished. I didn't want to go home. Amy was probably still downtown, and Renee would be raging around looking for prey to vent her spleen on. I drove past Rinconada on the way home, wishing I could swim, but the lap-swimming hours are curtailed on summer afternoons, and it was already too late. I could hear the kids yelling and splashing when I went by.

I wanted to get back to writing. I wanted to get on with the article for *Smithsonian*. I wanted to be free of sudden death and crime forever, though I'd settle for a few placid years.

Renee popped out of the house as soon as I drove up. "Where have you been?" She seemed more than usually agitated.

"Around." I got out of the bus, pushing past her.

"I need to call home. Why don't you have a phone, anyway? What are you trying to hide?"

"I'm trying to avoid expense," I said, remembering my vow to be civil, if possible. "There are pay phones downtown, Renee."

"Impossible. Too much noise. You used a phone to call me. Where is it?"

She'd been through the living room, that was certain. The Hide-A-Bed was still stretched out like a sleeping monster. My desk was disordered, the stacks of different projects askew on its scarred surface. The doors to the built-in bookcases next to the fireplace were swinging, and a couple of books had fallen to the floor.

Renee pushed in behind me. I turned and looked at her, and she took a step back.

"I—thought you must have a phone," she stammered, glancing at the disorder. Then she drew herself up. "I looked everywhere for it, and then Amy finally told me on her way out to goodness knows where that you didn't have one. Don't worry, I'll straighten your little place."

"You pawed through my desk."

"Don't be ridiculous." She glanced away, a spot of color on each cheek. "It's been a mess since I got here."

"It was my mess." I still haven't really adapted to having a computer. I had to print out each of my projects at every stage, instead of just doing the rewrite onscreen, like all the rest of the writers I know. That makes for a lot of paper, I admit; but I had developed a system for keeping track of each revision, and it was recycled micro-perf, anyway.

I sorted the pages of the article about spring perennials from the proposals I had been trying to finish for the last few days. Behind me, Renee huffed a little as she pushed the Hide-A-Bed framework into its womb.

When I turned, she was putting the cushions on—with the zippers facing out, I noticed. Considering that I had spent three years living in a Volkswagen bus, I was kind of embarrassed about my territorial feelings for my house.

Renee mistook my smile for a sneer. "Look, I'd leave in an instant if I could get Amy to listen to me." Her voice was loud, defensive. It was the tone of voice in which my family had always communicated; I supposed she learned it through seventeen years of close association. It made my soul wince.

"You said she'd do as she was told."

Renee collapsed onto the sofa, ignoring the little gouge she got from the zipper tab. "She doesn't understand," she wailed. "I want what's best for my daughter. How can she just walk away from me when I'm helping her for her own good?"

"Maybe she has her own ideas about her own good. Did she say when she's coming back?" I'd dropped her downtown before lunch; it was after two. She must have met some of her new friends.

"I don't know." Tears led Renee's mascara gently down her cheeks. She glanced around for a tissue. I handed her the box that was on my desk, and she clutched it, her shoulders shaking, wiping and blowing alternately. I turned away until the snuffling ended.

"You have to get this settled." I spoke without turning back. Behind me, there was a last trumpeting nose-blow.

"I'm trying." Renee's voice was wobbly. "I just don't know what else to do."

"Leave her here." I didn't mean to say those words. Once they slipped out, though, I couldn't call them back.

"I really do have to call home." Renee touched me on the shoulder. She was subdued, now. But more tears and hysteria were doubtless on tap.

Drake's car wasn't in his parking spot. If Renee called collect, he might never know she'd used his phone. I felt delicate about letting people use his phone when they weren't preapproved.

I sighed. "Okay. I'll show you the phone. Collect or credit-card calls only. Keep it short. And you can't use it again unless Drake's there, and you get his permission."

The key was in my pocket; I'd taken all the keys off the peg by the door when Renee had first arrived, in case her snooping led her into the few locked areas of my life.

The message light blinked rapidly on Drake's answering machine. I thought of leaving it alone, but one of those messages might be for me.

"Wait in the living room," I told Renee. "Don't snoop around; Drake's a cop, and he can tell when someone's been at his stuff better than I can."

She flushed. "What a rude thing to say."

"Snooping's a rude thing to do. Just have patience while I check the messages, and you can make your phone call."

The first message was from Drake to me. "Liz. I want to talk to you. I'll be back around two. Be there."

I didn't really want to talk to Drake, but he was using a tone of voice you can't argue with.

The second message was just a name, phone number, and "I'll call you back" for Drake. I made a note of it on the pad by the phone.

The third was a man's voice, hesitant. "Uh, I'm looking for Liz Sullivan." There was a weak cough. The man seemed to be whispering. "If you get this, Liz, it's Ed. I'm in the hospital. I need to see you." More hoarse coughing. "As soon as possible."

The answering machine beeped and fell silent. I rewound it and looked at the note I'd jotted about Ed's message.

Renee came in when she heard me punching the hospital's phone number. "Hey, I'm supposed to get to call."

"I'll just take a minute." The switchboard answered, and I asked for Ed Garfield's room. The phone rang four times before the operator came back on.

"He must be there," I told her. "He's sick."

"Maybe he's in PT or X-ray or something." She sounded bored. "I'll give you the nurses' station."

The nurses' station answered and put me on hold in one fell swoop. I waited. Renee waited, her fingers tapping impatiently on the little telephone table.

"This is ridiculous. How long are you going to wait?" Renee glanced at her watch. "Andy will be on the golf course pretty soon."

I hung up. "Go ahead. Make it snappy."

Turn about was fair play. I went in the living room to give her privacy. But that loud, defensive tone of voice was easy to hear. And Renee's voice got louder as she spoke.

"I'm telling you, she won't come! Short of handcuffing her, I don't know what to do." A pause. "Well, maybe you'd better just come on out and do it, then. I sure as hell won't! You don't know how stubborn she's being." Another pause. Her voice got lower, but I could still hear words.

". . . uncooperative . . . refuses . . . shack, really . . . can't understand . . . rest of the summer?"

Another pause. "Well, that's the best I can do," Renee said angrily. "Maybe I'll just stay here with her, and you can take care of yourself for a change!"

The phone crashed into its cradle. I went back in the kitchen as Renee stood up. Her mouth made a tight line, and her eyes were narrowed. I opened the back door. "Let's go."

She stomped out, still mad at Andy. I hoped she'd forgotten to memorize Drake's number. Our lives would be living hell if she had.

By the time I locked the back door she was halfway to my place. I let her get inside before I opened fire on my own.

"Amy will be home soon, most likely." I glanced at the clock in my kitchen. "You have until I get back to settle this with her. I can't stop you from staying in town, Renee. But you don't stay here. I'm not running a boardinghouse for warring relatives."

She tossed her head. "There are motels around, I'm sure. Apartments."

"That's right," I said pleasantly. "They're expensive, and around Stanford graduation, which is now, they're really booked up. But you'll probably find a place, although you may have to go to Redwood City."

She yammered while I got my bag and climbed in the bus. "Where are you going?"

"To visit a sick friend." I leaned out the window. "There's a grocery store about ten blocks downtown. You and Amy can walk down and pick up some groceries if you want. Looks like we're pretty much out of food."

I backed out the drive, getting a last glimpse of her standing in front of my house, hands on hips, glaring at me.

25 _____

THERE was space available in the hospital's pay lot, but Rule Number 14 is never to pay for parking. I cruised stubbornly around the long approach to the Stanford hospital, and off onto the side streets, looking for a free spot. Even on the curb, they ticket if you're parked a minute more than two hours. I had overstayed on the occasion of Bridget's latest baby being born and had been amazed at the cost of the ticket I'd gotten. Rule Number 15 is never to get tickets.

It was a long trudge back to the entrance from my parking spot. A silver-haired pink lady in the lobby told me where to find Ed, and I headed for the escalators. The hospital was huge, with corridors going everywhere, and that kind of high-tech, metal-and-plastic decor that public institutions like hospitals and airports have adopted.

I stepped onto the escalator, joining a stream of people moving up to the second floor. One of them was a tall, thin woman in a faded polo shirt and Levi's—Suzanne. I didn't speak. She looked preoccupied. I wondered if Ed had called her, too. Maybe she'd just come to soothe his fevered brow. Or maybe she was going to rectify the mistake that had left Ed alive.

Suzanne knew where she was going. There was no hesitation when she turned into another corridor, no slowing of her long legs. I had to trot a little to keep up. She rounded another corner, and I put on some speed.

She was waiting around the corner. I nearly bumped into her.

"I thought I recognized you. What are you doing here?" Her voice was not friendly, but not hostile, either. Remote.

"Trying to catch up to you." It wasn't really a lie. "Ed called and asked me to come in—said he had something to tell me."

Her expression stiffened further. "I see." She was silent a moment, not stirring, but when I moved she put a hand on my shoulder, holding me in place.

"Did Ed—tell you what it was about?" Her eyes were shadowed, but I saw the pain there.

I fidgeted under that heavy hand. "Not really. I don't know why he would call me, anyway. I'm not part of this."

She shook her head slowly. "You're deep in it now."

The words lifted the hair on the back of my neck. "What do you mean?"

Her lips smiled, but the pain in her eyes didn't go away. "If I were you," she said, her voice so soft I had to strain to hear her over the clatter of trays and squeaking of carts in the halls around us, "I would leave now. Don't visit Ed today. Come back tomorrow, when he's more himself."

I looked at her doubtfully. She was bigger than I was— taller, and in great shape. I could picture her at home on her cross-country ski machine or cycling miles on the weekends in Lycra shorts. On her they wouldn't even look that bad.

But I was scrappy, and I knew a few tricks. "Ed asked me to come today."

She took her hand off my shoulder. "Oh, well. It's your funeral."

She walked swiftly away, and I followed, turning her last words over in my mind. I didn't much care for them.

There was one nurse at the nurses' station, carrying on a conversation on two lines at once while a third line rang and rang. Suzanne strode through the area confidently. The nurse didn't stop us. I jogged along a step behind.

Ed's room was at the end of a corridor, several doors away from the nurses' station. It was isolated—across the hall was a linen room bursting with huge plastic bags of sheets and gowns. The room next to it had cupboards floor to ceiling. On the counter was a tray of little paper cups filled with pills, like pharmaceutical party favors.

The first bed in Ed's room was empty, its curtains pulled back. Ed was lying on the bed next to the window. He had an IV plugged into his right arm and tubes coming out of his nose. There were black circles under his eyes. He looked miserable.

He also looked surprised. "Suzanne! I thought you were coming later."

"That's what I said yesterday," she said composedly, "but I didn't suppose you'd remember, in your condition and all."

The look he gave her was a compound of fear and defiance. "You don't have to come at all."

"I know." She sat down in the chair, pulling it around so it was between the bed and the door, blocking the narrow aisle at the foot of the other bed. "How are you?"

Ignoring her, he turned to me. "I'm just glad to be alive. The doctors are amazed, frankly."

I stood, hemmed in between Suzanne in the chair and Ed's bedside table. This was cluttered with a cup and water pitcher and a couple of weird-shaped vessels whose uses make our bodily functions seem so alien. The table that was supposed to swing over the bed was pushed back against the window, displaying several flower arrangements and a potted Swedish ivy. "So," I said, "what was it? Strychnine?"

He stared. "How did you know?"

"I read mysteries. The symptoms are pretty easy to tell."

"I thought maybe the policeman told you. Paul Drake." He was gazing at me, almost anxiously, as if my answer mattered more than the words would indicate. "You seemed pretty chummy with him, and you're neighbors and all."

"He wouldn't tell me anything about a case." I thought that Ed's manner was oddly flirtatious, for someone who'd practically died.

Suzanne had her arms crossed in front of her, fingers

drumming impatiently on the opposite elbows. "So how long do you stay here, Ed?"

"Not long." He answered her civilly enough, though he didn't look directly at her. "They'll probably let me out tomorrow if everything checks out. Then I'm going to find the person who killed Jenifer and Larry."

Both of us were silent a moment. Suzanne bowed her head. Her shoulders shook, her voice was muffled. "I thought she was supposed to have committed suicide."

"It seems obvious now that she didn't." Ed's voice was impatient. "The same person who killed her just tried to kill me."

"That could be," I admitted cautiously. "Do you know who it is?"

Ed's gaze flicked to Suzanne. "I think so."

"Then you should have asked to see the police, not me." I edged back against the other bed. "Why don't you get in touch with Detective Drake or Morales? If you know who's trying to kill you, spit it out to the cops. It's stupid to sit on it."

"That's good advice." Ed glared at Suzanne. "Would you leave us for a moment, Suse? I have something personal I want to say to Liz."

I stepped sideways, between the other bed and Ed's bedside table. "Oh, never mind. You can tell me after you get out of the hospital." There wasn't room between the head of the other bed and the wall for me to slip out and get a clear shot at the door. I wanted out of that room; the vibes were too weird.

Suzanne dropped her hand and sat up, laughing. She had been laughing all along. She didn't sound particularly demented, just amused.

"That might be hard to do—to confide in the police. Right, Ed?"

"Suzanne!" Ed sat up, his tubes dangling. I suppressed a gasp of concern, but Suzanne was untouched.

"Tell her, Ed. Don't mind me. Tell her that you're the one who killed Jenifer, who killed her neighbor, who killed

196

Larry and faked your own poisoning to make yourself immune from suspicion. Tell her whom you are going to blame, Ed."

Both of them looked at me.

26 _____

ED scooted to the edge of his bed. "I meant to pin it on you, Suzanne," he snarled. "It's just like you to figure it out and get in my way. So help me, you're dead meat, Suse. I don't need you around that much. Not anymore."

"Yes, you do, Ed." Suzanne stood, her tall, strong body looming over him as he sat on the bed. "You always did. I've pulled many an iron out of the fire for you, haven't I?"

"It was no sacrifice for you." Ed's face contorted. "Nobody asked you to stick around. You did as well out of our association as I did." He looked at her polo shirt and jeans. "I don't know what you spend it on—certainly not your looks. I might have stayed with you if you'd just taken care of yourself."

They bent their energies on each other, both forgetting me. I didn't want to draw their attention—despite what he'd said, it wasn't clear to me if Suzanne was on Ed's side or not. They might be in it together, with me as the fall guy. I would look guilty if I were found dead in Ed's hospital room, if he said he'd barely managed to fight me off.

If I made a break for it by scrambling over the other bed, would Suzanne still do Ed's dirty work? Or would she stand by while he handled it? I didn't like either of those alternatives.

"Clarice takes care of herself." Suzanne kept her voice low, but she spoke with a force and venom I hadn't heard from her before. "You still left her."

"She was a nag." Ed's dismissal came easily. "That reli-

198

gious stuff got to me, too. Always saying we had to get married. She froze up on me."

"But it was Jenifer you killed. Why?" Suzanne seemed taller now, although Ed still strove to dominate the situation. I pushed gently against the other bed, with the idea that hospital beds roll easily, and maybe I could shove it around to clear a path to the door. The bed must have had its brakes on—it wouldn't move.

"I'm not going to talk about it anymore." Ed made the announcement as if it were a business decision. "I'll have to blame it on both of you after all, Suzanne. You and our sinister temp." He gestured at me.

I froze, petrified by the malice in his voice.

"Yes, you." Ed was looking at me know, directing all his negative charisma my way. "I was planning just to incriminate Suzanne, but then I thought you'd make a good murderer. A backup murderer—because Suzanne always nagged me to back everything up. You were there that afternoon—I heard you talking to Jenifer, though it took me a while to recognize your voice. It was like a present from the gods, to have two possible people to take the blame." His voice changed, became introspective. "I knew then that all of it was meant. I was right to clear these little annoyances out of my way. I just couldn't decide which one of you to set up for it."

Suzanne laughed again. Ed jerked around to look at her. "You won't need to decide now." She spoke almost indulgently. "You've said too much, Ed. And all that stomach pumping they did to you yesterday has weakened you. You're no match for two determined women." She glanced at me, pinned between the table and the other bed.

"I'll get help." I edged along toward the foot of the bed.

"No!" They spoke together. Suzanne stood in front of me, blocking the narrow path to the door.

"I can't let you interfere," she said.

Ed was out of bed, his IV pole rattling behind him, his hospital gown absurdly dainty on his hairy, muscular body. He yanked the tubes out of his nose, with a fleeting gri-

199

mace of pain when the adhesive tape took some of his nose hair with it. Then he grabbed a hypodermic syringe out of the bedside table's drawer.

For a moment everything stopped while Suzanne and I stared at him.

"This is just potassium," he said conversationally, waving the hypodermic. "I got it out of the medication room on my morning walk around the halls. A pity they're so under-staffed here, isn't it? Nobody noticed what I was doing." His charming smile appeared. "I was going to tell Liz about my fears of Suzanne, and then when you came later to visit me, Suse, there'd be a struggle, a shout for the nurse. They'd all think you were trying to kill me—again." He held the hypo up, squirting a few drops into the air. "Potassium's lethal, you know. An overdose just causes the heart to stop. It's untraceable injected into the IV, which is how you were planning to do it. I'll be very shaken by my second near-escape from death."

Suzanne drew a deep breath. "It won't happen that way, though. Now, there are two of us. One of you."

"There'll be one of you soon." He lunged at her, holding the hypodermic like a dagger, pointed straight at her chest.

Suzanne dodged; Ed grabbed her. They fell back together on the unused bed as if they were urgent lovers instead of enemies. Ed was on top of her, the hospital gown flapping open at the back.

His IV stand teetered. It was tall, with a heavy wheeled base. I took it by the waist and forced it over. It landed on Ed's naked backside.

He yelled and rolled aside, making a final effort to thrust the hypodermic home. Suzanne put out her hand to ward off the blow; the needle went into her palm, up to the hilt.

Ed didn't notice that he hadn't shot the syringe's plunger. He was off the bed, righting the IV pole and then reaching for the discarded tubes he'd ripped out of his nose. His face was intent, focused. He pulled the tubes taut between both hands and came at me.

I backed up, not taking my eyes off his merciless face.

The IV stand rolled meekly behind him. He held the clear plastic tubes like a garrote; his gaze measured my neck. The backs of my knees hit the chair behind me, and I fell into it.

Ed was on me right away, his knee pressed intimately between my legs, his weight holding me down. He raised his hands and yanked the tubing down behind my head, lassoing my neck. I felt the cold plastic on my nape. Leaning back, he crossed his arms between us, grunting in satisfaction when the tubing tightened and I gagged and choked.

My eyes were being forced from their sockets. Blinking away the red haze that clouded my vision, I saw Suzanne stagger to her feet behind Ed. She grasped the syringe that protruded from her palm. I could see the glittery point of the needle coming out the other side of her hand. She squeezed her eyes shut and the point disappeared. A moment later a bright red bead took its place.

I managed to get my hand between my neck and the tubing, and sobbed with relief from the pressure. Ed's look of concentration was replaced by a frown. He twisted the tubing together and transferred it to his left hand. Then he slapped me, hard. The pain exploded sharply inside my skull. My head rocked sideways against the chair's scratchy welting. Instinctively I put both hands up to my face. He twisted the tubing again, and once more I couldn't breathe.

"Ed." Suzanne sounded so calm, so normal. "You said this stuff is fatal in IV?"

Ed went very still. He dropped the tubing, and my chest heaved reflexively. He turned, crouched beside me on the chair. Suzanne stood beside the IV stand, holding the syringe.

The empty syringe.

"What did you do?" Ed's cry was heartfelt. He launched himself, but Suzanne stepped aside, and he ended up sprawled on his bed. "Take it out, take it out—" He pawed at the IV in his right arm. Suzanne grabbed his left hand and twisted it behind his back.

"It'll reach you pretty soon," she said in that soft, polite voice. He writhed and bucked, but she kept his hand wrenched up behind him. "Then you'll die, like they died. You're evil, Ed. You have to be destroyed."

The door banged open, and a nurse popped in. "What's all this commotion," she began. Her eyes widened. "Backup," she yelled, squeezing between the chair where I still sat, collapsed, and the end of the unused bed.

My foot was in the way. I truly didn't mean to trip her.

Ed screamed, a horrible sound. He tried to gnaw the IV out of his arm with his teeth. His eyes were frantic, bulging with fear. I felt as if there were some force in the room besides us—some implacable judge who constrained Suzanne to keep her grip on Ed's hand, who kept Ed from saving himself, who'd made me trip the nurse.

Then the nurse jumped up, another one ran in, and Suzanne, sighing, let go of Ed's hand. He didn't even notice. He still tried desperately to bite or pull out the IV line. The nurses rushed at him.

"Was he having a seizure? What happened?" The first nurse questioned us while she and the other one grabbed Ed's legs, strapped him to the bed, and then managed to pry his hands down long enough to give them the same treatment. His head flailed from side to side, his mouth working. It must have looked as if he had had a fit, and Suzanne had been subduing him.

"Potassium," he gasped out. "She—they—potassium in my IV line."

The nurses looked at him, then at each other. One of them examined the IV. "No sign of a puncture."

The other one shook her head. "Delusions. Sometimes an aftereffect of these poisonings."

Suzanne smiled wearily at me. "Okay. Call your cop friend." She glanced back at Ed. "I just wanted to let him know how it felt."

"You—didn't—" My throat was raw. It was hard to talk.

"Of course not." She walked toward the door. "I'll be in the waiting room down the hall. The air in here is too foul."

The nurses hovered busily over Ed, who still watched the IV line with a panic-stricken gaze. I picked up the phone, got an outside line, and called Drake at home. For once he was there.

"You sound like shit. Are you okay? I was just leaving for the hospital," he said as soon as he heard me. "For God's sake, Sully. I warned you to be careful. Don't you know better than to keep assignations with people who are mixed up in a murder case?"

"I didn't suspect Ed—he was poisoned," I pointed out. The words came out hoarsely. One of the nurses turned to look at me. "But as it turns out, he wasn't really."

Drake's impatient sigh hissed down the phone line. "That's why I left that message for you to stay put. We tested that tonic of his. It has minute amounts of strychnine in it—enough to make Ed's bodily fluids test positive, but not enough to cause any symptoms. He could have poisoned Larry's coffee and faked his own symptoms."

"Very clever, Drake." I felt tired. "Come on over to the hospital. Ed's pretty much confessed to the murders, in front of two witnesses."

Ed hadn't even heard me. He was still waiting to die.

"What's this about murder?" The first nurse scowled at me. "I understood this man was administered poison yesterday. This room is restricted. You shouldn't be here."

"I'm not." I followed Suzanne down the hall. It would do Ed good to expect death for a while longer.

27 _____

WE were crowded into Drake's tiny office, Suzanne with her long legs wound around a folding chair, Bruno Morales perched on Drake's desk. We'd had our statements taken separately, and then they'd herded us together. It looked like Suzanne was going to avoid an attempted-homicide charge. I hadn't mentioned the final twist she'd applied to Ed with the syringe. Evidently she hadn't either.

"I still don't get it," I said. "Why did he kill Jenifer? Why did he have to do that? Or did she really commit suicide after all?"

Bruno and Drake exchanged glances. "You know, Paolo," Bruno said, getting up from his desk, "we've been working on this for quite a while. I feel like taking a break, walking over to Jim's for some coffee. How about you?"

Drake grimaced. "How about Rodger's? Coffee's better."

"But they only have those fancy desserts, not doughnuts." Bruno grinned.

"Jim's it is." Drake got up and stretched. "We'll probably discuss the case. Unofficially, of course. If you ladies—women—want to listen in—"

"They may have insights to contribute, Paolo." Bruno held the door open courteously.

"And we're free—I'm free—to go?" Suzanne glanced at me, then at the policemen. "We can just walk out if we want?"

"If you're tired of our company, certainly." Drake strode down the corridor, not waiting for anyone else.

I trailed Suzanne out the door, and Bruno Morales followed, shutting it carefully behind him. He glanced at Drake's receding form and tsked, shaking his head.

"No excuse for rudeness," he murmured, walking up the hall between the two of us. When we reached the street, Suzanne hesitated, but shrugged and came with us. Drake slowed down, and she walked beside him, her lanky form nearly topping his. That didn't seem to bother him.

Beside me, Bruno kept up a gentle flow of conversation, centering around his three children, his wife's activities on the Children's Theatre board, the way his tomatoes were growing. The couple ahead of us turned at University, but Bruno held me back with a hand on my arm. "Miss Sullivan," he began, gazing earnestly at me with his soft brown eyes. "Paolo is—he's been very concerned about you getting mixed up in this case."

"I'm not really mixed up—my participation was totally involuntary." I didn't want to hear this—it was almost as bad as being called into the principal's office.

Bruno sighed. "That's true. I guess what I'm trying to say is that I was concerned for Paolo, and for you. And do not tell me to mind my own business. I will tell myself." He moved on down the sidewalk to the door of Jim's. I wanted to pull away and stalk on back to my house, but I knew it was still occupied by the invading relatives. And besides, I burned with unassuaged curiosity.

Once we were seated in the neutral territory of a duct tape–patched booth, with a plate of maple bars on the table and steaming cups all around, Drake picked up the story.

"You asked why Ed had to kill Jenifer." He gazed somberly from me to Suzanne. "At this point we're just conjecturing, because he hasn't given us a coherent statement."

I shuddered a little, thinking of Ed's panic-filled gaze, wondering if he'd become completely unhinged.

"But this is what we think, putting together what you've told us"—he nodded at Suzanne—"with what we've dug up. Ed wanted to take SoftWrite public after bringing out the new product. He wanted the money, he wanted the prestige. He wanted to be the Bill Gates of Palo Alto."

Suzanne snorted. "He got greedy. I kept telling him we weren't ready to go public till we had a bigger range of products, but he didn't want to listen. It took us so long to get profitable, and a couple of extra rounds of venture capital eroded our stock position. The VC wanted us to go public too, but I was totally against it."

"That's what we heard," Drake murmured, exchanging glances with Bruno. "Several people told us you were against both the venture financing and the public offering."

"Call me a stick-in-the-mud." Suzanne smiled tiredly. "Ed did. And then he wanted to bring out our new product right away. I was only doing the user interface. He had Jenifer working on the real guts. And I couldn't believe she could get it done so fast. I wondered about it—after all, she'd worked for MicroMax, although he tried to keep that quiet. She was his new software queen." Her face twisted with pain. "Last weekend I went in and checked through the code. I found places where the two of them had unplugged chunks of proprietary stuff from somewhere else and stitched them into our product."

"Why didn't he just ask you to write original code?" Drake leaned forward, the last bite of a maple bar waiting in his hand.

"Too slow." Suzanne shrugged. "When Ed and I started out, we were a scrappy team, making it up as we went along. Our first product, the screen saver with the thunderstorm that rained cats and dogs, was a kind of thumb-your-nose thing that we tossed off for fun. It made us a lot of money. Suddenly we had offices and staff and cash flow—and a high overhead. Ed changed. Our next product was complicated and took more time to develop. He was impatient. He wanted more money, fast. He wanted to release things before they were ready and bring out endless variations of what we'd already done."

She stirred her coffee, not meeting anyone's eyes. "He said I was holding him back by insisting on testing and quality. Our private relationship died, but I wouldn't let him get rid of me in the company." She glanced up. "I actually own more of the stock than he does—he made some bad investments, and I bailed him out in return for some of his options. He started doing little power plays—dating women we hired, making under-the-table deals with investors. I knew he'd find some way to force me out sooner or later—I'm not good with that kind of scheming political management. I was just hoping to keep the standards up a little longer."

"Why didn't you want him to go public? Then you could have recouped your investment and gotten out." Drake poured more coffee from the tall plastic pot. I fished the tea bag out of my little metal pot of lukewarm water and refilled my cup.

Suzanne put one hand over her eyes. "I just didn't trust him. And there's so much more scrutiny when you go public. Once I found he was pirating other people's software for our product, I was really frightened of lawsuits. I was trying to think of a way to postpone the new release, some way to let our investors know that Ed should be removed without causing everything to collapse. Like I say, I'm not good at these things, and I didn't know where to go for help. I just—withdrew, I guess."

"So Jenifer was helping Ed doctor the new release." I still didn't really understand. "Why? She didn't seem like that kind of person. Because they were in love, talking marriage?"

"She was," Suzanne corrected. "Ed never talked marriage. But he probably did use his personal—charisma—to overwhelm her into helping him. He probably let her think he would marry her. He might even have meant to, just to keep her quiet."

"And then she joined Clarice's religion," Drake said. He pushed his coffee cup away and folded his arms on the table. "Clarice was jealous of Jenifer for getting Ed after he'd ditched her. But her new religion didn't allow jealousy, so she decided that if her beliefs had driven Ed away from her, the same thing would happen if she converted Jenifer. And Jenifer was easy meat for Clarice. She'd already been influenced by a group in Seattle, several of whom blamed all their problems on child abuse they remembered. Jenifer's new 'memory' broke up her brother's romance, and she wasn't sorry."

"Yes," Bruno Morales put in. "Jason told us that she said she felt cleaner after she'd 'confessed' to his fiancée, and she'd feel cleaner yet once she was done. Obviously she had something more on her mind."

"Ed must have known she was getting ready to denounce him," Drake said. "The big scene at the office that morning wasn't really about their romance, but about her plans to confess to doctoring the software. The blackmailing note in the lunch bag just made Jenifer more determined. Ed couldn't allow it. He took her home, gave her a sedative, told her to rest up. He was probably already thinking how much better it would be if she were dead. After you came by, Liz, he gave her cocoa with a lethal dose of the sleeping pills—she would be groggy by then, unquestioning. When she passed out, he left her to die."

"And Bill Aronson photographed his car there." Bruno Morales took over the story. "He had a habit of keeping track of things, and he'd found out from one of Clarice's spiteful remarks about Ed and Jenifer. After she died, he got his pictures printed and tried to cash in on his knowledge. Ed agreed to meet him on Skyline to hand over the blackmail, but instead he just knocked Aronson out, put a hole in his exhaust pipe, and left him to die. Ed didn't really kill them, he says. They died when he wasn't there."

We were all silent for a moment.

"But I don't understand why he planned to pin it on me," I said, standing a maple bar up on one end like an office building. "I had no motive for any of it."

Drake gave me a look I couldn't interpret. "I don't think he really did. He felt you should be included in his scheme when he found out you'd been at Jenifer's that afternoon. But right up to the end you were just going to be insurance, an outsider to confirm that Suzanne was threatening him. And if something went wrong, you could be the backup suspect, in case we didn't buy the suicides or Suzanne didn't look guilty enough. That's why he made sure you came back to answer the phones after Clarice's big fit. He wanted you available."

"Why did he kill Larry?" Suzanne had a pile of crumbs in front of her from shredding her maple bar. "Did Larry know that Ed had—killed Jenifer?"

"He figured out that Jenifer and Ed were using MicroMax's proprietary code." Drake pushed his hair back and looked wearily at Suzanne. "Ed saw Larry as the last obstacle, and also an opportunity to divert suspicion from himself."

"What's going to happen to Ed?" Suzanne was trembling enough to shake the whole booth, but her voice was even. "Will he—be executed?" She smoothed the bandage that covered the hole in her hand.

Drake shrugged. "Not for me to say. He'll be remanded for trial. Your testimony will be important, and so will Liz's, that he attempted to intimidate and murder. As far as Jenifer and Bill and Larry, we'll find more evidence now that we know what to look for. Certainly he'll be brought up on capital charges."

Suzanne rubbed her thin arms. "I don't know what to do about SoftWrite," she said helplessly. "The new release is compromised, the investors will be frantic, and that public offering is looming over me."

"Call up Emery and ask him for some names," I suggested, feeling sorry for her. "You need a good lawyer. Maybe there are some consultants who can sort things out for you."

"We'll need a new receptionist, too," she said, glancing at me. "Sarah phoned in her resignation yesterday evening. She didn't have the flu after all. She's been in Tahoe, getting married to a guy she met last week and fell violently in love with, and they're moving to Phoenix." She hesitated. "Would—guess you wouldn't be interested in the job."

She was right about that. "No, thanks," I said gently. "I'm not cut out for the office life."

Drake shook his head in exasperation. "You could at least think about it. Would it kill you to have a regular job and benefits and a real salary?"

"It might kill me. In fact, it almost did." I slid out of the booth. "If you'll excuse me, I've got to get home and let my sister-in-law yell at me for a while. She's almost as good at it as you are, Drake. And if you don't clean those big old nettles out of your parking strip, I'm calling the city weed abatement people to come out and fine your ass."

Bruno laughed. Drake had to try hard not to smile. By the time I got to the door, he was behind me.

"Hey, Liz." He reached around to push the door open. "We planting that hedge tomorrow?"

"Sure. Right." He walked with me back to where I'd left my bus. Before I climbed into it he threw his arm around me for a brief hug. He traced a finger along the angry red line that bisected my throat. I had refused hospital treatment; it would fade soon enough.

"When I think of you taking these risks I just get all worked up." He paused, then pressed a gentle kiss on my lips. He'd never done that before. It was over before I had time to decide if I wanted it to go on. He walked on toward his office.

I tossed my tote bag onto the passenger seat. Something crackled when I reached into it for my car keys. It was the letter from my mother. I had forgotten about it in all the excitement.

I held it for a minute, then ripped it open and read it quickly.

Dear Lizzie,

I didn't answer your letter before because I didn't know what to say to you. I am sorry your marriage did not turn out, but as you know I do not believe in divorce, no matter what the bishop says. You must lie in the bed of your own making. Your Dad and I are getting old now and can't be traipsing around. Of course if you come to visit we will not turn our own child out of the house. We are not very well fixed so don't know what we could do for you. Amy is a Dear Child and is just mixed up. Do you think you are the right person to set her straight? Be very careful because you will be called to account for your actions at the Heavenly Tribunal.

She'd signed it, *Best wishes, your Mom.*

The paper was lined, with a border at the top of kittens frolicking with a ball of yarn. Her handwriting was shakier than I remembered. She was seventy-three. My dad was nearly eighty-four. They were old people, no longer the figures of powerful authority whom I'd been compelled to defy.

I put the letter back in my bag and drove home feeling exhausted. At least the cloud of suspicion and murder was gone. The census was almost finished. I was on speaking—or at least writing—terms with my family, even if I didn't care for what they wrote. If Renee would only leave, I could get down to my real work. I should have felt pretty good, and I did, really, except for a stupid desire to burst into tears.

The front door was open when I pulled up. Barker ran out at me, woofing like mad. There was a lot of commotion in the house. I stepped into the living room and slipped in a puddle of water, nearly skidding into the sofa.

Renee and Amy were sloshing around in the kitchen, with all the towels I owned lying in a heap across the doorway. Renee was on her hands and knees, sponging and wringing water into a bucket. Amy wielded the mop. The water was up to their ankles.

"What's happening?" I noticed that the floor, the water, and Amy's and Renee's feet were a streaky orange. "Not the water heater?"

Renee straightened and pushed her hair out of her eyes.

"It's the last straw," she raged. "I'm leaving as soon as I can get some dry clothes on. If Amy stays in this shack another minute, she's crazy."

"Sorry, Aunt Liz." Amy wrung her mop and leaned on it. "Mom was showering and it—the water heater—just, like, broke. I mean, it was like a tidal wave or something. It gushed all over the place. We managed to keep most of it in the kitchen, but I think it's going to take a while to clean this up." She looked down at the rust-colored water.

"Did you turn off the gas?" I sniffed, but couldn't smell anything.

"Of course. We're not morons," Renee snapped. Through the open door of the back porch, the perpetrator of this chaos stood silent for once, its feet drowned in a pile of rusty metal.

"There's another mop in the garage." I reached in and set my tote bag on the kitchen table. "I'll get it."

"And your 'friend' was looking for you." Renee managed quite a good sneer. "The policeman. Is he going to arrest you?"

"Not any time soon."

Amy looked relieved. "It's all okay?" She followed me to the garage. "I didn't tell Mom anything about the—you know."

"Thanks."

"Plotting?" Renee scowled when we came back in. "That policeman was really frantic to find you, and now you look like hell. What's that around your neck? What's the matter?"

"Nothing's the matter." I rolled up my jeans legs.

"Good. It's not pleasant having a jailbird for a sister-in-law." She stepped over the towels. "You two can clean up this mess. I'm going to pack." Renee looked at her daughter with a mixture of exasperation and respect. "Amy should come with me, but she insists on staying to do this internship thing. If that's okay with you," she added in a rare outbreak of manners. "I told her she shouldn't impose, but she said you wouldn't care."

"I don't mind." Oddly enough, it was the truth.

"Well, I hope I'm not making a terrible mistake." Renee eyed my dubiously. "If you get into trouble, what will Amy do?"

"She'll manage," I said, grinning at Amy, who sputtered a protest at her mother's words. "She's resourceful. So when does your plane leave?"

"She leaves in an hour and a half," Amy said, glancing at the kitchen clock. "After we drop her off, we should go to the grocery store, Aunt Liz. There's absolutely nothing to eat except peanut butter."

There would be green beans at my garden, and beets and carrots and lettuce. Amy could help weed. I smiled graciously at Renee.

"So glad you could visit," I murmured. "Please, get right on that packing. Amy and I will finish up here."

28 _____

I was sitting on my front porch steps, enjoying a balmy July evening—one of the rare six nights a year that aren't cold in the Bay Area. Barker ranged back and forth over the yard, digging at a fresh gopher mound, sniffing the base of the redwood where the squirrels always headed toward the canopy. Amy had stopped on her way home from work that afternoon to pick up a half-pint of cream, and I was savoring the luxury of strawberry shortcake with my own berries, sweet enough to need no sugar—although Amy had sprinkled hers liberally. I could hear her in the house behind me; through the screen door came a golden oblong of light and the sound of her humming as she got ready for a date.

We could shower now without fear. Suzanne had honored Ed's commitment to pay me double, and the check from SoftWrite had been more than enough to cover the cost of a new water heater. Amy had insisted on paying for the plumber out of her salary. I had felt bad about taking her money, but Claudia had urged me to let her pay. "It seems like a fortune to her now," she'd pointed out. "Real life is learning that it doesn't go that far."

Amy was pulling her weight, anyway, which was good, because I'd turned down all the temp jobs for the past month. I had sent off the *Smithsonian* article that afternoon, and was working on a go-ahead from *Forbes ASAP*—about the influx of temporary employees into the job market. Amy had suggested it, and *Forbes* had actually wanted the perspective of a temp instead of the employer. It was shaping up pretty well.

The evening star appeared in the west. I had been reading in the light from the door, but I let *Persuasion* slip out of my grasp while I counted stars. I was up to seven when Drake's headlights blinded me.

He pulled into his parking space and busied himself around his car for a moment. Then his dark form came toward me. He was carrying something that must have been heavy—I could hear him huffing. Barker raced over, and Drake stumbled at his enthusiastic greeting.

"Down, you dog!"

I called Barker to heel, and Drake came on up the walk. He plopped his burden down in front of me. It was a rosebush in a pulp pot, white blossoms luminous in the dark.

"For you," Drake said gruffly. "They were having a sale at Roger Reynolds when I drove past."

"Thanks." I had to clear my throat. "It's beautiful." I grinned at him. "We can plant it as the beginning of the hedge." I found the little metal tag at the bud union and tried to read it in the weak light.

"Margaret Merrill." Drake sounded proud of himself. "I asked its name. And put it wherever you want it. The hedge should wait until fall, according to the woman at the nursery."

I stood up and circled the bush, enjoying its graceful shape. "This is very nice of you, Drake. What's the occasion?"

He shrugged. "No occasion. Don't look a gift horse in the mouth, Liz."

"Sorry. I really do appreciate it." Awkwardly, because I wasn't used to making such gestures, I wrapped my arms around him.

I had wanted to do that for some time. Drake's teddy-bear quality was finally getting to me. But even though Californians hug at the drop of a beret, I don't know how to achieve that light, affectionate touch.

Drake stood still, and I thought miserably that I'd ruined

a perfectly good friendship. But when I dropped my arms, his came around me, hard. "You're welcome," he whispered in my ear. Then he kissed me, which I guess was what I'd wanted when I'd initiated the embrace. This time the kiss lasted long enough for me to know that I was enjoying it.

He quit just before I would have had to push him away from sensory overload. "You're very welcome," he repeated, and his voice wasn't quite steady. "I'll help you plant it tomorrow, if you want."

Then he left, crunching over the gravel to his back door. I sat on the steps again, face-to-face with one of Margaret Merrill's white blooms. It was open, revealing its fringed red heart to the whole world.

"Wow. Nice flowers." Amy came through the door, dressed in white for a change—a flowing white overshirt we'd found at the thrift store and skintight white leggings. "Can I have one?"

She tucked the bud I cut for her into her cleavage and floated toward the street, where Randy's car had just pulled up. "I'll be back by eleven," she called over her shoulder.

I sat there for a while longer. The sky had blossomed into stars, and the night fragrance seemed to be theirs, pulsing down with almost unbearable sweetness. I took a big breath of it and carried my book inside.